Praise for the novels of

JOAN WOLF

"Especially appealing..."
—*Booklist* on *White Horses*

"Wolf spins a very entertaining love story."
—*Romantic Times* on *White Horses*

"Romance writing at its very best."
—*Publishers Weekly* (starred review) on *The Guardian*

"Wolf...leaps into the contemporary romantic
suspense arena with this smart, compelling read."
—*Publishers Weekly* on *Silverbridge*

"A quick-moving, enchanting tale...An excellent
choice for readers who want an exciting epic."
—*Booklist* on *Daughter of the Red Deer*

"Captivating...endearing...heartwarming...
Wolf's assured storytelling is simply the best."
—*BookPage* on *Royal Bride*

"Fast paced, highly readable..."
—*Library Journal* on *The Gamble*

"An entertaining and thought-provoking read."
—*Washington Post Book World*
on *The Reindeer Hunters*

JOAN WOLF

To the Castle

MIRA®

ISBN 0-7783-2203-3

TO THE CASTLE

Copyright © 2005 by Joan Wolf.

www.MIRABooks.com

Printed in U.S.A.

For Joe, the bedrock of my existence.

One

The funeral mass for Sybilla de Bonvile was held in the cathedral of Lincoln on a day of high clouds and gusty wind. Nell de Bonvile walked with her parents behind the coffin of her only sister as it was carried by six knights up the aisle to the altar rail. The archbishop himself waited with holy water to sprinkle on it before he turned with majestic slowness to ascend to the altar where he would begin the funeral mass.

Nell knelt next to her mother and listened to the familiar Latin words, her eyes on the coffin that contained the eighteen-year-old remains of Sybilla. She felt immense sorrow engulf her as she thought of her sister's life, blown out like a candle by a fever and coughing illness.

If only they had called upon Sister Helen, perhaps she might have been saved, Nell thought. But Sister Helen, one of the nuns at the convent where Nell had lived since her eighth year, had not been called upon, and Sybilla had died.

Next to Nell, her mother raised a handkerchief to her face and began to sob softly. Nell wanted to comfort her mother, but hesitated to touch her. She wasn't sure if her mother would want comfort from her sole remaining child. Nell knew she could never take the place of her beautiful sister or her brilliant brother. Perhaps her mother would be hurt by the reminder that they had gone and all that was left to her was Nell.

She looked beyond her mother to the face of her father. The Earl of Lincoln's face was like stone. He made no motion to comfort his wife.

Tentatively, Nell reached out and touched her mother's arm. The countess gave no sign that she felt Nell's fingers; she continued to sob quietly into her handkerchief. After a minute, Nell removed her hand and folded it in prayer.

Dear God, she prayed, *please receive Sybilla into the joy of your presence and help Mama and Papa to find comfort from their grief.*

When the mass was over, they left Sybilla's coffin in the church, where she would be buried alongside her brother, and went out into the windy day.

Nell, her parents and her aunt had stayed overnight in the bishop's residence, but now that the funeral was over, Nell knew her father was anxious to return to his castle of Bardney, some twenty miles outside of Lincoln. He gave orders to the knights who had accompanied him to bring the horses around and, as Nell stood waiting in front of the cathedral, her eyes took in the unfamiliar part of Lincoln that lay within the outer walls of the castle.

Nell had spent most of her life within the confines of a convent, and this glimpse of the busy outside world was fascinating. People were going about their business, coming and going from the castle, which towered high above them on a rock, or buying and selling from the stalls that lined one of the walls of the Bail. Many cast curious glances at the funeral party—everyone in the town was aware of who was being buried that day.

What different lives people live, Nell thought wonderingly. *How different my own life would have been if my parents hadn't given me to the convent when I was a child.*

An old woman passed in front of the cathedral, turning her head to look straight at Nell. Nell could feel the sympathy in her gaze cross the distance between them. She nodded slightly, in acknowledgment, and the old lady nodded back and continued on her way.

The sympathy was kind, but Nell knew it should be directed at her mother and father, not at her. She had hardly known her sister. They had been separated when they were very young and Sybilla had rarely come to visit her in the convent.

"Nell, stop standing there staring and get on your horse." Her father sounded impatient. She went over to the small mare one of the knights was holding and let him help her into the saddle. She was still a little sore from the ride in yesterday; life in the convent had not included horseback riding.

Her father mounted his big chestnut stallion and the knights who were leading their party started off. Her father's stallion moved off behind them, followed by her mother, her mother's sister, Aunt Alida, and Nell. Behind them came another group of knights, to protect their rear.

Nell's veil blew in the wind and she reached up to anchor it more securely on her head. She would not profess her holy vows until she was eighteen, but the novices at the convent wore wimples and veils like the nuns. Her little mare was very quiet, paying no attention to the people who were staring at them—unlike her father's stallion, who was dancing and throwing his head around. Her father sat quietly and spoke to him. Nell watched with awe as he controlled the large horse with his voice and gentle hands.

The earl's cavalcade went down the old Roman road, Ermine Street, through the town with its shops, past the inns that accommodated visitors to Lincoln, past the church of St. Peter ad Placita, across the River Witham and out of the town. Bardney was southeast of Lincoln while Nell's convent was to the northeast. She had been fetched two days ago by five of her father's knights and she supposed she would be spending the night at Bardney, then returning to the convent in the morning.

The road to Bardney led through several small

villages huddled around their churches, and some fine pastureland where cows grazed peacefully. The castle could be seen from quite a distance, its turreted stone walls rearing up out of the ground with arrogant authority.

Nell had spent the first years of her life at Bardney, but her memories of life in the castle were dim. When she was eight her brother, the much-longed-for male, had been born, and Nell had been sent to the Convent of St. Cecelia in fulfillment of a promise her parents had made to God when they had prayed for a son. The life she knew was life in the convent; she had felt like a stranger when she had dismounted in the inner bailey of the castle two days ago.

She felt like a stranger still as she rode across the bridge, over the moat and under the great iron portcullis that sealed the gate at night and in times of trouble. The cavalcade of horses crossed the huge expanse of the outer bailey, passed through a second gate into the inner bailey, and came to a halt in front of the great stone castle. The knights, who wore mail shirts called hauberks and helmets with the nose guards up, dismounted, and one of them came to lift Nell down from her saddle. Her knees buckled a little when she touched the ground and he reached out quickly to steady her.

"I'm all right," Nell told the knight, who was young and brown-eyed. "I just have never had the opportunity to do much riding."

"You did very well, my lady," he said.

"Come along, Nell," her mother called. "Don't stand there dawdling."

Nell went immediately to her mother and aunt and followed them into the Great Hall, which took up more than half the space of the castle's ground floor. Nell had been awed by the size of the Great Hall when she had come home two days ago, and she looked around now, still surprised by its immensity and by the colorful painted wall hangings that adorned the high stone walls. At the convent, rooms were small and the stone walls were bare except for a crucifix.

Her father, Lord Raoul, and her mother, Lady Alice, moved toward the chairs that were pulled up in front of the fireplace and Nell and her aunt followed.

"I think we could all use some wine," Alida said.

"Yes," the earl said. "Send for some."

Two young pages sat on a bench along the wall and Lady Alice said peremptorily, "Robin, go and fetch some wine for us."

The boy jumped up and ran in the direction of the buttery, where the drinks were kept.

Nell looked at her father, who sat in the largest chair with his legs stretched out in front of him. He did not speak and the others respected his silence. Nell looked down at her lap and folded her hands.

The page came back bearing four goblets of wine on a silver tray. He served his lord first, then Lady Alice, Lady Alida and Nell. The earl and countess both took a long drink, but Nell sipped her wine tentatively. The novices in the convent drank ale with their meals; wine was something new to Nell.

"Well," the earl said, when he had put his drink on the small table next to him. "So that's that."

"I can't believe she's gone," Lady Alice said sadly. "I can't believe that God could be so cruel."

"God does what He damn well pleases," the earl said.

Nell looked at her father with horrified eyes.

He caught her look and said harshly, "Despite what you may have heard in your convent, it's true. There is no making sense of the tragedies in life. No religion can explain to me why I had to lose both my son and my daughter. God does what He damn well pleases and He doesn't answer any questions."

Nell tried to think what she could say to answer the earl's shocking words. "It's true that we can't know the mind of God, but we must trust that there is a plan that we can't understand," she said, echoing words she had heard more than once in the convent.

"I don't think I would want to understand a plan that would take my son and my daughter from me," her father said, turning his grim look on her.

Nell bit her lip. *He's grieving,* she thought excusingly. *He doesn't mean it.*

Once more silence descended on the small group by the fire. Tears ran from her mother's eyes and her father looked angry.

I wish I could comfort them, Nell thought with distress. *I feel so useless here.*

Her mother wiped her eyes and looked at her. "I don't know what we're going to do about clothes for you. You're quite a bit smaller than Sybilla."

"We can alter some of Sybilla's gowns," Alida said. "They will do until we can have her own clothes made."

Clothes? Nell thought. She looked from her aunt to her mother in puzzlement. "Why should I need clothes, Mama? I have my habit."

Her mother and father glanced at each other. Then the earl spoke. "You will not be going back to the convent, Nell. You are my only remaining child and you have a duty to your family. You will be remaining here at Bardney for the foreseeable future."

Nell's dark blue eyes grew huge. "I'm not going back to the convent? But I was to be professed as a nun in six months' time!"

"You are not going to become a nun. You are now the heiress to the Earl of Lincoln—a far more important position than a mere nun could ever hope to attain."

Nell felt as if she had been hit over the head. Her brain was utterly scattered. Not going back to the convent? But the convent had been her life!

The earl continued, "I will write to Mother Superior to tell her of my decision. We were wrong to send you there all those years ago. It's true that God gave us a son, but then He took him away. I don't owe God a daughter, as well. From now on you will be staying here, with us."

* * *

Nell sat in her sister's bedroom, surrounded by her sister's things. The wooden trunks along the wall held Sybilla's clothes; the coverings on the bed bore Sybilla's monogram; the hangings on the stone wall were the product of her sister's paintbrush. When her mother had put her in Sybilla's room, Nell had assumed it was because all the other bedrooms were full. Now she realized it was because she had been designated to take Sybilla's place.

But I'm not Sybilla, she thought rebelliously. *My life has taken a different path.*

She jumped up and went to the window. The busy outer bailey of Bardney lay spread before her, with men coming and going on castle business. Panic fluttered in her stomach.

I don't belong here. This is not my home anymore.
Mother Superior won't let me leave.

The thought took root in Nell's shocked mind. For the past nine years she had dedicated herself to God. To be ripped so abruptly from her sacred purpose and returned to the secular world had stunned her and destroyed her sense of who she was.

Mother Superior would intercede with her father, convince him to leave Nell in the convent, where she had been so happy and so secure.

I must find a way to see Mother Superior.

But Nell was canny enough to realize that her father would not let her return to the convent if he thought she wanted Mother Superior to intercede for her. She had to think of another reason for wanting to return to St. Cecelia's.

I'll tell Father that I want to say goodbye to the nuns. Surely he won't deny me that opportunity. After all, they have been my family for the last nine years.

Her idea had barely formed when the bedroom door opened and her mother came in.

"I don't want you to wear that wimple at dinner," Lady Alice said to Nell. "Take it off and let me see what your hair looks like."

Reluctantly, Nell slowly removed her veil and wimple. Her brown hair was pulled back tight against her skull and fastened in a braid at the nape of her neck. It fell halfway down her back.

"Thank God they didn't cut it," her mother said, relieved.

"It was going to be cut when I took my vows," Nell said.

"Well, you aren't going to make your vows, so you don't have to worry about that anymore."

Nell had never once worried about having her hair cut.

She thought she should try to get her mother on her side about visiting Mother Superior.

"Mama," Nell said, as Lady Alice began to unravel Nell's hair, "I want to go back to the convent to say goodbye to the nuns. They were very good to me and it would be churlish of me to go away without even a goodbye."

"Good grief," her mother said. "How often did you wash your hair? It's greasy!"

Hair washing had never been of great moment in the convent.

"I don't know," Nell said vaguely.

Her mother made sounds of disapproval. "Well, this needs to be washed before you can display it. I had better put the braid back in for now and we can wash it tomorrow."

"Did you hear me, Mama?" Nell said a little desperately. "I would like to return to the convent to say goodbye."

Her mother continued to braid Nell's hair. "Well, I suppose that can be arranged. We'll have to talk to your father."

"Can we ask him tonight?"

"We'll see."

Lady Alice finished braiding Nell's hair, then looked into her face. "Your life is going to be very different from what you are used to, Nell, and I realize it may be hard for you at first. I will do my best to help you."

Nell dropped her eyes. "Thank you, Mama," she murmured.

"It's important to you, saying goodbye at the convent?"

"Yes."

"Very well. I will speak to your father."

"Thank you, Mama," Nell said again. "Do you think I can go tomorrow?"

"That will depend upon your father."

"But you'll ask him?"

"I said I would," her mother replied impatiently. She

looked at Nell, her head tilted to one side. "I suppose you will have to wear that habit downstairs to supper. I'll have my ladies alter a few of Sybilla's tunics tomorrow. At least if we get the hems up you can wear them."

I don't want to wear Sybilla's clothes, Nell thought stubbornly.

"Come along," her mother said. "It's time to go downstairs to supper."

Two

Supper was served for the entire household in the Great Hall. Trestle tables had been set up in the main body of the hall with the high table set close to the fireplace, where in winter it was warmest. At the high table sat the lord and lady of the house, Nell, Lady Alida, Father Clement, the chaplain, and Martin Demas, who was the steward of Bardney Castle. Two squires stood behind the table to serve the great folk dining there.

Nell looked at the roast venison that was reposing upon her trencher of fine white bread and felt her stomach heave. She was far too upset to eat. Her mouth felt dry so she took a small sip of wine. She looked enviously at the lesser folk sitting at the trestle tables who were being served ale.

"Eat something," her aunt Alida said. "The food is good at Bardney. You should enjoy it."

Aunt Alida looked as if she enjoyed the food. She

was a small plump woman who reminded Nell of a pigeon. Alida had been one of too many girls and her family hadn't known what to do with her until Alice had said she could come and live with her.

It was not always easy these days for a noble family to find a suitable match for a daughter. Because of the Norman custom that decreed that all of a family's holdings be passed down to the eldest son, it was only the eldest son in a family who was eligible to marry. Penniless younger sons usually remained bachelors. This left a limited number of potential husbands for the daughters of the nobility, and competition was fierce. There had been several girls in Nell's convent whose families had not been able to give them a good enough dowry to purchase a husband.

Alida had been fortunate to have a sister who had married well enough to be able to offer her a home. Nell had only a dim memory of Alida from the time that she had lived at home, but her aunt's smile was friendly and she smiled back.

"I'm just not very hungry, I'm afraid," she said. "Too much has happened in the last few days. My stomach's all in a whirl."

Her mother turned to her. "Aren't you eating, Nell?"

Nell took a bite of venison and forced it down. "I'm eating, Mama."

Alice spoke to her sister across Nell. "Do you really think we can alter Sybilla's clothes to fit Nell? It isn't just the length that will have to come up; they will have to be taken in all over."

"We can do it," Alida replied. "We'll get started on it right away."

"We'll have to," Alice said. "She has to have something to wear besides this black robe."

Alida patted Nell on the arm. "Don't you worry. You're a pretty girl and we'll soon have you fitted out properly."

I hope not, Nell thought. She turned to her mother. "Mama," she said, "don't forget to talk to my father about my going back to St. Cecelia's."

Alice looked exasperated. "I told you I would talk to him and I will—in good time."

"Talk about what?" Alida asked her sister with all the confidence of a close companion.

"Nell wants to go back to the convent to say goodbye to the sisters," Alice said.

Alida nodded approvingly. "And so she should. It is the mannerly thing to do."

Nell gave her aunt a tremulous smile of gratitude.

Nell waited all through dinner for her mother to have a chance to talk to her father, but he was deep in conversation with Martin Demas and didn't look at his wife. Finally, when the main dishes had been removed and the sweet was being served, he turned to the three women who sat to his right.

"Did you enjoy your food, Nell?" he asked.

"Yes, Father, I did," Nell lied.

"Good. I imagine you did not dine like this in the convent."

"No, Father."

"My lord," Alice began, "Nell wishes to return to the convent so she may say goodbye to the nuns. I think it would be the mannerly thing for her to do—after all, she resided there for nine years."

He frowned and Nell held her breath.

"I don't think it's necessary," he said.

"Not necessary, but mannerly," Lady Alice said.

His frown smoothed out. "Oh, all right. I suppose I can spare a few knights to take her." He spoke briefly with Martin Demas, then turned back to Nell. "All right," he said, returning his gaze to the women. "You might as well go tomorrow and get it over with. I can send five men with you."

"Surely I don't need five men, Father," Nell said.

"Yes, you do," he returned. "The country is teetering on the brink of civil war and lawless men are taking advantage of the unsettled state of affairs." He looked at her grimly. "You are all I have left to me, Nell. I don't want to lose you, too."

For the briefest of moments pain flashed in her father's dark blue eyes, then it was gone. Nell felt a stab of guilt that she was working to circumvent him.

After dinner was over, the servants began the work of taking up the trestle tables and storing them against one wall of the Great Hall. They left a few benches in front of the fire and a number of knights gravitated to them and sat down. Someone took out a pair of dice. The earl went to join his men by the fire and Alice said to her sister, "Let us go upstairs to the solar. I have no heart for company tonight."

Nell followed her mother and her aunt up the stairs to the living room used solely by the family, her mind forming thoughts of what she would say to Mother Superior when she saw her on the morrow. Surely Mother Superior would be on her side. She had always liked Nell. She prayed she would tell her father that it was God's will that Nell remain in the convent.

It was late in the afternoon when Nell and her retinue arrived at the gatehouse of the Convent of St. Cecelia. The portress greeted Nell, then summoned grooms to take the horses.

The stones of the convent buildings looked so familiar to Nell, so comforting. There was the church, where the nuns heard mass from behind a beautifully carved screen; there was Mother Superior's house; there was the main residence where Nell had lived along with the nuns and the rest of the novices; and there was the guesthouse, where the Bardney knights would spend the night. Unseen from the courtyard was the herb garden, where Nell had spent so many happy hours learning from the convent's healer, Sister Helen.

Sister Helen had been like a mother to her. How could she bear to leave her?

Nell pointed out the guesthouse to the knights and told them to make themselves comfortable. Then she crossed the courtyard in the direction of Mother Superior's tall, narrow, stone house. Her heart was thudding.

A lay sister answered Nell's knock. Nell asked a little breathlessly, "Will you be so kind as to tell Mother that I wish to see her?"

"Of course," the lay sister replied and disappeared up the stairs. She returned a few minutes later and told Nell that Mother Superior would receive her in her sitting room. By now Nell's heart was hammering and she drew a deep breath to steady herself before she went up the stairs.

St. Cecelia's was a well-endowed convent and the Mother Superior could have afforded a decent degree of luxury, but Mother Margaret de Ligne made do with only the bare essentials: several carved wooden chairs, two chests and a wall hanging depicting St. George on a white horse. The stone floor was bare of rushes.

Mother Margaret herself was almost as austere-looking as the room she sat in, but her face softened as Nell came in. "So," she said. "You have returned from burying your sister."

"Yes, Mother. And something has happened that I must discuss with you."

"Come and sit down," Mother Margaret said. "How are your mother and your father? Such a terrible thing for them, to lose your sister at so young an age. I am praying for them."

"Thank you, Mother," Nell replied.

"I see you are not wearing your wimple."

Nell clutched her hands tightly together in her lap. "My mother made me take it off. Mother, something terrible has happened. My father has said that I can't remain at the convent, that I must stay at home and take Sybilla's place!"

There was a little silence, then Mother Margaret said softly, "I thought this might happen."

Nell stared at her in shocked surprise.

Mother Margaret went on. "Your father is a very important man, Nell. He owns extensive lands, castles and manors. He has lost a son and a daughter and he needs an heir to carry on the family's holdings and its bloodline. So I am not surprised that he wants you to come home."

Nell found her voice. "But I was dedicated to God, Mother! Surely I ought not turn my back upon Him!"

Mother Margaret said gently, "When you were dedicated, your father had a son and another daughter. Now he has only you."

Nell was stunned. Mother was sounding as if she approved of this change in Nell's status! She said tensely, "I was hoping that you would speak to my father. I was hoping you would tell him that the ways of God come before the ways of men."

Mother Margaret leaned a little forward. "My dear child," she said. "we will miss you very much. You have given much joy to this convent. But you must obey your father, Nell. The Commandments tell us, honor thy father and thy mother."

Nell felt betrayed. She had been so sure that Mother

Superior would fight for her. "If you could just talk to him, perhaps he will change his mind," she pleaded.

Mother Margaret shook her head decisively. Her light blue eyes held sympathy for Nell, but her words were adamant. "I will not interfere. You can continue to serve God, no matter what your station in life, Nell. You will be in a high position, a position where you can affect many lives—many more lives than you would affect in this convent. Perhaps God has had this plan for you all along. You learned here how to be a religious woman. Now it is time for you to take what you have learned and apply it to the life you will lead as mistress of many people."

"But I don't want to leave here," Nell cried in deep distress. "I have been happy here!"

Mother folded her hands in her lap. "I am glad about that, but now your duty lies elsewhere, Nell. Your family needs you more than we do."

There was a little silence. Nell hunched her shoulders and stared into her lap. "I thought you would take my side."

"Look at me," Mother Superior said.

Reluctantly, Nell lifted her eyes.

"Your job will be to work good in the world," Mother said. "That is a much harder task than praying from within the shelter of a convent, but I'm sure you're equal to it."

No, I'm not, Nell thought. *I don't want to go into the world.*

Mother Superior continued. "One thing you can do is bring healing to those who need it. Sister Helen tells me that you are almost as accomplished an herb woman as she is. We have Sister Helen—we don't need another healer. But many people in the world need the skill you have, Nell. That will be something you can do for God."

Nell stared into Mother's light eyes. She truly thought that Nell should go. *She's wrong,* Nell thought rebelliously. *I'm sure God wants me to stay here.*

"Be a good daughter to your parents," Mother Superior said. "They have need of you now."

Nell's chin set stubbornly and she did not answer.

Mother Margaret stood up and Nell followed. Mother Margaret was half a head taller than the girl. "I am sure you will want to say goodbye to all your friends. Come, have dinner with us in the refectory and I will relax the order for silence so you may converse."

There was nothing more that Nell could say. Mother Margaret's mind was clearly made up. Tears stung behind Nell's eyes. She was going to have to leave the convent.

Mother Superior said, "I am sure you will want to give your news to Sister Helen. I believe at this hour she is in the herb garden. Go and find her."

"Thank you, Mother." Nell pushed the words through the choking feeling in her throat.

She went back down the stairs and let herself out through the thick wooden door. *This is terrible,* she thought in panic as she crossed the courtyard and took the path that led between the convent and the squat storage building. *How can I bear to leave here? How can I bear to leave Sister Helen?*

The path descended gently to the convent's large kitchen garden. At the far end of the garden was a fenced-off area and a small hut with smoke coming out of the smoke hole. Nell crossed the kitchen garden, went through the fence and into the hut.

A nun was standing with her back to the door, watching a glass pot as it cooked on a small stove. At the sight of the familiar figure, tears flooded Nell's eyes.

"Sister Helen," she said.

The nun turned. "Nell! You're back. How are you? How are your parents?" She left the burner and came to stand beside Nell and look into her face.

Sister Helen was small, like Nell, and their eyes met easily. Nell looked into the pretty, unlined face of the person she loved best in the world and felt her stomach clench. The tears spilled down her cheeks.

"Oh, Sister Helen," she cried. "Something terrible has happened. My father has said I must leave the convent and go to live with him and my mother. They want me to take my sister's place!"

There was a moment of silence. The mixture of herbs gave off a pungent smell that filled the hut.

"Oh, my dear," Sister Helen said, her voice full of aching sympathy.

Nell's sobs broke loose. "I asked Mother Margaret to intercede with my father, but she won't! She says I must obey my parents and leave the convent."

Sister Helen took Nell's hands into her own small work-worn ones. She spoke soberly, "Mother Margaret has no say in your future, Nell. You are the daughter of a powerful man. If the earl wants you home, then home you must go."

"But he gave me away!" Nell cried through her tears. "He and my mother. They didn't want me, Sister Helen. They still don't want *me*. They need a daughter, that's all. It isn't fair that my life should be turned upside down because they have changed their minds."

Nell flung herself forward and Sister Helen's arms closed around her. There was a long silence where the only sounds were the pot boiling on the burner and Nell crying. Then Sister Helen said quietly, "Listen to me, Nell. It may very well be that God has other plans for you than the convent. You will join the world of the great. You may be in a position to do much good. Perhaps that is God's plan for you."

Nell said into her shoulder, "That is what Mother Margaret said. But I don't think it's true. I think I was meant to be a nun."

Sister Helen patted Nell's back between her shoulder blades. "I think you should listen to Mother. She is a very wise woman, Nell."

"I don't want to leave you!" Nell cried passionately. "You have always been my best friend. You have been more my mother than my real mother ever was."

Sister Helen put her hands on Nell's shoulders and held her away. She looked into her streaming eyes. "God knows, I will miss you very much. Very much. But we must bow to His will, my dear. That is what we are put on this earth to do."

"It is the will of my father," Nell retorted through her tears. "I'm not so sure it is the will of God."

Sister Helen tightened her grasp on Nell's shoulders. "Listen to me, Nell. I know this is hard for you. Your life is going to be very different from the life you have known. But it's important that you feel you are doing God's work in your new life. It is easy to be religious in the convent—much harder in the world. But that is now your calling and you must embrace it, however hard it may be. Are you listening to me?"

Nell said in a trembling voice, "I am listening, Sister."

"Good. Take pity on your father instead of blaming him. He is a man who has lost two children. And your mother, too. Show yourself to be a good daughter to them—they need you now."

They never needed me before.

"Have you heard me, Nell?" Sister Helen asked gently.

Nell tried hard to stop crying. "I heard you, Sister. But I still think this is the wrong thing to do."

"It is important that you make the best of the life that has been chosen for you," Sister Helen said soberly. "Promise me you will think about what Mother Margaret and I have said."

Nell didn't answer.

"Nell?"

"I promise," Nell said in a low voice.

Sister Helen squeezed Nell's shoulders then dropped her hands. "I will miss you," she said painfully.

"Oh, and I will miss you!"

At that, Sister Helen held out her arms once again and Nell went into them. Sister Helen held her tight. Nell could smell the faint aroma of herbs that always clung to Sister Helen's clothes. "Can I come and visit you?" she asked.

"You will always be welcome."

Finally Sister Helen relaxed her arms and Nell stepped back. The nun said briskly, "It is time for dinner. Let me take this pot off the fire and we can go up to the refectory."

Nell sniffed and nodded and waited while Sister Helen turned off the stove and removed the pot. Then the two women walked up the hill together.

Three

It was late in the afternoon and the Earl of Wiltshire and his grandson were returning from inspecting the defenses of the many castles and manors whose lords owed fealty to the earl. The Earl of Wiltshire was one of the most powerful men in the kingdom, the overlord of demesnes in Wiltshire, Dorset, Somerset, Hampshire, Surrey, Buckinghamshire, Hertfordshire and Oxfordshire. As the country was braced for a civil war to break out between King Stephen and his cousin, the Empress Mathilda, the earl had thought it important to visit the lords who owed their feudal duty to him and to remind them that the earl had pledged his loyalty to King Stephen.

As the contingent of knights crossed Salisbury plain on their return to the earl's main castle of Wilton, the sun shone on polished helmets and hauberks and shields, and the sheen of the horses' coats almost equaled the brightness of the men's armor. The summer day was breezy and the flag carried by the leading knight flew bravely. The jingle of the knights' spurs and armor could be heard all along the road as they passed. Behind them came the pack horses carrying the household goods the earl considered necessary when he traveled: one horse was loaded with his dismantled bed, sheets, blankets and mattress, another with his wardrobe, another with the wine he favored and others still with the various items that contributed to his comfort.

The old man turned to his twenty-two-year-old grandson and said, "It will be good to get home. We've been away a long time."

"It was early spring when we left and now it's deep summer," Roger replied. "But we had a good tour, I think."

"It is wise to show your face once in a while," the earl advised. "Remember that, my boy. There's nothing like a little inspection to keep a man honest."

"Yes, sir," Roger said.

"I'm looking forward to sitting in my own hall, though," the earl said. "I'm getting too old to be putting in so many hours in the saddle."

Roger grinned. "You have more stamina than half of the knights, sir."

"I put up a good front," the earl grunted. "When we get home we can turn our thoughts to your wedding."

Roger shifted his grip on the reins. "Ah, yes. The wedding. I still can't believe you got the king to agree to it."

"It was an enticement. He knows he needs to keep me loyal. If Wiltshire should go over to the empress it would be a catastrophe for Stephen. We hold sway over too much land for him to lose us."

Roger shook his head in amazement. "But to join the earldoms of Wiltshire and Lincoln! The de Roches will be the most powerful family in the kingdom."

The earl gave his grandson a sly smile. "I know. We will control all of Lincoln, as well as Wiltshire. We will sit astride the kingdom, Roger, as powerful as the king, and the Earl of Chester will be furious."

"The present Earl of Lincoln is still very much alive, sir," Roger pointed out. "The union of the two lordships won't happen until he is dead. Only then will his daughter inherit."

"Raoul de Bonvile wants what we want. He wants his blood to be foremost in the kingdom. That's why he agreed to the marriage."

They rode for a little way in silence, Roger's thoughts on his upcoming union to this unknown girl. At last he said, "I hope Sybilla is pretty."

"It doesn't matter what she looks like," the earl said. "What matters is what she brings to us. Earls do not marry for a pretty face, my boy, and you are the future earl."

There was a little silence. Then Roger replied, "Yes, sir, I know. But it would help if she was pretty."

"There's no reason why she shouldn't be pretty. Her mother is a very good-looking woman."

They rode in more silence until the earl said with satisfaction, "There is Wilton."

Roger looked up from his thoughts to the castle that had just come into sight. The first thing one saw upon approaching Wilton was the massive stone battlemented curtain wall, with its twin gate towers. Four other towers were set at the corners of each of the outer walls, and from the crenelated crests of each of these towers flew a crimson flag displaying the de Roche signature of a leopard.

"It's impregnable," the earl said with great satisfaction. It was a remark he made rather frequently. "The walls are fifteen feet thick. No siege artillery can breach them. Of all the castles we have seen in the past two months, nothing can match Wilton."

Roger nodded, sharing his pride. The home of the Earl of Wiltshire was the greatest castle, outside the royal castles, in the country. It was one of the reasons why his grandfather was so powerful.

Within a few minutes the earl's party passed over the moat, between the gate towers, under the raised portcullis and into the outer bailey. This courtyard contained stabling for the knights' horses, as well as the usual storehouses and buildings for workmen and castle defenders. There was even enough room in the huge bailey to house additional troops, should they be necessary for the castle's defense.

While the knights dismounted in the outer bailey, Roger and his grandfather continued on horseback toward the inner wall, which was also built of thick stone, with a second gate barred by another iron portcullis. A square tower stood at each of the four corners of these inner walls.

The knight on guard called out, "Welcome home, my lord," as the earl and his grandson rode through the gate and into the inner bailey. This courtyard surrounded the keep, a square stone edifice, four stories high, with four towers that rose another two stories above the main building.

Grooms came running to take the earl's and Roger's horses and the two men went up the steep stone ramp that led to the main door of the keep.

The first floor of the castle was given over to store-rooms, the second floor to guardrooms, where the knights lived, and the third floor to the Great Hall. Roger and his grandfather climbed one set of narrow stairs and entered into the hall where most of the activity in the castle took place.

The room was empty now, and no fire burned in the immense stone fireplace that was set on the far wall. The three other walls were hung with large wall hangings to keep out the damp and the floor was strewn with rushes and herbs. Two heavily carved chairs were placed on ei-ther side of the fireplace and in front of one of them a dog was sleeping.

"Gawain!" Roger cried, and the dog lifted his head. "It's me, fellow," Roger said. "I'm back."

As he recognized the beloved voice, the dog stood

up and raced across the floor to his master, barking excitedly as he ran. Roger squatted on his heels and the rush of the dog almost knocked him over. Roger laughed and tried to pat the dog, but Gawain was too excited to stand still. He circled Roger, still barking excitedly.

The earl said indulgently, "You would never know he was eleven years old."

Roger laughed. "He's like you, sir. He wears his age lightly."

Finally the dog calmed down enough to stand and let Roger pet him. "I'm sorry I had to leave you for so long," Roger said into the adoring brown eyes of the black-and-white mongrel. "But you're too old to come anymore. You couldn't keep up, fellow."

"It's just as well he doesn't come," the earl said. "I can imagine what my vassals would think when they saw that my grandson's dog is a notched-ear mongrel."

"He's the best dog in the world," Roger said without heat.

"He is a good dog," the earl agreed. "He's certainly devoted to you."

"He knows who loves him." Roger stood up and pulled off his helmet, revealing his dark gold hair. "It's still two hours before supper. Would you like a drink of wine, Grandfather?"

"That sounds like a very good idea. My poor old bones are sore from so many hours in the saddle."

The two men moved toward the chairs in front of the empty fireplace. The shutters were pushed back on the high, narrow windows to let in the afternoon sunlight. The door to the hall opened again to admit two pages.

"Come over here, lads, and disarm us," the earl called, and the two pages hurried over to them. Both men stood patiently while the boys undid the laces on their mail hauberks and pulled them over their heads. Each hauberk was made of leather, with more than two hundred thousand overlapping metal rings sewn on it for protection. Neither man was wearing the long-sleeved mail shirt or mail leggings that made up full armor.

When they had been stripped to the comfort and the coolness of their tunics, the earl and his grandson relaxed with their wine and enjoyed the comfort of their own hall. The door opened again and an elderly man came in.

"Simon," the earl called. "Come over here and tell us what has been happening in our absence."

Simon, who had been the earl's squire when he was a youngster and was now his steward, crossed the floor, a smile on his face. "My lord, how happy I am to see you safely returned."

"Thank you, it is good to be home."

Simon turned to Roger. "It is good to see you, also, my lord."

"How are you, Simon?" Roger returned. "How have your joints been holding up?"

"I am well, my lord. The sore joints, well, God has seen fit to burden me thusly and I must live with it."

The earl said, "Has anything happened in my absence that I should know about?"

"You received a missive from the Earl of Lincoln, my lord. It came last week. I knew you were coming home soon, so I didn't try to send it on to you. Shall I get it for you?"

"The Earl of Lincoln." The earl glanced at his grandson. "I wonder what this can be about."

"Perhaps it's something about the marriage," Roger said.

"Get the letter, Simon," the earl said.

"I have it in my own room, for safekeeping." The man began to move stiffly in the direction of one of the towers and Roger and the earl fell into conversation.

"The wedding must take place soon," the earl said. "Everyone will want it done before the empress Mathilda and her half brother, Robert of Gloucester, land in England to take up arms against King Stephen."

Roger agreed with his grandfather, agreed that the marriage was a great coup for the family, and was faintly ashamed that the idea of it made him so nervous. He was more comfortable talking about the political situation. "*If* the empress and her troops can land," he said. "Stephen is having all the major ports watched."

"England has too long a coastline to watch all the places where a ship might land," the earl said. "They will make the crossing from Normandy and land somewhere that Stephen isn't watching. Then they will make their way to Bristol, which is Robert's stronghold. From there they will send out their summons to those they hope will support them."

"Who do you think will answer that call, sir?"

"Brian fitz Count will probably join them, but most of the earls will play a waiting game. Men like Rannulf of Chester will want to see which side can offer him the most. They have no honor, men like that. They all swore an oath to uphold Stephen and now they are only looking out for themselves."

Didn't you do that, Roger thought, *when you forced the king to give the heiress of Lincoln to me in marriage to keep you loyal?*

But Roger would never say that to his grandfather.

The earl was going on. "Rannulf of Chester owns a quarter of the kingdom already, and he will be looking to increase his holdings. He will be furious when he learns that Stephen is giving us the earldom of Lincoln. Rannulf was hoping the prize of Lincoln would go to his half brother, William of Roumare. William has a number of castles in Lincolnshire."

Roger said, "You are supporting Stephen because you think he will be the best king for England, isn't that so, Grandfather?"

"Certainly," the earl replied. "Stephen is a man and a warrior and as direct a descendant of the Conqueror as Mathilda is. Mathilda may be the daughter of the old king, and Stephen just the nephew, but undoubtedly Stephen is the best man for England. The empress has never lived in England—the old king sent her to Germany to marry the emperor when she was a young child, and she has lived in Normandy ever since the emperor died. Her second husband, Geoffrey Plantagenet, is fighting for the rule of Normandy—he has little interest in England. It is Mathilda who wants England for her son."

At this point, Simon exited from the tower staircase and hurried toward them, a rolled piece of parchment in his hands. The earl gestured for him to give it to Roger.

"My old eyes can't see to read these days," he said. "Read it to me, my boy."

Roger read aloud: "Greetings to the Earl of Wiltshire from his brother, the Earl of Lincoln. I bring you sad news. My daughter Sybilla went home to God on the third of June of this year."

My God, she's dead! Shocked, Roger looked up from the letter and over to his grandfather.

The earl glowered. "Hell and damnation," he said. "This will spoil all our plans."

Roger shook his head as if to clear it, then looked back down at the paper. "There is more," he said, and began to read again. "Fortunately, this tragic news will not force us to cancel our plans. My other daughter Eleanor will take Sybilla's place. The marriage between Lincoln and Wiltshire can go forward as planned."

Roger looked up once more in bewilderment. "Another daughter? I thought the earl had only one."

His grandfather raised his thick gray brows. "So did I. I wonder where this Eleanor came from."

Roger felt a pang of uneasiness. There was something strange here. "Do you think there might be something the matter with her? That they kept her hidden for a reason?"

"I don't know," the earl said. "But I'm damned glad they had an extra daughter! This marriage will be the making of our family. I would be loath to give it up."

Roger wasn't listening. "I don't want to marry someone who is not right in the head! Or is deformed!"

The earl said crisply, "I don't care what is wrong with this girl, you will marry her because it is your duty to your family. All you have to do is get children on her. You can continue to pursue your other interests—like the silversmith's widow that you see in town. But marry the heiress to all of Lincoln you will."

"How do you know about Tordis?" Roger asked in surprise. "I never told you."

"I know everything," the earl said complacently. "Knowledge is power, my boy. That is another thing for you to remember.

"I will reply to Earl Raoul and tell him that we shall be happy to accept this other daughter," he continued. "I will also suggest that we get the two of you wed as soon as possible." The earl shuddered. "God, after all our careful plans, the whole scheme might have been lost because the girl died. How fortunate that they had this other daughter to bring forth."

Roger was having a hard time sharing his grandfather's enthusiasm. The thought of wedding a girl who had something wrong with her repulsed him. "Yes," he said glumly. "Very fortunate."

"Drink up, my boy, and don't look so disheartened,"

the earl recommended. "I married, like you, to advance the family, and the marriage turned out very well."

"What about my parents?" Roger asked. "Did my father marry for the sake of the family?"

"Your father never did anything but thwart me in every way he possibly could. We won't discuss him. You are the son of my heart, Roger. You are the child who will carry our name into the future." The earl lifted his cup. "God bless you, my boy."

It was the usual dismissive reply Earl William gave whenever Roger asked about his father. After so many years of being rebuffed, he knew enough not to pursue the subject.

Four

The first thing Lady Alice did to reclaim her daughter was to give her a bath and wash her hair. Nell had never been so embarrassed in her life. In the convent they had worn bath sheets, which went over the head and covered the sides of the tub like a tent, so that they could not see themselves naked. Lady Alice scorned the bath sheet. She had the servants set the big wooden bathtub up in a splash of sunshine from the window, and she herself set to work on her daughter. It was as if she thought she could scour all the years in the convent away from Nell if she scrubbed hard enough. Her hair was washed and rinsed three times before Lady Alice was satisfied.

The castle ladies had done a hasty job of taking up and taking in one of Sybilla's gowns, and Lady Alice dressed Nell in it once she had come out of the bath. Then her hair was toweled briskly and braided into two long plaits that would fall over her shoulders when they had completely dried.

"Take a look," Lady Alice said, handing Nell the first mirror she had ever seen. Nell peered in it cautiously, a little afraid of what she was going to find.

A girl with large, wary, dark blue eyes looked back at her. She had delicate eyebrows and a small, straight nose. There was color from the bath in her cheeks and her lips.

I'm pretty, Nell thought, and tried to squash the pleasure she felt at this discovery. Mother Margaret would say that worldly looks were not important and certainly were no measure of the worth of a person.

"You're a very pretty girl, my dear," Lady Alida said.

"Yes, you are," Lady Alice agreed. "You don't look like Sybilla, you look more like your grandmother—my mother. She was small and delicate, like you. But she ran a great household and raised a family at the same time, and so will you, Nell."

I'm not Sybilla, even though I am wearing her dress, Nell thought, clenching her teeth. *I'm Nell. I was brought up in a convent. I know nothing of how to run a great household. I don't want to be married. I don't want to run a great household. I want to go home.*

But the convent was closed to her. As miserable as it made her, she was going to have to remain here at Bardney.

Over the next week, Nell attended meals and helped her mother and the ladies sew her new wardrobe. In the evenings she sat in front of the fire and listened to one of the squires play the lute. Outwardly she was docile and obedient to her parents, but inside she was grieving for the loss of her old life, for the loss of Sister Helen. At night she would kneel on the wooden floor of her room to say her prayers and ask the Lord to send her back to St. Cecelia's. Then, almost as an afterthought, she would pray dutifully, *If it is your will that I stay here, Lord, help me to learn to love my mother and my father. Help me to be a good daughter and to do good works in this strange place.*

Then she would get into bed, loneliness engulfing her heart, and cry herself to sleep.

Ten days after Nell's arrival at Bardney, the Earl of Lincoln's usher approached the high table to tell the earl that his messenger had returned from Wiltshire with a reply.

"Send him to me," the earl said, returning the piece of meat he had been about to eat back to his trencher. Nell, who was sitting between her mother and her aunt, heard the usher's announcement but didn't think much of it. She chewed slowly on her beef and didn't notice the way her mother had stiffened.

The messenger came into the hall still wearing his spurs and carrying his helmet under one arm. He threaded his way between the trestle tables where the household was dining until he stood in front of Lord Raoul. He bowed his head. "My lord," he said, "I bring you the reply to your missive. The Earl of Wiltshire bade me give it directly into your hand."

"Thank you, Waldo," the earl replied and took the rolled parchment from his messenger's hand. "Sit you down and have some dinner."

"Thank you, my lord."

Nell watched as the messenger found an empty place at one of the tables. He was greeted genially by his fellow diners, and a servant came scurrying with a trencher for him to put his meat upon. Another servant poured him some ale.

Nell looked back at her plate. There was so much meat served in her father's house! In the convent, meat had been a luxury. Fish had been the food of choice, either caught fresh from the river or salted and dried.

Conversation at the high table was suspended while the earl read his letter. Then he rolled it up again and put it on the table next to his wineglass. He turned to his wife.

"All is well," he said. "They want to proceed as quickly as possible."

Lady Alice glanced at Nell. "It might be wise to wait a little, my lord."

The earl shook his head. "This is a great matter, not something to be delayed because of a girl's sensibilities. I will write to Lord William that we will be ready to receive him in two weeks' time."

Lady Alice did not reply.

"You haven't seen the falcons yet, Nell," Alida said

brightly to Nell. "After dinner why don't you come with me to look at them?"

Nell looked at her aunt. "That would be nice, Aunt Alida. Thank you."

There was a smile on Lord Raoul's lips. "A little more wine here, if you please," he called heartily. One of the squires who was standing behind the table hastened forward with the wine for his lord.

Lord Raoul took a deep swallow, then he turned to Nell. "Never mind the falcons. Your mother and I want to talk to you after dinner, Nell. You will attend us in the family solar."

"Yes, Father," Nell said with some surprise. Her father had paid very little attention to her since she had come home.

When dinner was finished, mother, father and daughter climbed the stairs to the tower room that was the private family solar. The room was well furnished and comfortable, with a charcoal brazier for heat in the winter. The earl sat in a wide, carved, high-backed chair and his wife sat beside him. Her father waved Nell to a third chair that faced his. The chair was so high that Nell's feet would not reach the ground, so she placed them on the embroidered footstool that was in front of it.

The earl began. "Nell, have you heard that your sister was betrothed to the grandson and heir of the Earl of Wiltshire?"

Nell clasped her hands tensely in her lap. She sensed

that something big was forthcoming. "No, my lord," she replied. "I did not know that."

"The earldom of Wiltshire is very large," her father explained. "And once the holdings of Wiltshire are combined with the holdings of Lincoln… Well, the man who holds that combined title will be almost as powerful as the king. So you can see that this marriage is a great thing for our house."

Nell's heart had begun to thud. She glanced at her mother. The countess was looking at her with an expression of pity in her eyes. Terror struck Nell's heart. She thought she knew what was coming.

The earl continued on. "Sybilla's death was a blow to my hopes, but fortunately I have another daughter. I wrote to the Earl of Wiltshire and today I have had his response. He is willing to see you wed to his grandson in place of Sybilla."

Nell felt herself grow icy cold. She tried to speak and found she could not.

Her father said, "Earl William wants to see this marriage accomplished as soon as possible. I am going to write to tell him that we will be ready to receive him in two weeks' time, on the date we set for the original wedding."

"Her wardrobe will not be ready, my lord," her mother interjected. "Surely we can put it off for a month at least."

"That is not possible," the earl said. "You were making clothes for Sybilla. Nell can wear those."

Nell turned to her mother. "Mama, I am not ready to get married!"

Her mother said softly, "I am sorry this must come upon you so quickly, Nell. But you are the daughter of a great house. You must do your duty, I'm afraid."

Nell could feel herself trembling. "You didn't care about me when I was a child—you sent me away to the convent and forgot about me." Her voice shook with anger. "And now you talk to me about my duty to my house? My duty is to God."

The earl's face darkened with anger. "Your duty is to obey your parents. I believe the Commandments—*God's* Commandments—are very clear about that. And I tell you that you will marry Roger de Roche in two weeks' time. That is all I have to say on this matter." The earl stood up. His dark blue eyes looked very cold.

"Talk to your daughter," he said to his wife.

Both women sat in silence as the earl exited from the room. Then Nell turned white-faced to her mother. "I don't want to get married so soon, Mama! I don't know anything about men. I have scarcely left the convent."

Lady Alice leaned over and patted Nell's clasped hands. "I know, my dear. But your father is set upon this great dynastic match and he won't risk something happening to stop it. There is nothing I can say or do that will make him change his mind."

Nell started to tremble all over. "I still feel a stranger at Bardney, and I have you and Aunt Alida. It will be terrible going to another castle, where I won't know anyone."

"Girls do it all the time, my dear. Perhaps Alida would go to stay with you for a few months."

Nell didn't say anything, she just continued to tremble.

"Sybilla was looking forward to this marriage," Alice said brightly. "You will be a very great lady, Nell. You will have brought Lincoln, with all its castles and manors, into your husband's keeping. He will reverence you for that."

This can't be happening, Nell thought with terror. She looked imploringly at her mother. "I'm just not ready for this, Mama," she whispered.

Lady Alice came to sit on the arm of Nell's chair and hugged her. "I will help you get ready," she promised. "And, Nell, you must know it was very painful for me to send my little girl off to the convent. If I hadn't thought that it was God's will I could never have done it. And I missed you. Sybilla and Geoffrey could never fill the gap that you left."

Nell turned her head and looked into her mother's eyes. "Is that true?"

"Yes."

"You used to come to visit me, but then you stopped."

"Your father thought that I should leave you to the convent and not keep reasserting other ties. I could see that you were happy where you were, so I left you to immerse yourself in convent life. It was hard for me to do that, Nell. You may not believe that, but it was. Just as it was hard for me to send Geoffrey to be a squire in the Earl of Hertford's castle. But that is the fate of a mother. You will find that out for yourself one day. We bear children, we love them, and then we must send them away to be brought up by other people. That is the way of the world, my dear. There is no use in railing against it."

Nell thought it sounded like a dismal life. The convent, with its structured life, its warm, continuing friendships, was much more desirable.

"I don't think I like the world, Mama," she said in a little voice.

Her mother smiled. "You know nothing about the world, my dear. It may not be as safe as your convent, but it is brimming with life and love. Open yourself to life, Nell. Embrace it. Don't look backwards. Don't be afraid. Your future is an adventure where you might find happiness you never dreamed of. Give it a chance. Will you do that for me, sweeting?"

They're making me marry a stranger, they're sending me away again, and they want me to be happy?

Nell stared at her lap and didn't answer.

Lady Alice started toward the door and after a moment Nell followed. *I don't want to get married,* she thought desperately. *I don't want to get married.*

But it was clear that her thoughts and feelings were of no matter to her father. *It would serve him right if I died, too,* she thought.

She fought back tears as she went with her mother

down the stairs to the Great Hall. In her mind she turned for solace to the only friend she had. *Dear God,* she prayed, *if it is your will that I marry this man, please give me the courage to face what must be faced. I beg you to help me, Father. I don't know how I will be able to get through this alone.*

Five

For Nell, the time until the date set for her marriage went by far too quickly. Every morning she woke up thinking, *I'm another day closer to my wedding.* And her stomach would churn and wouldn't stop churning until she finally fell asleep again at night. She had no appetite and she lost weight, to the dismay of the ladies who were altering Sybilla's clothes to fit her.

"You must eat," her mother scolded her one afternoon as they sat at the table for dinner.

Nell looked at the food on her plate and her stomach heaved. "I'm not hungry, Mama," she said.

Her mother said worriedly, "You didn't have any weight to spare when you first arrived here, and this refusal to eat is making you look like the daughter of a poverty-stricken house."

The earl, who had been in conversation with his

chaplain, turned his head. "What is the matter here?" he asked his wife.

Lady Alice hesitated, then she said, "Nell is not eating properly, my lord. She grows too thin."

The earl frowned at Nell. "What is the matter with you? The food at Bardney is of the best."

"The food here is wonderful, Father," Nell said quickly. "It's just that I am not hungry."

"If you are fasting, I am here to tell you that this is not the time. You are not a religious any longer, Nell. You are my daughter and I want you to eat."

He turned to the chaplain. "Tell her, Father, that it is not appropriate for her to fast."

Before the priest could speak, Nell said quickly, "I'm not fasting, Father. I'm just not hungry."

"I don't care if you are hungry or not. You will eat," the earl said.

Nell's stomach heaved at the thought. "I don't think I can," she said.

"Nonsense." The earl scowled at her. "Pick up a piece of pork and eat it."

Nell picked up the pork with her fingers. She looked at her mother. "It won't harm you," Lady Alice said. "Go ahead and eat it."

Nell put the meat into her mouth. She chewed twice. Her stomach heaved and she shoved back her bench, got up and ran for the stairs. She threw up in the rushes before she was halfway there.

She heard her father curse.

Nell wrapped her arms around herself and stayed where she was. She had never felt so humiliated in her entire life. She had vomited in front of everyone! She shuddered and squeezed her eyes shut so she wouldn't have to look at the disgusting mess on the floor.

"It's all right, Nell." It was Aunt Alida's voice close to her shoulder. "Martin will have someone clean it up. Come along with me and we'll go upstairs."

"You will both stay right here." It was her father's voice. "Nell may have gotten away with such behavior in the convent, but it won't work here. If she doesn't want to eat, that's her choice. But she will sit with her family at dinner regardless of what she eats herself."

Aunt Alida took her hand and squeezed it gently. "Come and have something to drink," she said in a low voice. "Your mouth must taste terrible."

I hate him, Nell thought. *He doesn't care about me at all. All he cares about is getting the earldom of Wiltshire.*

She dropped her head so she would not have to look at anyone and let her aunt turn her and lead her back to the table.

The wedding party arrived at Bardney two afternoons before the wedding was to take place. Nell was in the ladies' solar when a page came to inform them of her bridegroom's arrival and to summon Lady Alice and Nell to the Great Hall. Nell was already dressed in her new finery, a fine white linen undertunic with embroidery at the cuffs and neck, and over it a dark blue overtunic, fitted closely to the waist from which it flowed out freely. Wrapped twice around her narrow waist she wore a jeweled belt and her two long brown plaits fell across her shoulders and almost touched the belt.

Nell felt numb as she walked with her mother down the main staircase that led into the Great Hall. She could scarcely even pray; all she could think was *Please God, please God, please God...*

The visitors were standing with her father in front of the fireplace. One of the men was tall; the other was of medium height. And slim.

That must be Roger, Nell thought.

With her eyes on the floor, she walked with her mother across the hall. When they had almost reached the fireplace her father stepped forward and offered her his arm. Thus supported, she was brought to meet her bridegroom.

"Earl William and Lord Roger," her father said. "I am pleased to introduce to you my daughter, Eleanor."

Nell curtsied to the earl, then turned to Roger. For the first time she lifted her eyes.

He was very handsome. His hair was dark gold and his eyes were golden, as well. She thought they bore an expression of relief.

"My lord," she managed to say. "You are welcome to Bardney."

"I am pleased to be here, my lady," he replied, and smiled at her. He had a nice smile; his teeth were white and even.

Nell tried and failed to smile back.

Everyone, including the pages who sat on a bench along the wall, watched the two of them. Nell turned to her mother for help.

"Nell, why don't you show Lord Roger around the bailey?" Lady Alice suggested. "I'm sure you two young people would like to spend some time together."

The last thing Nell wanted was to be alone with her future husband. She gave her mother a reproachful look, but it was too late. The words had been spoken.

"Would you like to see the bailey, my lord?" she asked Roger. Her eyes were on a level with his mouth. At least he didn't tower over her, like her father did.

"I would like that very much," he said. He sounded courteous and she peeked a look upward. His eyes were grave.

"Go along, Nell," her father said. "Be sure to show Roger my horses."

"Yes, Father," Nell said. Then to Roger, "Will you come with me?"

He fell in beside her and together they crossed the wide expanse of the Great Hall. Nell could feel everyone watch them as they went.

"I'm afraid I'm not overly acquainted with the bailey, my lord," Nell said as they approached the door, "but I'll do my best to show you around."

"Are you called Nell?" he asked.

"Yes. My given name is Eleanor, but I have always been called Nell."

He nodded. "Well then, Nell, why are you not acquainted with the bailey of your own castle?"

Her name sounded strange on this strange man's lips. She said, "I have only been home for a month, my lord, and we have been busy making wedding clothes the whole time."

They had arrived at the front door of the castle, which was open to let in the air. He looked at her curiously. "If you were not at Bardney all this time, then where were you?"

They walked through the door and started across the inner bailey, toward the portcullis gate. She shot him a swift, upward look. "They haven't told you?"

He shook his head. Gold glinted from his hair in the sunlight. "They have told me nothing," he said. "It seemed as if your father produced you out of nowhere, like a magician. My grandfather and I had always thought that Sybilla was an only daughter."

Nell drew in a deep, steadying breath. "I was in the convent," she said. "My parents sent me there when my brother was born. Then, when Sybilla died, they changed their minds."

Roger was silent as they passed under the lifted portcullis gate. As they emerged into the large enclosure that was the outer bailey, he said slowly, "So that was the mystery. We wondered where this other daughter had come from."

"I can't imagine why they didn't tell you," Nell said.

He looked down at her. "I suppose your parents

didn't think it was important and my grandfather didn't care. All that mattered to him was that there was another daughter." He gave her a fleeting grin. "But I wondered where you had come from. I had a few unpleasant ideas, I can tell you that."

He had a very nice speaking voice, very clear but not harsh. Not like her father's.

He continued to look down at her. "Were you a nun?" he asked.

She shook her head. "I was due to be professed at the end of this year."

The August sun shone brightly on the packed-dirt ground of the bailey. The blue flags flying from the towers fluttered in the afternoon breeze. The men guarding the main gate watched them as they turned left to follow the line of the wall. "How old were you when you were sent to the convent?" Roger asked.

"Eight," she replied.

"You were there a long time," he said, sounding surprised.

"Yes. It is the only life I ever knew until I came to Bardney a few weeks ago."

He looked at her thoughtfully. "Did you want to leave?"

She returned his gaze straightly. "No, I did not."

Wonderful, Roger thought ironically. *They are marrying me to a girl who wants to be a nun.*

Nell looked around. "My father wants me to take you to the stable, but I've never been out of this front part of the bailey. I don't know where the stable is."

Roger looked around at the storage sheds and craftsmen's workshops that lined the stone walls in this part of the bailey. He said, "Let's walk around the whole bailey and we're certain to find it."

They began walking toward the east side of the bailey, with Roger accommodating his stride to Nell's shorter step.

Roger said, "Have they explained to you the reason for this marriage?"

"Yes," Nell said shortly. "It is political."

"It's more than political," he explained. "It's dynastic. One day your son will be the Earl of Wiltshire and the Earl of Lincoln. It will be a position of unparalleled power in the kingdom. When Sybilla died, I imagine your father could not give it up."

"No, he couldn't," Nell said bitterly. "And I don't care much about dynasties." She glanced up at him. He was looking straight ahead. His profile was cleanly cut, with high cheekbones and a strong jaw. He really was extraordinarily good looking.

"You would care if you had lived in the world," he said.

They passed the mews, where the earl's falcons were housed. The head falconer was standing in front of it with a bird perched on his wrist. He tugged at his forelock as Nell and Roger went by.

"Do *you* want this marriage?" she asked directly.

"Yes," he replied quietly. "My grandfather says it is a great opportunity for our house, and I agree. It is a great opportunity for both our houses, Nell."

They walked in silence for a few paces.

In two days time I will be married to this man, Nell thought. A panicky feeling tightened her chest and her stomach. *I will have to go with him back to his castle.*

They turned the corner of the inner wall and saw several small fenced-in enclosures where horses were turned out. "Here are the stables," Roger said, sounding relieved.

They walked up to the wooden building that was built against the stone outer wall of the bailey. It was a large structure that held the horses of forty knights. The smell of manure hung in the warm summer air. Two grooms were carrying water buckets from the well and Roger called to them, "Find me the head groom. We are here to see Earl Raoul's horses."

"Yes, my lord." The grooms carried the water into the stable building and shortly thereafter a thin, red-haired man dressed in a plain brown tunic and cross-gartered leggings came out and hastened to join them.

Roger said, "I am Lord Roger de Roche and Earl Raoul has sent me to see his horses." His voice was pleasant, not demanding.

"Yes, my lord." The red-haired man beamed. "Lord Raoul's mount is the finest stallion you'll ever have seen, my lord. And he has a colt out of him by a splendid mare. Those are the horses you'll be wanting to see."

The horses were brought, the big chestnut stallion immediately intimidating Nell by rearing, and a bay mare with a chestnut colt at her side that was the image of his sire.

Nell kept her distance from the horses, making sure not to come too close to those iron-shod hooves. Roger walked right up to the stallion however, and got him to stand by simply telling him to do so. Nell couldn't help being impressed. He then went over the entire animal, even running his hand down each hard leg. He checked over the mare and the colt in the same fashion.

"You're right," he said to the head groom. "These are superior horses. No wonder Earl Raoul is proud of them."

The redhead grinned.

"Thank you for showing them to us," Roger said.

Nell looked at him. She liked it that Roger had thanked the head groom. Her father never thanked the people who worked for him, but Mother Superior always did. She had said that everyone is loved by God, and we should never forget to give people the respect that they deserve.

They continued their walk around the bailey, past the archery butts where the knights were practicing, past the kitchen garden where the vegetables for the household were grown, past the lines of laundered clothes that were hung out to dry.

As they walked, Roger's mind grappled with the situation that faced him. He was to wed a girl who might not be willing. This was not a possibility that had ever occurred to him. In its own way, it presented as many difficulties as if she had turned out to be strange in the head.

He had to address it. She was very pretty and he

would like to marry her, but something in him recoiled from taking a woman against her will.

He put his hand on her arm and stopped her. They turned to face each other in the sunshine. "Nell," he began carefully, "I don't know if you know this, but the Pope has ruled that a woman cannot be forced to marry against her will. You can appeal to the church if that is the case. So let me ask you now, are you making this marriage willingly?"

No, I'm not, was her immediate reaction.

But she couldn't answer him that way. The convent was closed to her; there was no place else for her to go. She shuddered at the thought of confronting her father with the news that she had told this man she wouldn't marry him. She couldn't defy her father. She didn't have it in her.

She looked at her hands, which were clasped over her gold belt. "Yes," she said in such a low voice that he had to bend his head to hear her. "I am marrying you willingly, my lord."

"Are you sure?"

Tears stung behind her eyes. It occurred to her that he was the only person so far who had cared how she felt. "Yes," she whispered. "I'm sure."

"All right," he said. He lifted her chin with his thumb, so she had to look up into his face. He smiled at her. "I'm not such a bad fellow, Nell. There's no reason why we shouldn't get along."

Her lips trembled and she blinked away her tears. "I will try to be a good wife to you, my lord."

"And I will try to be a good husband to you." He bent from his superior height and touched his lips to her cheek. "You're a beautiful girl," he said. "I consider myself a lucky man."

Nell didn't feel lucky, but it occurred to her that things could be worse. At least Roger seemed kind.

She said in a low voice, "You will have to be patient with me. I know very little of the ways of the world."

He took her hand into his. "Don't worry, little Nell," he said. "I will take care of you. Everything is going to be all right."

Six

Nell retired to her bedroom that evening with a hard knot of tension in her stomach. What had once been marriage in the abstract had suddenly become very real.

Gertrude, the handmaid who had been serving her since she'd come home, helped her to disrobe. Most of the Norman upper class slept naked, but Nell had worn a nightgown in the convent, and she continued to cling to this custom.

Gertrude was brushing her hair when her mother came into the room. "I want to talk to you, Nell," Lady Alice said.

Gertrude curtsied to Lady Alice and left mother and daughter alone.

Lady Alice went to sit beside Nell on the bed. She picked up her daughter's hand. "Roger is a very handsome lad," she said. "I foresee a happy future for you, Nell."

"He seems nice," Nell said woodenly.

"Tomorrow we will go into Lincoln and the day after that you will be married. This may be the last time I have a chance to speak to you privately." She squeezed Nell's hand gently. "I think I should tell you about what happens between a man and a woman when they are wed. I have a feeling that you are completely innocent of this matter and I don't want you to be shocked on your wedding night."

Nell looked at the flowing white linen that was draped over her knees and didn't answer.

Lady Alice said, "Do you know how a man and a woman make a baby?"

Nell shook her head and continued to look at her lap.

Her mother then described the act of lovemaking, and what Nell was to expect on her wedding night. Nell was speechless, unable to comprehend what she was hearing.

"It's not so bad," her mother said. "I know it probably sounds frightening to you, but it can be pleasurable, Nell."

Nell thought it sounded terrible. This man, whom she scarcely knew, was going to do this to her? She looked at her mother. "Mama," she said hoarsely, "I'm not ready to do that yet."

Lady Alice shook her head. "I wish we could have waited for a while to have this wedding. You are too new from the convent to appreciate how lucky you are to be marrying a fine young man like Roger. But the men wouldn't wait and you are just going to have to resign yourself, my dear. You are going to have to let Roger do what he wants—that is the nature of marriage, I'm afraid."

Nell's stomach heaved. "The basin," she said. "Mama…"

Lady Alice grabbed the washbasin that reposed on Nell's side table and Nell vomited into it.

"You can't do this tomorrow, Nell," she said sharply. "I sympathize with you, but you are going to have to do your duty. At least you are not going to an old man with sour breath and no hair. Your bridegroom is the kind of young man that most girls would give anything to marry. Show some backbone."

"I'm sorry, Mama," Nell said miserably.

"Perhaps I shouldn't have spoken to you tonight. Perhaps I should have let you find out for yourself."

Nell shook her head. "No. I'm glad you told me. At least I can prepare myself now."

"That's my good girl." Lady Alice stood up. "Now let's get Gertrude to clean up this mess."

After Lady Alice had left and the washbasin had been removed, Nell crawled into bed and curled up into a tight little ball. Roger's words from this afternoon kept going through her mind. *The Pope has decreed that no one can force a woman to marry against her will.*

What if she cited this proclamation by the Pope? What if she refused to make this marriage?

She thought of how angry her father would be.

She thought of what Mother Superior and Sister Helen had said to her.

She thought of her mother.

Show some backbone, her mother had said.

She shut her eyes tightly. She would have to go through with it. There was really no choice.

Roger awoke with the sun the following morning. Today he, his grandfather and their retainers would process into Lincoln to spend the night at the sheriff's quarters in the castle. They would be followed an hour later by Nell and her wedding party, who would spend the night in the bishop's lodging. On the morrow the bishop would perform the ceremony that would wed him to Nell de Bonvile.

She's so pretty, Roger thought as he stretched his arms comfortably above his head. Her eyes were beautiful—so dark and yet so blue. And she was shy.

I can handle shyness, he thought. *I'll get Lady Mabel to take her under her wing and show her what her duties will be as my wife.* Lady Mabel was married to Simon Everard, the earl's steward, and she was in charge of the few ladies who currently resided at Wilton castle.

Roger was placed next to Nell at the high table for breakfast. He smiled down into her pale face. "Just think, tomorrow at this time we will be getting married."

Nell went even paler. "Yes," she said faintly.

His smile faded. "Are you ill? You don't look well."

"I'm fine. I didn't sleep well, that is all."

Roger had slept soundly; he usually did, no matter where his bed might be. "We're leaving right after breakfast," he said now. "I won't see you again until we meet at the church."

Nell nodded. She had taken scarcely a bite of the fresh white bread that was in front of her. "Are you nervous?" Roger asked.

She produced a faint smile. "Yes. I'm not used to being the center of attention."

He gave her a reassuring smile in return. "Everything will be all right. You'll see."

"I'm sure it will be," she said in a low voice.

She was as pretty this morning as he'd remembered, he thought. Her skin was flawless in the sunlight coming in through the high windows of the hall. *She's frightened,* he thought. *I'll have to be very careful with her.*

The bridegroom's party left Bardney directly after breakfast. Nell looked out the window as the wedding party lined up in the outer bailey. The knights leading the party wore armor, but Roger and his grandfather were dressed in fine tunics, flowing mantles and low, soft boots. Their heads were bare and Roger carried a bag of coins to fling to any bystanders they might pass along the way.

The sun reflected off Roger's hair, making it shine like one of the golden coins he carried.

"He's so handsome." Marie, one of the ladies, came up behind her. "You're so lucky, Nell."

She sounded wistful. Nell realized that Marie wished *she* was the one marrying Roger tomorrow. Well, Nell wished that, too. "Yes," she replied quietly. "He is very handsome."

Lady Alice came into the room. "Come along, Nell, and get dressed. We have to make a show for the common folk. They will be lining the road to see you."

"Yes, Mama," Nell said dully, and turned to follow her mother out of the room.

Nell's wedding day dawned overcast and damp.

"At least it isn't raining," Lady Alice said brightly as she and Lord Raoul walked beside Nell to the cathedral. They were all dressed in their best finery, with Nell wearing a deep blue overtunic over a red undertunic. It was Sybilla's dress, redone to fit Nell. Lord Raoul and Lady Alice also looked richly colored and sumptuous. They all wore mantles suspended around their shoulders by gold chains, and Nell's braids were entwined with gold thread and fastened with golden balls. She was bareheaded while Lady Alice wore a small veil anchored by a thin gold circle.

Lord Raoul looked down upon his daughter with approval. "You look very nice, Nell," he said. "Roger will think himself a lucky man to be getting such a pretty bride along with an earldom."

"Thank you, Father," Nell said in a voice that was scarcely audible.

"You need some color in your cheeks, though," he said.

"Here." Lady Alice stepped in front of Nell so she had to stop, then she pinched her daughter's cheeks. "There," she said. "That's better."

The Bail of the castle was filled with people waiting

to catch a glimpse of the bride. *Thank goodness the bishop's residence is right next to the cathedral,* Nell thought. She didn't feel prepared to run the gamut of a large, noisy crowd.

"Ah, isn't she lovely," a woman's voice called out. "Good luck to you, dearie."

The crowd murmured agreement.

Then they were walking up the steps of the cathedral and into the large stone building. Martin Demas, Bardney's steward, was standing in the vestibule waiting for them. Lord Raoul cracked the door into the church and peered in.

"It's full," he reported proudly. "Looks like all of our and Wilton's vassals in the area came."

"That they did, my lord," Martin said.

Nell shivered a little and crossed her arms over her blue tunic.

This can't be happening to me. I can't be standing here, waiting to get married. Oh, God, why did Sybilla have to die?

Nell wet her lips with her tongue. "Where is Roger?" she asked.

Her father looked through the door again. "He just came out to stand beside the altar."

Lady Alice said, "I should take my place."

The steward came to her. "I will escort you down the aisle, my lady."

"Thank you," Lady Alice said.

Nell stood, her arms crossed over her chest, as her

mother left the vestibule to walk down the church aisle. Lord Raoul watched through the partially open door. When Lady Alice was finally seated, the cathedral choir began to sing an unaccompanied Gregorian chant.

"That's our signal," the earl said. He offered Nell his arm. She put her small hand on it and together they entered the church and began to proceed down the aisle.

Nell felt like a helpless animal being led to the slaughter. She could feel the people looking at her from either side, but she stared ahead at the bishop, who was waiting for her at the top of the aisle. He was magnificently dressed in gold vestments, with his white miter hat making him look very tall. He was flanked by six altar servers who were dressed in crisp white cassocks.

What if I told the bishop that I was being coerced into this marriage? What would he do?

Nell and her father stopped before the bishop and Roger came to join them.

The bishop raised his hands and the singing stopped. He spoke clearly, so he could be heard throughout the church. "We are gathered here today to join these two young people in a yoke of concord and an indissoluble chain of peace. This union is blessed by God and is as holy and sacred as is Christ's love for his bride, the church. It is not to be taken lightly or unadvisedly." He looked from Roger to Nell. "Do you understand this?" he asked, his face stern.

"We do," Roger said and, after a brief moment, Nell echoed his words.

The bishop next looked at Lord Raoul. "Who is it who gives this woman in marriage to this man?"

"I do," Lord Raoul said firmly.

"Do you swear that there is no known reason why this couple may not be joined in holy matrimony?"

I could speak up now, Nell thought wildly. *I could tell the bishop I am not willing....*

She almost opened her mouth, but then her father said, "I swear that there is no reason why this couple may not be joined in holy matrimony."

The words of denial just wouldn't come.

The bishop looked to Roger. "You may take the bride's hand."

I am being handed over from one to the other, just like a piece of chattel, Nell thought despairingly.

Roger reached out and took Nell's hand into his. His large grasp felt warm around her frozen fingers.

She stood next to Roger and they listened as the bishop read to the church the Old Testament passage about the creation of the world: "God created man in His image, in the divine image He created him, male and female He created them. God blessed them, saying, 'Be fertile and multiply; fill the earth and subdue it.'"

The bishop made the sign of the cross over them, and Roger and Nell turned to take their places at the kneelers on the altar. The bishop started the mass.

The familiar Latin words rolled over Nell, but her mind was on the reading the bishop had just given. The purpose of marriage was procreation. She remembered what her mother had told her about how babies were conceived, and she shuddered. How could she endure such a violation of her modesty?

Her attention went back to the mass when the bishop mounted the pulpit.

The bishop began reading from the book of Matthew: "When Jesus finished these words, he left Galilee and went to the district of Judea across the Jordan. Great crowds followed him, and he cured them there. Some Pharisees approached him, and tested him, saying, 'Is it lawful for a man to divorce his wife for any cause whatever?' He said in reply, 'Have you not read that from the beginning the Creator made them male and female and said, "For this reason a man shall leave his father and mother and be joined to his wife, and the two shall become one flesh?"' So they are no longer two, but one flesh. Therefore, what God has joined together, no human being must separate."

Marriage is a sacrament blessed by God, Nell told herself. *This is a holy thing I am doing.*

But I always thought I would be a bride of Christ, not of a man! Sybilla should be making this marriage, not me. I should be back in the convent, where I belong, not here, being wed to this stranger.

Now the bishop was coming to the center of the altar to stand in front of them. "My brother and sister in Christ," he said. "You have come here today to ask the church's blessing on your marriage. Marriage was ordained by God for the procreation of children, to avoid fornication and for the mutual help and comfort that one might have of the other. Therefore I must ask of you, do you Roger de Roche, take this woman to be your wedded wife?"

"I do," Roger answered firmly.

"Do you pledge to care for her, to comfort her, to be faithful to her all the days of your life?"

"I do," Roger answered again.

The bishop turned to Nell. "Do you, Eleanor de Bonvile, take this man to be your wedded husband?"

There was a pause. *I could say no*, she thought. But she didn't have the nerve. "I do," she said in a voice that was scarcely audible.

"Do you pledge to care for him, to comfort him, to be faithful to him all the days of your life?"

"I do," Nell said.

"Do you have the ring?" the bishop asked Roger, who took a plain gold band from a pouch on his belt.

"You may put it on her finger," the bishop said.

Roger took Nell's small, cold hand into his and slid the ring on her finger. It was too big and she had to close her fist to keep it on.

The bishop then spoke to the assembly in the church. "In as much as Roger and Eleanor have consented together in holy wedlock, and have witnessed to it before God and this company, and have given and pledged their lives to each other, and have declared the same by the giving and receiving of a ring, I pronounce that they be man and wife. In the Name of the Father and of the Son and of the Holy Ghost. Amen."

Roger turned his head and smiled down at Nell. She did not smile back.

It's done, she thought bleakly. *It's been sealed by the bishop in front of all these people. I'm married to Roger de Roche.*

Nell listened to the familiar prayers, but she felt detached from it all. She felt numb. It was as though all of this were happening to someone else and all she was doing was looking on. Even when she received the host upon her tongue and bent her head to pray, she felt a distance. This had always been one of her favorite moments of the day; she had felt so close to Christ when she received Him into her own body. But now her words seemed perfunctory, not deeply felt as they usually were. "Help me, Jesus," she prayed automatically. "Please help me."

Finally the mass was over and the bishop was coming to stand before them once more. It was time for the last blessing. He raised his hands and began to pray.

The spectator that was Nell bowed her head. Then the six altar servers lined up to process out, and the bishop fell in behind them. Roger gave Nell his arm and they took their places behind the bishop. The choir once more began to chant as the procession moved down the center aisle of the cathedral.

The wedding was over. They joined their families in the vestibule and, after much congratulations, they walked over to the bishop's residence where the wedding supper was to be held. Nell's hand rested on the fine linen of Roger's sleeve. *It's done,* she thought sadly. *I'm married.* She walked beside Roger like an animated doll. *I've been handed over from my father to Roger. The life I knew is gone for good.*

Seven

The wedding supper was held in the bishop's private dining room and was attended by the bishop, Nell and Roger, Earl Raoul, Lady Alice, and Roger's grandfather, Earl William. The rest of the congregation was being fed in the sheriff's quarters in the castle. Behind each of the guests was a squire from Bardney, ready to serve each course as it came out of the kitchen, to fetch more wine, and to bring ewers and basins so they could wash their hands. The Norman aristocracy was fastidious about cleanliness, and since they ate with their hands and shared dishes, etiquette decreed that hands and nails must be kept scrupulously clean at table.

The men carried on the conversation and the talk was about the expected landing of the Empress Mathilda on English soil.

"Stephen has men in position at all the main ports," the bishop said. "If she tries to land, she will be turned back."

"There are dozens of small ports along the English coast where she may come in," Lord Raoul said. "I doubt she'll try to land at some place like Dover."

"Robert of Gloucester is too smart to try to come in at a main port," Lord William agreed. Robert, Earl of Gloucester, was the empress's powerful bastard half brother. He was the chief English champion of her cause and her main adviser.

"How many men do you think will come with her?" Roger asked.

"I don't know," Lord Raoul said. "I don't think her husband will want to give up any of his men, not while he is engaged in the conquest of Normandy. It's Mathilda who wants England, not Geoffrey Plantagenet."

"She wants the crown of England for her son," Lord William said.

"Aye," Lord Raoul agreed. "Just as Stephen wants to keep it for his own son."

Roger dipped his meat into the dish of sauce that was between him and Nell. "What do you think will happen when she does land?" he asked.

"We'll have to wait and see how many barons go over to her side," Lord Raoul replied.

Roger brought the piece of meat back to his trencher. "Brian fitz Count has always been one of her supporters."

"Yes," Lord Raoul said. "And a few men from the west may go over to support Gloucester. That's where she's going to find her chief support—in the west."

Nell listened to the men talk, but the reality of what

they were saying didn't penetrate her tense self-absorption. All she could think of was what was going to happen between her and Roger when the feast was over.

"Civil war is an ugly thing," Roger said somberly.

"We have the power to protect our own," Lord William said.

"Yes, there will be few who will want to antagonize us, not with this alliance we have forged." Lord Raoul sounded very satisfied.

The bishop had been largely silent while the earls spoke, but now he said, "The Bishop of Winchester is Stephen's brother. That will help him with the church."

The conversation continued as the meal was served: soup, roasted pork and mutton with various sauces, green beans and green leaves for a salad, all served on fresh white-bread trenchers and washed down with red wine.

Nell could barely eat. Her mother looked at Nell's almost-full plate and started to urge her to eat more, then fell silent. Instead, she reached over and squeezed Nell's hand, where it lay loosely in her lap. Nell turned to her mother in surprise and Lady Alice gave her an encouraging smile.

The meal was finally finished and all the men turned to look at the two women who were seated side by side.

"I believe it is time for you and your daughter to go upstairs," Lord Raoul said to his wife.

"Yes," Lady Alice said. She stood up. "Come along, Nell."

Nell stood up, as well. Lady Alice took her hand in a warm, reassuring grip, and Nell followed her to the door and up the stairs to the bedroom where she had slept alone last night. Gertrude was there, waiting for her.

"You must disrobe," Lady Alice said. "Then the bishop will come to bless your bed."

Nell stared at her mother out of enormous dark blue eyes. "I can't do this, Mama. Please don't make me do this."

"This is something that all women of your class must do," Lady Alice said briskly. "Believe me, Nell, having a husband is far better than not having one. Every one of my ladies would give the world if they could change places with you."

"I would change places with them happily," Nell said despairingly.

Lady Alice's voice sharpened. "Remember who you are, Nell. You are the daughter of the Earl of Lincoln. Don't shame your father and me by playing the coward. You are wed to a fine young man. You should appreciate that."

Nell was silent. It was clear that she wouldn't get any sympathy from her mother. Her mother thought she should be happy about this wedding.

I have to do this, she thought. *Please, Lord, please help me to be brave.*

Lady Alice and Gertrude stripped Nell down to her chemise and her drawers. They would have gone further, but Nell wrapped her arms around herself. "Can't I wear my nightgown?" she pleaded.

"No," Lady Alice replied. "But I have brought a night robe with me. Put it on and you can finish undressing underneath it."

She handed Nell a rich blue velvet robe that was open in the front and tied around the waist with a matching velvet belt. Nell put it on, turning her back on her mother and her maid, and slipped off her chemise and her drawers and drew the robe close around herself.

The velvet was very warm. Too warm for the bedroom, but Nell didn't care. It covered her up; that was all that was important to her.

There was a silver pitcher of wine on the table under the window and Lady Alice poured Nell a glass. "Here, drink it. It will help."

Nell still wasn't used to wine, but she took the glass and swallowed a sip. Her eyes watered and she handed the silver goblet back to her mother. "It tastes terrible," she said.

"You will learn to like it," Lady Alice said.

I don't think so, Nell thought rebelliously. *I don't think I'll learn to like anything about what is happening to me tonight.*

The sound of men's voices floated through the thick wooden bedroom door. Involuntarily, Nell tightened the robe about herself. There was a knock on the door. Lady Alice called, "Come," and the men entered the room.

The first thing Roger thought when he saw Nell was how lovely she looked. Her hair had been taken out of its braids and it flowed in a loose silken stream down her back. She was wearing a blue velvet robe, like the light woolen robe that covered his own nakedness. She looked so small and delicate as she stood next to her mother. She wasn't looking at him.

The bishop stepped forward. He was carrying holy water in a small gold bucket and he dipped the shaker into it and sprinkled the bed. "I bless this bed and this marriage," he said as he sprinkled. "May Roger and Eleanor follow your will, O Lord, and be fruitful and multiply. May they see their children like olive plants around their table. May the Lord so fill them with all spiritual benediction and grace, that they may so live together in this life, that in the world to come they may have life everlasting. Amen."

"Amen," everyone in the room with the exception of Nell echoed.

"It is time for us to leave," Lady Alice said firmly.

Roger watched Nell as the room cleared. Her long brown hair was tucked behind her small ears and spread in a smooth fan to her waist. The pure oval of her face was regarding the floor with grave absorption.

Then they were alone.

He crossed the floor to where she stood. "You are so beautiful, Nell," he said.

She cast a quick upward glance at him, then looked away.

A shy one, he thought.

"Everything will be all right," he said reassuringly. "I'm not going to hurt you."

She nodded slightly.

He put a finger under her chin and lifted her face up, so she would have to look at him. Then he bent his head and kissed her.

She gave him no response. He deepened the kiss and she hung like a doll in his arms. He could feel her trembling.

He lifted his head. "What is wrong?"

She didn't answer, but a tear crept its way down the ivory of her face.

Roger muttered a curse word to himself.

"What is wrong?" he repeated, more strongly than before.

"I'm sorry, my lord," she said. She spoke so low that he had to bend his head to hear her. "I know I should be brave but I just can't seem to be."

"Brave?" he said. "You said you entered this marriage willingly."

She stared at his chest. "Everyone told me I had to do it. Even Mother Superior told me it was an opportunity for me to do good in the world. There was no place else for me to go...." Her voice ran out.

"I see," he said quietly. And suddenly he did. They had all pushed her into this marriage for their political ends and no one had cared that she was a convent-raised girl who knew nothing of the world, nothing of men. Even he—he had asked her if she was willing and he had been very happy to accept her weak assurance that she was.

"Come sit beside me," he said, and moved to sit on the side of the bed. Slowly she came to join him. The bed was so high that her feet didn't touch the floor. He picked up one of her icy hands and held it between his two.

"What do you know about human coupling?" he asked bluntly.

He felt her hand grow rigid. "My mother told me last night," she said tersely.

He sat there, thinking about what he should do next. He was a young man, with all a young man's passions, but it occurred to him that if he took her tonight it would be nothing less than an act of rape. She was so frightened, this little girl from the convent. And he was a perfect stranger to her.

He inhaled deeply. "Would it be easier for you if we waited for a while?" he asked. "Perhaps, after you get a chance to know me better, all of this won't seem so terrifying."

She turned to look at him. "Do you mean that?" she asked breathlessly.

"I don't want a wife who has to be brave to make love with me," he said wryly. "I want a willing partner. The act of love can be a very beautiful thing, Nell, but I don't think you're ready to find that out yet. Get to know me. Get to be my friend. Then we will accomplish the marriage act and get to work on all of those olive plants around our table."

For the first time that day color flushed into her cheeks. "Oh, my lord, that would be wonderful!"

"Call me Roger," he said.

Her lips parted a little. She was really very lovely. "Roger," she said shyly.

He smiled at her. "Nell. I am not such a bad fellow, but I will let you find that out for yourself. In the meantime, I think we should keep our little arrangement to ourselves. I have a feeling that our elders would not approve."

"My mother would, I think, but not my father," Nell said, her voice stronger now. "Mother wanted the marriage to be delayed to give me a chance to adjust to life outside the convent, but Father wouldn't hear of it."

"My grandfather also wanted the marriage to take place quickly." He grinned at her. "I was nervous, too, you know."

"You were?" she looked at him wonderingly.

He nodded. "I was afraid you were going to be ugly and that I wouldn't be attracted to you at all. I was much relieved when I saw how pretty you are."

A little more color came to her face. "It is vain of me, I know, but when I saw my face in the mirror I was happy that I looked nice," she confessed.

He stared at her in astonishment. "You sound as if this was a recent occurrence."

"Since I came home, a few weeks ago. There were no mirrors in the convent."

"You really didn't see yourself until a few weeks ago?"

She nodded. Then she offered, "My mother's ladies were all agog about how handsome you are. They all of them wished that they were marrying you."

"But my looks didn't sway you."

"I prayed that you would have a kind heart," Nell said. She actually smiled at him. "And you do. I thank you, my lord, for your consideration of my feelings."

"Roger," he said.

Her smile stayed in place. "Roger." Her hand loosened its clutch on her robe and the top of it opened a little, giving him a glimpse of her long, delicate throat. She said, "I hope I am not going to be a disappointment to you. My mother has been trying to teach me how to run a castle, and I have learned somewhat, but much of it is still unknown to me."

"You will do fine," he said cheerfully. "My grandfather's steward, Simon Everard, is in charge of all the domestic staff in the castle, and things run like clockwork. Lady Mabel, Simon's wife, is in charge of the women. Will you be bringing ladies with you?"

"My aunt, Lady Alida, will come with me and stay a few months until I am settled in. How many ladies do you have in residence?"

"Not very many, I'm afraid. We are very much a bachelor household. My grandfather has been a widower for many years."

"How old is he?" Nell asked.

"Seventy," Roger replied.

"He seems very young for his age," Nell said.

"He is. This year he insisted on going on a tour of his vassals that took us almost two months. He bore up wonderfully."

"You sound as if you love him very much," Nell said softly.

"My own father died when I was an infant and he is the only father I have ever known," Roger replied matter-of-factly.

"What about your mother? She doesn't reside at Wilton?"

"No. After my father died, my mother went to live at the convent in Cirencester."

"Is she a nun?"

"No, she is still a laywoman, but she chooses to live there instead of at Wilton."

Nell gave him a shy smile. "You seem to be surrounded by convent-dwelling women—first your mother and now your wife."

"Yes." He returned her smile. "It is odd."

Her eyes slid away from his and her fingers once more clutched the front of her robe. "I have always slept in a nightgown," she said. "Do you think I can sleep in this robe tonight?"

"I think you will be very uncomfortable if you do," Roger said. "Velvet on a summer night, no matter if it is a bit chilly, is too warm. Besides, they will think it odd in the morning when the servants come in. I won't look if that's what you want."

"That would be…good," she said, relieved. "Should I get into bed now?"

"Go ahead," he said. "I'll just wait here."

She slid off the bed and went to the other side. The

cover had already been turned back and she quickly folded her robe at the bottom of the bed and slipped in between the sheets, pulling them up to her chin.

"It's all right, I'm in bed," she said to Roger.

He turned to look at her and smiled. *I have a long way to go here,* he told himself. Then, unselfconsciously, he shed his own robe and walked to the opposite side of the bed. He slipped in under the covers and pulled them up to his waist. Then he turned to Nell. She was staring resolutely at the ceiling.

"You can look at me," he said softly.

She shot a swift look in his direction, then returned her stare to the ceiling.

"Will it be all right if I kiss your forehead?" he asked.

"Yes," she said on a soft breath.

He moved closer to her, pushed himself up on his elbow and leaned over her. He bent lower and touched his lips to her forehead. Her skin was soft as silk and her hair smelled like lavender. He inhaled. "Your hair smells nice," he said.

"Mama washed it in lavender soap," she said.

"I like it."

"I'm sure I can make some myself if you really like it," she said.

He flopped on his back. "I like it on you. I'd lose all my status with my knights if I showed up smelling like lavender."

She chuckled.

It was a charming sound, he thought. He was relieved to find she had a sense of humor.

"Good night, Nell," he said.
"Good night, Roger," she replied softly.
With a wry smile, he settled himself to sleep.

Eight

Nell, who had scarcely slept at all the night before, slept deeply and was surprised when it was a male voice that called her back to the world.

"Nell, wake up," Roger was saying. "Your maid is here to help you dress."

She opened her eyes and looked into the dark gold eyes of her husband. He smiled at her. "Wake up," he said again. "We are going to be late for mass."

Nell started to sit up, then belatedly realized that she was naked. She clutched the covers to her breast.

Roger was already dressed. Nell looked from him to Gertrude, who was laying out her clothes on the bottom of the bed. She could feel herself begin to blush.

"We have to go together," Roger said in a low voice so Gertrude could not hear him, "but I will occupy myself while you dress."

"Thank you," Nell said.

Gertrude approached with her long chemise in hand and Roger moved over to the window and turned his back on her. "My robe," Nell said to Gertrude.

"Now, my lady, we don't have time for that," Gertrude said. "Just put on your chemise and I'll fetch the water for you to wash."

Nell took advantage of Gertrude's turned back to hurriedly pull her chemise over her head. Gertrude returned promptly with a bowl of warm water and Nell hastily washed her hands and her face. Next Gertrude handed her a pair of green stockings with garters to hold them up below the knee. After that came a white embroidered long-sleeved undertunic and a green overtunic made of the finest wool. The clothes had all originally belonged to Sybilla. Nell let Gertrude help her dress, then Gertrude said, "Now let me braid your hair," and at the window Roger turned around.

Nell gave him a faint smile as Gertrude pulled a comb through her hair and swiftly plaited it to form two braids, which she arranged to fall over Nell's shoulders.

"Quick work," Roger said admiringly as he regarded his bride.

Nell slipped her feet into a pair of soft leather low boots and stood up straight. "I'm ready," she said.

"Don't forget your mantle," Gertrude said. Nell stood quietly as the maid hung a dark green mantle around her shoulders and fastened it with a golden chain.

"You should have awakened me sooner," Nell said as

they left the room and went down the stairs to the bishop's hall. "I hate to be late for mass."

"I thought it would be a good idea if I got dressed first," he replied.

There was a little silence, then Nell said, "Thank you, my lord...Roger. That was thoughtful of you."

He smiled at her.

The rest of the wedding party was already seated in the front pews of the cathedral when Roger and Nell came in. They walked down the aisle together and slipped into the pew next to Lord William. Roger and his grandfather exchanged low greetings. Lady Alice, who was seated directly in front of Nell, turned to give her a searching look.

Nell smiled at her mother, trying to indicate that everything was all right.

Lady Alice smiled back, then turned around to face the front as the bishop came out upon the altar and began the mass.

Breakfast was served in the bishop's dining room. The meal was the usual Norman breakfast of white bread and ale and for the first time in a very long time Nell was actually hungry. Lady Alice watched her daughter eat with relief and some surprise. The haunted look that Nell had been wearing of late had quite gone. After breakfast was over, Lady Alice maneuvered so she had a chance to be standing next to Nell at a little distance from the rest of the party, who were preparing to return to Bardney.

"Are you all right, Nell?" she asked in a low voice.

"Yes, Mama," she replied in the same tone.

"You were so distraught—I am much relieved to see you looking so relaxed," Lady Alice said.

Nell thought for a moment about what Roger had said about keeping their arrangement to themselves, then surmised that he had meant for them to keep it from the earls. Her mother had been so worried about her— it was only fair to let her know what had happened.

"Roger said we can wait a little while before we consummate our marriage," she said. "He said he will give me time to get to know him better."

Lady Alice stared into her daughter's face, then put her hand on Nell's arm. "Bless the boy," she said. "There are not many men who would be so considerate of a young girl's feelings, Nell. I hope you appreciate that."

"I do, Mama," Nell said. Then, urgently she added, "Don't tell my father. Roger said not to tell anybody, but I knew how worried you have been about me…"

"Don't worry, your secret is safe," Lady Alice promised. "What you do in your marriage is between you and your husband. But I'm glad you told me. I have been worried about you."

Nell kissed her mother's cheek.

"The horses are waiting for us," Lord Raoul said, turning to look at mother and daughter.

"We are ready, my lord," Lady Alice said, moving forward. Nell followed and the whole party went out to

the courtyard. Tomorrow, she and her husband would
depart for Wiltshire, and Nell's new home.

They had ridden away from Bardney as two separate
companies, but they returned as one. Roger rode beside
Nell and the bells on their horses' bridles gave evi-
dence to the world that a newly married couple was
traveling past. As they went by the several small villages that lined the road from Lincoln to Bardney,
Roger once more distributed coins to the onlookers,
who shouted their thanks and their congratulations to
the noble pair.

Roger said to Nell as they were winding through a
swampy meadow, "The ride from Bardney to Wilton
will be a lot different from this one. The countryside is
unsettled because of the coming strife and all our men
will be in full armor."

"Will we be in danger?" Nell asked, concerned.

"No one will attack as large a party as we are, but I
wouldn't want to be traveling alone," Roger said.

"I am not accustomed to the saddle," Nell confided.
"I will try not to hold you up."

"You don't ride?" Roger asked in surprise.

"There was no necessity for me to ride in the convent. I never went anywhere."

"Well, I know the first thing we're going to do when
we get home," Roger said. "I'm going to teach you to ride
properly."

Nell turned to look at him. He was sitting perfectly

upright in his saddle, with his legs hanging straight down under him as if he were standing on the ground. The horse he rode was a big gray, with an arched neck and sloping shoulders. Horse and rider looked perfectly in harmony with each other. "I would like that," Nell said, pleased.

"Do you like animals?" Roger asked.

"Oh, yes," Nell answered. "We had a dog once in the convent and I took care of him. He was a stray and Sister Helen and I kept him in the herb shed. We had him for a year before he died."

"We have many dogs in the kennel at Wilton, but I have a special dog who lives with me," Roger said. "He's not very fancy—he's a mongrel, as a matter of fact, but he's been my dog for eleven years. I hope you won't mind sharing a room with him."

"Oh, no," Nell said. "I will like that very much. I was very sad when our Bruno died."

Roger nodded.

"My father keeps dogs also, for hunting. Do you hunt, Roger?"

"We go out almost every day," he answered. "Wilton supports a very large household."

"Is it as big as Bardney?"

"Bigger," Roger said.

Nell digested that in silence. They rode for a little while longer, then Nell asked, "What do the women do while the men are out hunting?"

"They do whatever it is you did at Bardney."

"The whole time I was at Bardney we were preparing for the wedding."

Roger's brow creased as he tried to think of the things the women did at Wilton. "Some women hunt and many women hawk," he said. He thought some more. "They take charge of the entertaining. Whenever we have notable guests, Lady Mabel does all the arranging. And, of course, they sew." He held out his arm and showed her the fine embroidery on the sleeve of his undertunic. "See—the ladies of the castle did this."

"I did some embroidering at Bardney," Nell said, grateful that she at least was familiar with something the women did at Wilton.

Roger thought of something else. "They also make wall hangings. We have several wonderful wall hangings at Wilton that were made by the ladies of the castle."

"I've never done that," Nell said.

"Lady Mabel can show you," Roger said.

"Do you think Lady Mabel will mind giving up her position to me?"

"Not at all," Roger said.

"I think I might like hawking," Nell said. "Do you think I could learn?"

"I'll teach you," Roger said. "Hawking is great fun. I have a wonderful gyrfalcon and I'm sure we can find a smaller falcon for you. You have to carry them on your wrist and they can be heavy."

"I would like that," Nell said.

They arrived at Bardney without incident, and Nell

and Roger dismounted in the inner bailey and went into the castle where food was being set out for supper. Lord Raoul was as genial as Nell had ever seen him as they sat at the high table. He even recommended several dishes to Nell and told her marriage must agree with her—she finally had some color in her cheeks.

Nell blushed at this, adding more color to her face. "Thank you, Father," she replied faintly.

After supper was cleared away, they had singing around the fire, which was lit to take away the damp of the stone castle on this early autumn day. One of the Bardney knights, who had a true tenor voice, gave them the note and the rest of the company joined in. It was not a song that Nell knew—her repertoire ran mainly to hymns—but she listened with delight as the large group in front of the fireplace, which included her family, Roger, Lord William, her mother's ladies and a contingent of her father's best knights, all sang lustily. It was the first time since she had come home that she had seen her mother and father really looking happy.

I wish I could be as happy about my marriage as my parents are, Nell thought. Still, it could have been worse. She could have married a man who had no respect for her feelings. *Thank you for giving me Roger, Lord,* she thought. *I will try to be a good wife to him, truly I will.*

The song died away and Lord Raoul said, "You weren't singing, Nell."

"I don't know the song, Father," she replied.

"Then give us a song you do know."

"All I know are hymns."

"Give us a hymn, then."

Nell looked at her mother.

Lady Alice smiled encouragingly. "You must know how to sing. So much of liturgy is singing."

In fact, Nell had a beautiful pure soprano voice that had been much appreciated by the convent choir. She had sung solo many times.

"All right," she said. "I'll sing a song about our Blessed Lady."

"Let's hear it," Lord Raoul said.

Nell folded her hands in her lap, took a deep breath, and began:

"I sing of a maiden
That is matchless;
King of all kings
To her son she chose.

"He came as still
Where his mother was,
As dew in April
That fallith on grass.

"He came as still
To his mother's bower,
As dew in April
That fallith on the flower.

"He came as still
Where his mother lay
As dew in April
That fallith on the spray.

"Mother and maiden
Was never none but she;
Well may such a lady
God's mother be."

There was a little silence when she had finished, then Lord Raoul said, "That was lovely, Nell. Thank you."

Nell flushed with pleasure at this rare compliment from her father.

By the time the singing was finished, it was time for the household to go to bed. Nell and Roger retired together to Sybilla's old room and Nell went this night with a much lighter heart than she had the night before at the bishop's house.

Roger's squire, a blond, blue-eyed, freckle-faced boy who had been absent last night, awaited Roger, and Gertrude awaited Nell. Nell stopped at the door. Surely she wasn't expected to get undressed in front of this young boy!

"I don't believe you've met Richard, my squire," Roger said to Nell. The sixteen-year-old bowed to her. "My lady," he said.

"Hello, Richard," Nell managed. She looked at Roger pleadingly.

He said, "I'll get undressed first—how is that?"

"That would be fine," she answered a little breathlessly.

She sat on her bed while Roger undressed. When Richard had gone, Gertrude undressed Nell, then left bearing Nell's clothes with her. Roger turned away from the window, went over to the bed, matter-of-factly shed his robe and got in.

Nell did not have a chance to look away and her eyes widened at her first glimpse of a naked man. It was just a glimpse; he slid under the covers quickly, but she had definitely seen all of him.

That's not so frightening, she told herself. Then she blushed. He definitely did look different from her.

She got into the bed and managed to shed her robe under the covers, which she then pulled up to her chin.

"Good night, Nell," Roger said. Amusement sounded in his voice.

"Good night, my…Roger," Nell replied. She didn't at all mind the amusement. Better that he found her amusing than irritating or exasperating.

Roger went to sleep first. Nell lay awake and listened to him breathe. *He's a good man, Lord,* she prayed. *Help me to appreciate him. And help me in my new life in this strange castle I am going to. Help me to do my job and to find some friends. Amen.*

Nine

The Wilton party left Bardney the following day directly after breakfast. At the last moment, Alida became ill and was not able to go with them. Lady Alice volunteered to go in her place, but Lord Raoul would not hear of it.

"You have your duties to do here," he said. "I cannot spare you for any length of time. Besides, we expect the empress to be landing any day now. The traveling could be dangerous after that."

"I will be fine, Mother," Nell said with a great deal more confidence than she felt. "Roger says that his steward's wife is in charge of the ladies and that she is very nice. I will rely on her to show me what I must do."

"It is not right, sending you off by yourself," Lady Alice fretted.

Nell felt badly, too. She had been counting on the companionship of her aunt. But she put a brave face on it for her mother. "I will be fine," she repeated.

Lady Alice squeezed Nell's hand. "You are a valiant girl, Nell. Your father and I are proud of you."

Tears clogged the back of Nell's throat so that she couldn't answer. She wished badly that her father had let her mother go with her.

Roger came over to them. "The horses are waiting, Nell."

Nell forced a smile and kissed her mother. Then her father joined them. "You're a good girl, Nell," he said. "I know you'll be a credit to Bardney."

"I'll try, Father," Nell replied.

Lord Raoul bent and kissed her forehead. "Goodbye, my child."

A squire was waiting to help her on her horse. Nell put her foot in the stirrup and swung easily up. It was not the getting on the horse that was her problem; it was what to do once the animal started moving.

She arranged her skirts so that they were under her and when she had finished, Lord William said, "Ready?"

"Yes, my lord," Nell replied.

Lord William called to the cadre of armed knights riding in front of them, "Go on," and the entire party moved out.

I'm leaving, Nell thought. *I'm actually leaving Lincolnshire to live in a place I have never seen before with people that I don't know.*

Pain wrenched at Nell's heart. While she was at Bardney she had been comforted by the thought that Sister

Helen was only a few hours away. But the Convent of St. Cecelia would be a ride of several days from Wilton. Nell wondered sadly if she would ever see Sister Helen again.

The ride was physically difficult for Nell. The walking wasn't so bad but the periods when they trotted were more than painful; they were scary. The horse bumped under her and she was afraid she was going to come off. It got better when Roger came to ride beside her and give her encouragement.

"Put some weight on your stirrup," he said, "so you're not sitting so hard in the side saddle. And take a hold of the mane for balance."

When Nell did this the bumping became easier to tolerate.

"Good girl," Roger said encouragingly.

At a little before darkfall they stopped at an abbey for the night, where Roger stayed in the men's guesthouse and Nell in the women's. The following afternoon they arrived at Wilton and for the first time, Nell laid eyes on the great stone walls of her future home. She looked up and saw fluttering from all four of the high towers the scarlet flag bearing its emblem of a leopard. It was the same flag that the man at the forefront of their party was bearing.

"My father doesn't have a flag like that," she remarked to Roger.

"It's a new thing," Roger replied. "Some of the earls have made their own insignias. We've had ours for a few years now."

They rode in under the two portcullises to the inner bailey and Roger came to lift her off her horse. Surprised, Nell put her hands on his shoulders as he swung her down. Her knees buckled when her feet hit the ground. If Roger had not been there to support her, she would have fallen. She leaned against him for a moment, then straightened away. He had felt very solid and strong against her.

"It's been a long ride for you," he said.

Nell nodded. She ached all over, especially in her back and her legs. Her arms hurt from hanging onto her horse's mane.

"How do you feel?" Roger asked.

"Like someone has been pummeling me," she replied frankly. "I'm not sure I want to learn how to ride if it leaves me feeling like this."

He laughed. His teeth were very white in his tanned face. "Once you know how to ride, and are riding regularly, you won't hurt at all. I promise."

Lord William came to join them. "I am pleased to welcome you to your new home, Lady Eleanor," he said courteously. "Will you come indoors with us?"

"Thank you, my lord," Nell replied.

She accompanied the two men as they approached the castle and restrained herself from groaning aloud as she toiled up the ramp. Then they were going in through the door and into the Great Hall.

It was bigger than Bardney's. There was a massive lit fireplace at the far end of the room and there were several servants sweeping dirty rushes into the fire. A dog was lying in front of the fireplace and his head lifted as he heard the door open.

"Hullo there, Gawain," Roger called.

The dog leaped to his feet in a flash and tore across the room, barking excitedly. Roger bent to pet him, but the dog was too energized to stand still. Instead he raced around the whole party three times before finally coming to rest in front of Roger, who bent once again.

Nell laughed watching the two of them. "My," she said. "That is some greeting!"

Roger looked up at her with a smile. "Gawain is very attached to me."

"I can see that," Nell said. "Can I pet him?"

"Certainly," Roger said.

Nell bent stiffly and began to rub the dog behind his ears. "Hello there, fellow," she said. "I hope we're going to be friends."

The dog reached up and licked her face.

Nell laughed again.

"That dog lives a better life than our castle knights," Lord William commented.

"He's a good boy," Roger said, still patting. After a few more moments he straightened up. The dog stood close beside him, his tail wagging so hard it could have created a breeze.

Roger said to Nell, "You should have a hot bath. That will help your sore muscles. Come along with me and I'll show you to our room."

They crossed the floor toward one of the towers and

went by a line of pages sitting on a bench along the wall, waiting to be given errands. "Three of you—make yourselves useful and bring up Lady Eleanor's baggage," Roger said to them as they went by.

Three boys popped up as one. "Yes, my lord," they chorused.

Roger's dog trotted at their heels as they went up a spiral staircase to two rooms at the top of the tower. "My grandfather gave us this tower because there is a bedroom and a solar here," Roger explained. "My old bedroom was in his apartment and he thought we would want more privacy."

Nell went first as they climbed the stairs to the first level, where Roger's new apartment was.

They passed through a small anteroom and into a medium-sized solar with one window whose shutters were open to let in the early autumn air. The room was furnished comfortably, with two high-backed carved armchairs with footstools, a backless chair against the wall, and a table with four narrow chairs set around it. A multicolored rug lay on the bare wood floor. The stone walls were whitewashed, with a painting of a stag in the woods on one wall.

"Come and look at the bedroom," he said.

The bedroom was smaller and was dominated by a large curtained bed. Nell had never before slept behind curtains, but she instantly deduced that getting undressed and dressed in privacy would be greatly assisted by them. Aside from the bed, the room was furnished with two large chests for clothing, a table and two chairs, and a backless bench that was pushed up against the wall. The floors were bare.

"This is very nice," Nell said to Roger.

"It will do," Roger said. "Perhaps we can find a rug and some wall hangings to make it more cozy."

The first of the pages came into the room carrying a large leather bag that contained Nell's clothes. "Where do you want this, my lady?" he asked.

"Put it on the bed for now," Nell said.

The other two boys came into the room carrying similar bags that had been carried to Wilton by the packhorses. Nell had everything put on the bed.

"I'll unpack them and put my clothes into one of the trunks," Nell said to Roger.

"Your maid will do that," Roger said. "I want you to take a bath first. It will help your muscle soreness." He turned to one of the pages. "Have a bath brought for Lady Eleanor."

Nell had to confess that a bath sounded attractive. *I am going to have to get used to the ways of the world,* she told herself. *The maids have probably seen dozens of naked women. They won't be overly interested in me.*

"Who will be Lady Eleanor's handmaiden?" one of the pages asked.

"Ask Lady Mabel," Roger returned.

"Yes, my lord," the page said. "I will have the bathwater brought up right away."

"I'll leave so you can have some privacy," Roger said.

"Thank you," Nell said.

Roger left and a few minutes later a servant came in with a large wooden tub, which he set up in a patch of sunshine coming in through the window. Then he fixed a canopy over the tub to help keep the water hot. A stream of servants bearing buckets of hot water began to file into the room. A maid who introduced herself as Rose came in and helped Nell into the tub. Nell let herself be undressed and actually luxuriated in the water until it began to grow cool. Then she got out and put on the dress that Rose had laid out for her. As Rose continued to unpack, Nell stood uncertainly in the middle of the bedroom.

"It's almost time for supper, my lady," the maid said.

"Oh, thank you, Rose," Nell replied. "I shall go down to the Great Hall then."

"Yes, my lady," Rose said.

Wishing that Roger were there to accompany her, Nell left the bedroom by herself and began to go down the stairs.

Ten

In the hall, the area around the dais was wainscoted with Norwegian fir and whitewashed. The wood was painted with large blocks of red and within each block was painted a picture of a rose. Nell looked at the paintings curiously; they had not had such a thing at Bardney.

"Nell, this is Lady Mabel," Roger said and Nell turned to face a small stout woman with graying blond hair. Her pale blue eyes did not look overly friendly as she greeted her new lady.

Nell's seat was to the right of Roger, with Lady Mabel seated next to her. Lord William sat on Roger's other side.

The squires came out with ewers of water and bowls so that they could wash their hands.

The immense hall was packed with people. *How can I possibly be in charge of such great numbers?* Nell asked herself with a flash of panic. Then she glanced at the woman beside her. Roger had said that Lady Mabel would help her.

Nell turned to Mabel and made a comment about the size of the hall.

"Wilton is the largest earl's castle in the kingdom," Lady Mabel replied. Her voice had a definite chill to it. "It is probably larger than what you are accustomed to."

"It is larger than my father's hall at Bardney, that is true, " Nell said softly.

The woman nodded and turned away.

The meal had not yet been served before Roger's squire began to cough. Lord William turned to him with a frown. "Richard, you should not be standing so close to us if you are ill. Go and sit at a table and send someone to take your place."

"Aye, my lord," the boy replied.

Nell turned to Roger. "Do you have someone to prescribe medication for those in the castle who are sick?" she asked.

"Not really," Roger replied.

"In the convent I was an apprentice to our herbalist," Nell said eagerly. "I know somewhat of healing— enough to know that that boy should be given chestnut mixed with honey for his cough. If you have chestnut available, I can mix an elixir for him."

"I don't know what we have in the stores," Roger said. "You will have to ask Lady Mabel."

Nell turned to the woman beside her. "You and I will

have to go over your store of herbs, Lady Mabel. I would like to mix a potion for that cough."

"What are you looking for?" Lady Mabel asked sharply.

"Chestnut and honey is a good remedy."

"I don't know if we have chestnut."

Nell looked steadily at the woman. "Do you have an herb garden?"

Lady Mabel raised her brows. "Of course."

"Perhaps you could show it to me," Nell said.

"If you wish, my lady."

Nell looked back to her trencher. Despite what Roger had said, it didn't seem to her as if Lady Mabel were anxious to assist her.

I will have to try to win her over, Nell thought. *I need a friend, not an adversary.*

Lord William leaned across Roger to talk to her. "What convent were you in, Lady Eleanor?" he asked courteously.

"The Convent of St. Cecelia," she replied. "It was about twenty miles north of Lincoln."

"It must have been a surprise to you, to have your future change so quickly," he said in the same courteous voice. He sat very upright at the table and Nell thought he most definitely did not look his age. "Yes," she replied politely. "A very great surprise."

"To go from being a lowly novice to the future countess of Wiltshire and Lincoln. You have come a long way up in the world."

He sounded as if he thought she should be enraptured with her change in status. "It was a surprise," Nell repeated in the same carefully expressionless voice.

"You are a very important person, you know," Lord William said seriously. "Because of you, our two families will become the most powerful force in the kingdom, eclipsing even the Earl of Chester."

"The king will be more important, surely," Nell said gently.

The earl smiled. "The king will have to consult us before he scratches his head. The only men Stephen controls are his mercenaries. We control the feudal armies he will need to defend his monarchy."

Nell thought about what he had just said. "How can the king be our leader, then, if he is eclipsed by the Earl of Wiltshire and Lincoln?" she asked, surprised.

Lord William's smile widened. "The king will still lead, he will just lead the way we want him to," he replied with a wink.

Privately, Nell wondered if this was such a good idea. Someone should make decisions based on what would be good for England; the earls seemed to make their decisions based on what would be good for the earls.

Roger joined in the conversation. "Are you teaching Nell about politics?" he asked.

"I am just telling her what an important link she is to a grand dynastic plan," Lord William replied. He looked again at Nell. "Your job, my dear, will be to provide Roger with an heir. Your son will be the first earl born with both de Bonvile and de Roche blood in his veins—the culmination of all our plans."

Nell could feel herself blush. "All in due time, Grandfather, all in due time," Roger said patiently.

Throughout supper, Lord William told Nell all about the history of Wilton Castle and the earls of Wiltshire who had held it. Nell listened attentively and at the end of the meal earned an accolade from Lord William. "You are fortunate indeed in your bride," he said to Roger. "She seems like a very intelligent girl—as well as being very pretty."

"I think you are right, Grandfather," Roger said.

The room began to empty as people got up from the trestle tables and left the Great Hall. The earl stood up and everyone else at the high table followed his lead. Nell turned to Lady Mabel.

"Would it be possible for me to see the herb garden?" she asked

A faint line appeared between the woman's brows. "Now?"

"If it would not be too much trouble," Nell said.

There was a silence. "Very well. I will take you," Lady Mabel said a little impatiently.

"Thank you, Lady Mabel," Nell said.

"This way," the woman said. "It's quickest if we go through the kitchen."

Nell followed Lady Mabel across the Great Hall, where the cloths were being removed from the tables. Lady Mabel went down a corner staircase and Nell found herself in a big, warm room with an immense fire-place on the outside wall. A goodly number of servants were sitting at a large table having their meal. They all jumped up when Lady Mabel and Nell came in.

"Sit down," Lady Mabel said. "We are just passing through."

All of the servants were staring at Nell. She smiled a little nervously and said, "How do you do? I am Lady Eleanor, Lord Roger's new wife."

Heads ducked and the man at the head of the table, whom Nell assumed to be the chief cook, said, "Welcome to Wilton, my lady."

"Are you the cook?" Nell asked.

"Aye, my lady."

"The meal was excellent."

He smiled, showing one missing front tooth. "Thank you, my lady."

"This way, Lady Eleanor," Lady Mabel said, and Nell followed her out a door and into the early evening air.

The large kitchen garden was situated not far from the kitchen door and contained many of the same veg-etables as were grown at St. Cecelia's: onions, garlic, turnips, peas, cabbage, radishes, carrots and beans. Nell inspected the rows and rows of vegetables. "The herb garden is over here." Lady Mabel led Nell to a smaller garden that was planted closer to the castle walls.

It was an adequate garden, much the same as the one her mother had at Bardney. It was a start, Nell thought, and she immediately began to plan in her head how she would enlarge it. She would send to Sister Helen for some cuttings.

It was unfortunate that she couldn't plant until the spring. But she could prepare the land now, before the frosts came. That way she would be all ready when the weather grew fine again.

Nell thought about Richard's cough and turned to Lady Mabel. "Do you have almonds?" she asked.

"Of course we have almonds," Lady Mabel said, sounding a little offended. Most castles stocked such important luxuries as almonds, rice, figs, dates, raisins, oranges and pomegranates.

"I can make an elixir from almonds instead of chestnuts that is also very good for coughs," Nell said. "If you will show me where the almonds are I can get started."

"My lady, you will be expected to join the company around the fireplace," Lady Mabel protested. "The squire will survive another day without your help."

Nell explained, "My lady, I studied under a very great herbalist and I would like to bring my healing arts to the people of Wilton."

"That's all very well, Lady Eleanor," Lady Mabel said tartly. "But your first job is to be the lady of this castle. Did I hear Lord William say that you lived in a convent before you married Lord Roger?"

"Yes," Nell said.

"Then you clearly do not know that it is your place to join your lord at the fire after dinner."

Nell lifted her chin. "I will join him *after* I have mixed the elixir for the squire."

Lady Mabel stared at her, her blue eyes like ice.

"Show me the almonds, please," Nell said firmly, and started off toward the kitchen.

Nell was right about the bed curtains. She undressed inside the curtains and handed her clothes to Rose who stood on the other side. Roger had given her time to get to bed and he came in with his squire and dog after Rose had gone. Nell heard the two men talking as Roger was undressed. Her husband appeared to have a friendly relationship with his squire.

Then Roger parted the curtains and joined her in bed.

"Well, how did you get through your first day at Wilton?" he asked. It was dark inside the curtains and Nell could not see him—she could only hear his voice.

"Very well, thank you," she replied. She told him about making the elixir for Richard's cough. She did not mention Lady Mabel's chilly attitude.

"Do you think it would be possible for me to go to St. Cecelia's and pick up some medicines from Sister Helen?" she asked. "It is too late in the year for me to plant, but I'm sure she would give me some potions. With winter coming on, you will have sickness within the castle."

"Travel is going to be dangerous once the empress lands," Roger said carefully.

"I don't understand why," Nell said.

"Because King Stephen is going to be busy protect-

ing his territory and there will be no one to stop greedy
knights from plundering the lesser folk. Every man is
going to be out for himself and the losers will be the folk
with no means of defending themselves. The roads will
be unsafe for small parties."

"That sounds terrible," Nell exclaimed.

"It *will* be terrible," Roger said.

"What if the empress doesn't come?"

"She will come. The question is, how much support
will she draw?"

It was actually cozy inside the curtains and Nell felt
comfortable about questioning Roger. She knew instinctively that he would not make fun of her ignorance.
"Stephen seems to be doing a good job as king. Why
would anyone declare for the empress?"

"For their own profit," Roger answered. He added a
little ironically, "Why else does anyone act politically?"

"Your grandfather and my father acted for their own
profit when they arranged our marriage."

"That is indisputably true." His voice sounded a little ironic.

"Don't you think it was a good idea?" she asked
curiously.

"Men will ever strive for power, Nell. That is the way
of the world."

She was silent for a moment. Then she asked, "So
you think that men who believe they will have more
power with the empress than they have with Stephen
will declare for her?"

"Exactly."

"You have sworn your loyalty to Stephen, have you not?" Nell asked.

"I have. When Stephen agreed to our marriage I swore my loyalty to him. Now he can count on the support of Wiltshire and Lincoln both, with their large feudal armies. It was a move that benefited Stephen, as well as us."

"What about this Earl of Chester that everyone talks about? He seems to be your rival."

"Chester not only controls his own huge county, but he inherited large estates in Lincolnshire. Also, his half brother, William of Roumare, has a string of estates and castles in and around Lincolnshire. If Roumare had become the Earl of Lincoln, he and his brother would have controlled a huge autonomous triangle in the heart of the kingdom. Instead of that happening, however, the earldom and the power went to us."

Nell thought about this for a while. "The Earl of Chester must be angry at this move of the king's. Will he declare for the empress?"

"I think Chester will wait and see which way the wind blows before he declares for anybody. But he is married to a daughter of Robert of Gloucester, the empress's half brother. That is one tie he has to the empress."

Nell was curled up on her side, facing Roger's invisible bulk. "My father is not an old man," she pointed out. "He is not likely to die soon. The earldom of Lincoln should remain in his hands for many years."

"Your father and I have both sworn oaths to support Stephen."

"And will you honor your oath even if it is not to your advantage?" Nell asked.

"A feudal oath is an oath to God," Roger said soberly. "I will honor my oath no matter what."

Nell tucked her hand under her cheek. "Do you think I could go to St. Cecelia's right away, before the empress lands?"

A little silence fell. Then Roger said, "Give me a list of the things you want and I will send some knights to St. Cecelia's."

Nell wanted to see Sister Helen. "I could go myself," she said.

"You don't ride well enough. You will hold the knights up." He sounded adamant.

Nell had to admit that this was true. "Thank you very much, Roger," she said softly. "This is important to me."

He had been lying on his back and now she felt him move to face her. "I gathered as much," he replied.

"I have been thinking about another thing," she said.

"Yes?" He sounded faintly amused.

"Shouldn't we go to see your mother? She was not at our wedding, but I think she would like to meet your wife."

Roger rolled onto his back and when he spoke his voice was carefully neutral. "I have never met my mother. She doesn't want to see me."

In the dark, Nell's eyes widened with surprise. She

hesitated, not knowing what to say. Finally, "Why?" she murmured.

"I don't know. She left here when I was but two months old and she hasn't seen me since."

Nell felt a sharp pang of sympathy. She felt a desire to reach out to him, but then she didn't. "I'm sorry, Roger," she said instead. "I know how awful I felt when my mother stopped coming to see me in the convent."

"You don't miss what you've never had." His voice sounded stronger. "I always had my grandfather. He was both mother and father to me. He didn't even send me away to be trained by another lord. He kept me at Wilton and trained me himself. He was on the Crusade, you know. He is a very great knight."

"And your father?"

"He died right after I was born."

"He was a young man to die."

"Yes." He hesitated. "My grandfather will never speak of him so I don't know how it happened."

Nell thought that Roger's family sounded very strange. She said gently, "You were practically an orphan, then. That must have been hard."

"You were separated from your parents, too," he said.

"Yes. And it was hard at first. But then I had Sister Helen and things got much better."

"And I had my grandfather."

"You were lucky to have him," Nell murmured.

"Yes, I was. I'd do anything for him."

A little silence fell, but neither of them settled themselves to sleep. Finally Roger said, "Were you happy in the convent, Nell?"

"Yes, I was."

"I hope you will learn to be happy here at Wilton."

"I will try," Nell replied. "Sister Helen told me that God's plan for me may be for me to do good in the world and I will try to do that. That is one of the reasons I would like the medicines. I can help the people in the castle and in the surrounding area, too. Sister Helen always doctored the village that was close by St. Cecelia's."

"Give me a list of what you want and I will send some knights," Roger promised.

"Thank you, Roger. I will write out a list tomorrow."

"Where are you?" he asked, reaching out to her. "I want to kiss you good-night."

"Here." She reached out and touched his bare arm.

She felt his hand touch her face, then his lips were coming down on hers. Their touch was gentle and tender. It was nice. She wouldn't mind kissing him if it was like this. He smelled nice, too. And he had been very good to her. Being married to Roger might not be so bad.

"Good night," Roger said.

"Good night," Nell replied.

Finally they both settled themselves to sleep.

Eleven

As promised, Roger sent a party of knights to St. Cecelia's and Nell looked forward to receiving a bounty of medicines from Sister Helen. She also talked to the castle gardener about clearing more space for an expanded herb garden.

From the look on Lady Mabel's face, it was clear she did not approve.

The castle ladies—there were seven of them including Lady Mabel—were all a great deal older than Nell. The youngest was about the age of Nell's mother. Lady Mabel had acted as lady of the castle since Roger's mother had left for the convent twenty-two years ago and it was plain to Nell that she was loath to give up her position. The rest of the women took their cue from Lady Mabel, and treated Nell as if she were a child. Nell was used to living with women, however, and she thought that if she showed herself willing to learn from Lady Mabel, that perhaps she would come around.

One of the things Nell enjoyed about her first days at Wilton was her riding lessons. Roger put a sidesaddle on an older horse from the stables and started her in an enclosed horse corral inside the bailey so that the horse could go in a circle along the fence while he stood in the middle and gave instructions.

Once Nell realized that the horse wasn't going to do anything scary, she relaxed and was quick to learn. She had good natural balance and by the fifth day she had progressed to a canter. Roger was full of praise and she was pleased with herself, as well.

"I like it," she said to him when she had come down to a walk. There was color in her cheeks. She patted the black neck of her faithful steed. "He's so smart! He knows what you're saying when you ask him to walk, trot and canter."

"I insist that all my knights' horses be well trained. In battle your life can depend on how obedient your horse is."

"Is Onyx one of the knights' horses?"

"He used to be. He's retired now. I keep him in case one of the ladies might want to go out hunting with us— although none of them has in years."

"They are all rather…old," Nell said.

"They are from my grandmother's and my mother's day," Roger said. "I shall have to talk to my grandfather about perhaps getting some younger women in to be companions to you."

"That would be nice," Nell said fervently.

A few of the knights came over to lean on the fence and one of them called, "She'll soon be riding better than you, my lord."

The rest of the knights hooted.

"Is Lord Roger a good rider?" Nell asked the assembled knights.

"He's the best," a young knight returned emphatically. "You have to see him ride Bayard at the lists. They have perfect timing."

"You have to see my lord's archery," another one of the knights called. "He is the best at that, too."

"My goodness," Nell said with a smile. "I seem to have married a very talented man."

Roger smiled, unembarrassed by all this praise. "They are prejudiced."

"When we had a tournament here last year, Lord Roger took all the prizes," a knight said proudly.

"You had a tournament?" Nell asked Roger. "I have never seen a tournament."

"The king has banned them, but my grandfather held one last year anyway. He called it a festival," Roger said.

"Will you have another one this year?" Nell thought she would like to see a tournament.

"Not with the state the country is in. No one will want to turn their backs on their castles with civil war looming."

"Wilton won the melee, my lady," the same knight who had mentioned the tournament said. "Lord Roger led us well."

Nell turned to her husband. He looked all gold as he stood there in the afternoon sunlight: gold hair, gold eyes, gold skin. She realized she *liked* to look at him. She thought he was beautiful.

Roger looked at the group of knights who had been watching them. "Don't you have anything else to do?"

At his words, the knights melted away.

"They're very proud of you," Nell said when they had gone.

"A lord has to do everything better than his knights," Roger said matter-of-factly. "That is the way to earn their respect." He reached for her hand. "Come along and I'll show you the mews."

The mews at Wilton was a large building—large enough to allow limited flight to the birds that were housed within. "Henry," Roger called and a man came out. "My lady would like to see Adela."

The two of them waited for perhaps two minutes until Henry came out carrying a falcon on his wrist. There was a leather strap under where the bird was standing.

"My goodness," Nell said in awe. "She's enormous."

"She's a gyrfalcon," Roger said. "We'll find you something smaller." He turned to the falconer. "Do we have something that would be suitable for Lady Eleanor?"

"We have a nice sparrow hawk, my lord."

"Yes, I know the one you mean. He would be perfect," Roger said.

Nell enjoyed being outdoors and she liked to be with

Roger. She had begun to feel very comfortable with
him. He was her only friend at Wilton. It was with re-
luctant steps that she went back into the house to join
the group of elderly ladies in their solar.

The castle was at dinner on the second of October
when a squire approached the high table to announce to
Lord William that a messenger from the king had just
arrived. Lord William bade him approach.

The messenger bore all the signs of having ridden
hard. "My lord," he said when he had reached the front
of the dais. "I bear news from my lord, the king. Two
days ago the Empress and the Earl of Gloucester landed
at Arundel and sought refuge in the castle of Adeliza of
Louvain."

The Great Hall fell into a profound silence.

"How many men came with them?" Lord William
demanded.

"One hundred and forty knights, my lord."

Nell heard Roger let out his breath.

That's not so many, she thought.

"My lord, the king bade me tell you one more thing.
One of the knights accompanying the empress is your
son, Guy."

Nell's eyes widened in surprise. *I didn't know Lord
William had a living son*, she thought. She turned to look
at Roger.

He was deadly pale.

No one moved in the room. Even the servers were still.

Nell's eyes moved to Lord William. He was almost as pale as Roger.

"Guy is here?" he asked in a choked voice.

"Yes, my lord. He came with the empress."

As Nell watched, Lord William stood up. Roger said in a strangled voice, "Grandfather, how can this be?"

Lord William opened his mouth, as if to answer, then grabbed at his chest. His eyes widened and slowly he collapsed back into his chair. He slumped forward and his head hung forward onto his chest.

Roger jumped to his feet. "Grandfather!" he cried.

Nell was at Lord William's side before anyone else. She bent her head to listen to his chest. His heart was beating, but faintly and irregularly.

"It's his heart," she said to Roger. "He's had a seizure."

Lord William lay sprawled in his chair, his eyes closed.

"What should we do?" Roger asked wildly.

"Get him into bed," Nell answered. "I have something I can give him."

Roger called a few knights' names and himself slipped an arm around Lord William's shoulders. Three knights came to help him and together they carried the earl out of the Great Hall and up the stairs to his bedroom. Nell ran to the pantry to get her hawthorn seeds, which she mixed into wine. Then she followed the knights upstairs.

Lord William was stretched on his bed, his color a

deadly white. Roger looked frantically at Nell as she came in the door.

"Is he going to die?" he asked anxiously.

Nell came to the bed and once more bent to listen to Lord William's heart.

She raised her head and looked at Roger. "It doesn't sound good," she said. "Hold him up while I try to get him to swallow this wine."

She got the wine into him, then Nell took off his belt and his mantel and his shoes. She looked at Roger. "All we can do is wait."

Roger felt as if he were living in a nightmare.

How can my father have landed with the empress? He's supposed to be dead.

And yet the news of that landing had given his grandfather a heart seizure.

He sat beside his grandfather, praying for him, his mind filled with confusion. Nell sat on the other side of the bed, monitoring the earl's heart and looking very grave. Father Ralph sat in the corner, his head bowed in prayer. He had already anointed the earl.

I'm glad Nell is here, Roger thought. *There is no doctor close by. At least she knows what to do.*

It was deep in the night when Lord William finally opened his eyes. "What happened?" he asked faintly.

Roger was on his feet in a flash. "You had a heart seizure, Grandfather," he said. "How are you feeling?"

"A heart seizure," Lord William repeated weakly.

"Yes."

There was silence. Roger kept his eyes trained on his grandfather's face. *He looks so old,* he thought.

"Yes," Lord William said at last. "I remember now. A messenger came from the king." His hand plucked at the cover that had been pulled over him to keep him warm. "Guy is back."

"You told me my father was dead," Roger said hoarsely.

"No," Lord William gasped. "Dead to me. Banished. And now he is back. Like a vulture."

Roger didn't say anything. Couldn't say anything.

Lord William raised his eyes to search Roger's face. "You must promise me one thing." There was an unmistakable note of urgency in his faint voice.

"Anything," Roger replied. He sat on the side of the bed and took his grandfather's cold hand into his.

"Do not let him take the earldom. That is for you, not him. Whatever happens, don't let him take that from you."

Roger looked across his grandfather to meet Nell's eyes. She looked gravely back.

"Promise me." The earl's fingers fluttered and Roger increased the pressure of his own hand. "You must promise me, Roger." The urgency was even more pronounced. "Don't let Guy have Wilton."

"I promise," Roger said shakily.

The earl's thin hand returned his pressure slightly. Then suddenly Lord William's hand relaxed.

"Grandfather?" Roger asked sharply.

Nell stood up to lean over the earl's prostrate body. She listened to his chest for a full minute, then looked up. In a gentle voice she said, "He's gone, Roger."

Roger held his grandfather's hand for a few more moments, then put it down to rest on his chest.

"I can't believe that this is happening," he said hoarsely.

"It was the shock of the news," she said. "His old heart couldn't take it."

Roger stared down at his grandfather's body. "All my life, he has been there for me. I never left home. I never left him."

"I am so sorry, Roger," she said.

"Is it over?" The voice belonged to Father Ralph.

"Yes, Father," Nell said.

The priest came forward to stand beside the body and Nell moved around the bed to stand next to Roger. He was staring at his grandfather's face. The priest made the sign of the cross on the dead man's forehead, lips and chest, murmuring some prayers. Roger said blankly, "My father is alive."

"So it seems," Nell said cautiously.

He turned to look at her. "But why would he have let me believe he was dead?"

"He said your father was dead to him," Nell said softly.

"But to tell me he was really dead!"

Nell shook her head. "I don't know why he did it, but he must have had his reasons," Nell said.

Roger drew a deep, shuddering breath. "What do we do now?" he asked hoarsely.

"We must have a funeral," she said, in the same soft voice.

He ran his hand through his hair, mussing it. "Do you know how that should be done?"

"No, but Father Ralph will."

They both looked at the priest, who was still praying over the earl. "My father isn't dead," Roger repeated. He sounded as if he couldn't believe it.

"Talk to Father Ralph. Or Simon, " Nell said. "He has been here a long time. Perhaps he can explain why your grandfather behaved as he did."

"I will," Roger said tensely.

The priest was making the sign of the cross over the whole body, signaling that he was done. Nell said to her husband, "Would you like to be alone for a while?"

Roger nodded mutely.

"Come along, Father," Nell said. "Roger wants to be alone with Lord William."

The priest crossed the floor to her side and both of them moved toward the door. When they reached it, Nell suddenly turned back and returned to Roger. She kissed his cheek. "I'm sorry," she whispered.

He made no response.

Twelve

The funeral was held the day after Lord William's death, in the chapel at Wilton. The earl's coffin reposed at the top of the central aisle and the benches were filled with all the folk from Wilton Castle, from Roger down to the lowliest scullery maid.

Roger had watched over his grandfather's body the previous night, but he didn't feel tired at all as he listened to Father Ralph recite the familiar Latin of the mass.

How could you have kept this from me? he thought as he looked at the coffin. *For all these years you let me think my father was dead when he was really alive. Why would you do such a thing? How could you let me find out like this?*

He thought of his grandfather's last words and the promise he had extracted from Roger. *Grandfather thought that my father has come back to claim the earldom. What if that is true?*

What could have happened to cause his grandfather to disinherit his only son? he wondered. What could his father have done to cause his grandfather to behave so?

The priest turned to face the congregation. *"Dominus vobiscum,"* he intoned.

"Et cum spiritu tuo," the altar servers responded.

The congregation stood.

Roger looked at the coffin. *I'm the earl now,* he thought. He had been preparing for this role all his life; he was not afraid of shouldering the burden of authority.

But his father was still alive. His father had come back to England.

What can it all mean? he thought. *What is my father planning to do?*

He glanced down at the top of Nell's head, which reached just to his mouth. *I have Nell,* he thought. *At least I'm not completely alone.*

The funeral feast was largely silent. Roger couldn't eat any of the food that was set in front of him. The only words he spoke were to Simon Everard. "We must talk."

Simon, his face white and strained, bowed his head. "Yes, my lord."

"Come upstairs with me," Roger said to the steward when the meal was finally finished. The two men left the hall, Simon trailing a little behind Roger as they went to the stairs that would take them to Roger's apartment. When they entered the solar, Roger gestured Simon to one of the high-backed chairs while he took the other one. The shutters were open to let in the light from the chilly October day. The brazier had not been lit.

"Tell me about my father," Roger said.

The older man sighed. "My lord, I was never in favor of this deception but your grandfather insisted."

"Why did he do such a thing? What did my father do to cause him to be cut off like this?"

Simon sighed again, more deeply than before. "Guy was trouble from the day he was born," he said. "He couldn't stand authority. Even as a boy he flouted it as often as he could."

"Some boys are just naturally rambunctious," Roger said. "I have seen that in some of the squires. But they grow out of it."

"Guy was more than rambunctious. He always had to have his way. He thought the world revolved around him. And as he grew older he grew worse. He and Lord William were always at odds."

"But what did he *do*?" Roger persisted.

Simon nervously slid his hands up and down the arms of his chair. His gaze moved from Roger's eyes to the cold brazier. "For one thing, he seduced one of the castle ladies and got her with child. She was under Lord William's protection so he couldn't just ignore the situation and send her home. Guy had to marry her and that made Lord William furious. He had been planning a grand dynastic marriage for his son."

There was a little silence. "Was that my mother?" Roger asked in a low voice.

"Yes."

Roger was silent again. Then he asked, "And was that all he did?"

"No." Simon's lips tightened and his eyes sought Roger's again. "He drew his sword on Lord William."

Roger's breath caught audibly.

"They were arguing, as usual, and Guy drew his sword and held it to Lord William's throat. We all saw it."

"He wouldn't have used it!" Roger said.

"I don't know. When Guy was infuriated he would do anything. Fortunately, I was standing behind Guy and I pulled my own sword and held it to his back. I told him that if he didn't drop his sword I would run mine through him."

There was a tense silence. "And that was when my grandfather banished him?"

"No. He waited until you were born before he did that."

Roger frowned. "What difference would that make?"

Simon answered simply. "You gave Lord William an heir besides Guy."

Roger's face was somber. "Where has my father—" he had difficulty saying the words "—been all these years?"

"In France. He became famous at the tournaments. He is a formidable fighter. Like you, he was always the best knight in the castle. And he was a leader—again, like you. Men just naturally did what he said. He would have made an excellent earl, if it wasn't for that temper of his."

Roger shook his head slowly. "I don't understand—why did my grandfather let me believe he was dead?"

Simon leaned a little forward. "When you were born it was like a second chance for Lord William. He vowed he would mold you into the perfect successor to him." Simon leaned a little more. "You gave him much joy, Roger. You are as talented a knight as Guy was, but you don't have his temper. You are kind, you care about your people. Lord William was so proud of you!"

"But I still don't understand why he couldn't have told me!"

"I can't answer that question, my lord. I can only say that Lord William made the decision and he bound all of us to keep the secret. I am sorry the truth had to come as such a shock to you."

Roger was quiet for a few moments. Then he asked soberly, "Do you think my father came back to claim Wilton?"

"Yes, I do. The empress probably promised him the earldom if ever she wins the kingdom from Stephen."

"My God," Roger said feelingly.

"I am sorry all of this has descended on you at once," Simon said. "I think your grandfather meant to tell you one day about your father, but he never seemed to find the right time."

"I am twenty-two years of age!" Roger cried. "What was he waiting for?"

Simon sighed. "I don't know, my lord."

Roger ran his fingers through his hair, something he only did when he was deeply distressed. "Guy couldn't have come with a following. There were only a hundred and forty knights with Stephen."

"I think you should go to the king right away, my lord, and pledge your allegiance to him as the Earl of Wiltshire. Better to make certain of the earldom before anything else."

"Stephen wouldn't give the earldom to Guy!" Roger said sharply.

"No, Guy is pledged to the empress. But I don't trust him, my lord. He has a silver tongue and he can be very persuasive. He's a dangerous man, my lord. Never forget that. Make certain of the earldom."

Roger said, "The king will besiege Arundel Castle. Perhaps my father will be captured and sent back to France."

"That would be the best thing for all of us," Simon said fervently.

"Thank you, Simon," Roger said.

Recognizing a dismissal, Simon stood up. "I'm sorry, my lord, that you had to find out this way."

"Yes," Roger said grimly. "So am I."

That night in bed, Roger told Nell everything he had learned from Simon.

"I don't understand what my grandfather could have been thinking," he finished. "Why didn't he just tell me?"

"Perhaps he didn't want you to worry that someone

else may have a claim to the earldom," she said. She was sitting up against her pillows, with the covers pulled to her chin. Roger had left the curtain open a little and a candle lit so they could see each other.

He didn't reply.

"Or perhaps he didn't want your loyalty to be divided," she suggested next.

He said slowly, "I wonder if that was why he didn't send me to another great household to be trained. He didn't want me to learn that my father wasn't dead."

"Perhaps," Nell said.

"I'd like to meet him, Nell," Roger said in a tight voice. "I know Simon wouldn't agree, but I'd like to meet him. He had a temper when he was a boy. He could be different now that he is a man."

"Perhaps," Nell said again.

"And my mother...for all these years she has been separated from her husband."

"I wonder why he never sent for her."

"You can't drag a wife around the tournament circle," Roger said. "And the tournaments were how he made his living."

"I wonder..." Nell said slowly. "Do you think your grandfather might have been deliberately keeping you separated from your mother?"

He turned his head to look at her. "What do you mean?"

"I mean, I wonder if she didn't want to see you or if Lord William didn't *want* her to see you."

"My God," Roger said as he considered the possibility.

"It would be worth finding out."

"Nell..." His voice sounded strangled. "I loved m..."

She reached over and found his hand. She took it into a comforting grasp. "It's only natural that you should be," she said. "He kept things from you—very important things—and he left you to find out the truth in a horrible way. You can love and be angry at the same time. I was angry at Sister Helen and Mother Superior but that didn't stop me from still loving them."

Roger's hand returned her grip strongly. "Simon says I should go to Stephen and make my homage for the earldom."

"That is probably good advice."

"I want to be the earl," he said. "It's what I was raised for."

"You should be the earl. Your grandfather had the right to choose his successor, and he chose you. Nothing has changed about that."

There was a long silence.

"I will go to see Stephen," he said at last.

She patted their clasped hands with her other hand and slowly he released his grip. She settled down under the covers and fixed her pillow the way she liked it.

"You should get some sleep," she said. "You have had an emotionally exhausting day."

"Nell..." he said.

"What?" She looked at him in innocent expectation.

...nes of her cheekbones
...as long and slender, and h...
...kiss it. He wanted...
...into her an...
Fo...

...of his strength...
...have stayed...
...glad I have...
"I onl...
...murmur...
...eyes...
Nell. Le...
S...

"Pleas...
...the tension...
a little long...
The silen...
right," he said

Roger rode in...
of Arundel late in...
his entire army, al...
undel to capture the...
stepmother, Adeliza o...
Stephen was sitting...
...nished tent when Roge...
knights were in the tent,...
said, going down on one k...

all the women in the castle and now she had alienated Roger, her only friend.

She wished her mother had never told her what happened between a man and a woman when they made love. It was an ugly picture she just couldn't get out of her mind. All of her modesty recoiled from it.

But she had liked Roger's kiss. If only that was all that lovemaking involved, holding each other and kissing! She would like that very much.

It took two weeks for all of Roger's vassals to visit Wilton and swear their allegiance to him. The last one to come was Sir Humphrey Bouvay, who held the castle and manor of Claver, near Malmesbury.

"Humphrey was a friend of your father's when they were young," Simon told Roger. "If he doesn't come to swear allegiance we might have to move against him."

But Humphrey finally came, excusing his delay by saying that he had been ill.

Humphrey Bouvay was a slim man of Roger's own height. His black hair had a sprinkling of gray and his eyes were a pale blue in color. Roger invited him to sit next to him at supper and, as the soup was served, he said, "I understand that you used to know my father."

Sir Humphrey lifted his spoon to his mouth and took a swallow of soup. "Yes. I was a knight in service here when Guy was still at home."

"I have never met my father," Roger said.

"You were just a babe when Earl William banished him," Sir Humphrey replied cautiously.

"I have never heard why he was banished," Roger said frankly. "Do you know the reason?"

Sir Humphrey shrugged. "Guy had a temper, all did know that, but as far as I know, he never did anything that would justify the sentence that Earl William passed on him." He drank some more soup. "You know that he has come back with the empress."

"So I have heard." Roger's hand tightened on his knife. "My grandfather was a fair man. Guy must have done something unforgivable for my grandfather to have banished him like that."

Sir Humphrey shook his head. There was the faintest trace of bitterness in his voice as he replied, "There was nothing that I know of, my lord. I think it was just that they did not get along and once you were born Sir William had an acceptable replacement for his son."

Roger didn't answer and after a minute Sir Humphrey turned to the man on his other side, who was asking him a question. Roger ate in silence, his mind going over what Sir Humphrey had said. Evidently the fact that Guy had drawn a sword on his father was not common knowledge. How many other men thought like Sir Humphrey, that Guy had been badly treated by his father? How many men thought Guy to be the rightful earl?

The vassals all went home and life at Wilton returned to normal. Roger took Nell out hunting a few times and she found she liked it very much. If someone had told her a few months ago that she would enjoy a wild gallop through the woods, she would have said that they were mad. She still tended to hold onto her horse's mane a great deal, but she found the swiftness of the pace exhilarating, not frightening, and Roger was proud of her.

On the surface her relationship with her husband seemed to be unruffled, but in some significant ways Nell noticed that he had changed. His temper was shorter than usual with his knights and often he seemed to be on edge. She thought he was worried about his father, but he didn't talk to her about Guy anymore. At night he got into bed and blew out the candle immediately, not attempting to talk to her the way he used to. He also tended to lie as far away from her as he could.

Nell was lonely. She found herself missing Sister Helen desperately and shed many tears in the privacy of her own room. Roger had once said that he would try to get some younger women to be companions to her. Finally she decided to ask him to follow through on that promise.

She found her husband by the archery butts in the outer bailey. The knights were taking practice and Roger was watching. When Nell came up, Roger went over to her and the knights redoubled their efforts. Nell watched with admiration as they pulled on the great bows, sending arrows thudding into the target that was attached to the butts. They were all consistently around the center of the target. When one of them shot outside the arrows of the other men, they hooted and teased him until he shot again and did better.

"Shoot, my lord," one of the men called when all of the knights had finished. "Show my lady how good you are."

Roger looked at Nell.

"I'd love to see you shoot," she said, her eyes sparkling.

"Where is my bow?"

One of the knights came running, holding a huge bow in his hands.

"Can I see it?" Nell asked.

Roger held it out for her to run her hand across the smooth wood.

"My lord's bow has a draw weight of a hundred and fifty pounds," one of the knights told Nell proudly. "It's the most in the castle."

"A hundred and fifty pounds!" Nell looked at her slender husband. "Can you pull that?"

"Aye, he can," one of the knights answered her. "My lord is very strong."

Roger went over to toe the line. He stood for a moment, his arms lowered, and then began to raise the bow, all the while pushing the stave and pulling the string to bring the bow into a position of full draw. For the briefest of moments, he stood in the classic position of the archer, string near his ear, his head framed by the bow and the string. Then he let the arrow fly.

It buried itself in the dead center of the target circle.

A number of other arrows were in the circle, but none in the dead center.

The knights cheered.

Roger smiled and turned to Nell.

"Do it again," the knights demanded.

Roger shook his head. "Once is enough. The rest of you get on with your practice. I want to talk to Lady Eleanor."

He took her arm and steered her back toward the castle. "What brought you looking for me?" he asked.

"I just had a question and I thought it would be nice to get outside in this fine weather."

"What was your question?"

"I was wondering if it would be possible to get some younger women to come to the castle and serve as my ladies. We talked about it once before, remember?"

He walked for a moment in silence. "I suppose I could send word around to my vassals to see if they have some younger sisters or daughters who might come to Wilton to serve as companions to you. You should have reminded me when they were here. I could have asked them then."

"I didn't think of it."

Roger said, "I don't think I can get rid of the ladies who are already here, Nell. They have been at Wilton since my grandfather was young. I know they're old and set in their ways, but…"

"I would never ask you to get rid of them," she said quickly. "Wilton is their home and they have a right to live out their lives here. I would just like to add some younger ladies to our circle."

"I own, it would be nice to have some younger women here," Roger said. "The knights would be thrilled. Why, we haven't danced at Wilton in ages."

"I think it will even be good for the older women," Nell said. "Young blood will help enliven them."

He looked at her. "Are you having a problem with the women, Nell? Hasn't Lady Mabel been a help to you?"

Nell did not want to burden him with more problems and so she just shrugged. "She doesn't like it when I do new things. For example, she can't understand why I want to enlarge the herb garden. And she is scandalized that I am out there, supervising the work myself. But I don't let her bother me, Roger."

"Good for you," Roger said. She smiled up at him. He looked very handsome, with the October sun shining on his dark gold hair and his glinting golden eyes.

In so many ways she was lucky to have him, she thought. She had met his vassals and the thought had struck her more than once that she would be miserable if she had been married to one of them. Roger was beautiful to look at and he was kind. She always felt happy when she was in his company. And she couldn't deny the pleasure when he kissed her. She would have asked him to kiss her more if it weren't for her fear of what came after the kissing.

If only the consummation of this marriage didn't hang over her like a dark threatening cloud.

She was going to have to give in one of these days.

I will do it soon, she thought. *It will make Roger happy and he deserves to be happy.*

Her stomach tightened.

"Thank you, my lord, for listening to me," she said a little breathlessly.

"I am always happy to listen to you, Nell," he replied gravely. "And I will see about finding you some younger companions."

Fourteen

That afternoon, after dinner had been served and the trestle tables were being taken up, Roger asked Nell if she would like to see the small lake that lay in the woods to the west of Wilton.

"You said you wanted to get out of the castle and it's a beautiful spot, one of my favorites," he said. "I go there whenever I need to think."

"I would love to see it," Nell replied, delighted to be asked.

Roger had their horses brought and they rode out together, across the cleared fields surrounding Wilton and into the woods. Roger didn't talk as they rode along and Nell respected his silence. Instead she listened to the noises of the woods: the sound of squirrels scurrying through the undergrowth, of birds fluttering through the trees, of leaves rustling in the breeze. A rabbit ran across their path and Gawain chased it. The autumn leaves were turning and the red and gold colors overhead and drifting down were brilliant.

Nell inhaled deeply and thought, with a little surprise, that right now she was content.

Thank you, God, for this day.

She saw the reflection of water through the trees ahead and in a moment they came out on the shore of a small lake. The water glistened in the sunlight and the brilliant trees surrounding it were reflected back in the still water.

"Oh," Nell breathed. "It's beautiful."

"It's beautiful all year long, but particularly in the autumn," Roger said.

They rode out onto the shore and Roger slid to the ground. He turned to Nell, fitting his hands around her waist to swing her down.

His hands felt so strong around her waist, she thought. She remembered how he had pulled the bow.

"Come and sit down," he said. "There's a log that makes a good seat."

She trailed along after him, to a fallen tree that lay on the rocky shore. They both sat facing the water while Gawain went to sniff along the edge of the woods.

Roger took her hand into his. Nell's heart hurried a little at his touch. His hand was hard and callused across the palm. She drew a long breath and curled her fingers around his. "I can see why you like to come here," she said. "It's like a balm to the soul."

He looked at her. "I knew you'd feel like that."

His hair was as deeply gold as the leaves. Nell loved looking at him.

"I like knowing how to ride," she said. "I like being able to go to different places."

"With this war, it's a little difficult to travel." He looked down at their clasped hands. "Do you like it here at Wilton, Nell? Are you happy?"

"I still miss Sister Helen," she said honestly.

"In the spring I will send you to Sister Helen to pick out your herbs."

She turned to face him, her face aglow. "Do you mean that, Roger? Truly? I can go myself?"

"If the roads are safe," he said.

She gave him a radiant smile. "Thank you!"

He ran his thumb over her knuckles. She felt a strange shiver go all through her. He said, "I came here to think about what I should do about my mother."

She nodded gravely.

His eyes were dark and troubled as he looked out over the water. "Do you think I should write and ask her if I could come to visit her?"

"Yes," she said. "I do."

There was a little pause. "What if she responds that she doesn't want to see me?"

"You will be hurt," she said.

His mouth set in a straight line. He was still looking out over the water. "I don't know if I want to be hurt like that, Nell."

"I understand," she said softly. "But I still think that you should give her a chance."

He tightened his hold on her hand and turned to look at her. "But why would my grandfather have wanted to keep us apart?"

A strand of hair had slipped over his forehead, spangling it with gold. She said, "I'm sure he must have been afraid that she would tell you the truth about your father being alive."

He nodded slowly, then he looked back at the lake, showing her his profile. "Of course, it could just be that she didn't want to see me."

"I have a feeling that it is not," she said gently.

Gawain came to lie at Roger's feet. He said, "So you think I should write to her?"

She repeated, "I think you should give her the chance."

He took a deep breath. "All right, I will. I shall send to my mother tomorrow."

Silence fell again. Nell regarded the long cross-gartered legs stretched out next to hers. She listened to the lake water lap against the shore. She found herself wishing that Roger would kiss her and she blushed at the thought. He didn't kiss her, however. Instead he kissed her hand and returned it to her, her fingers tingling where his lips had been.

Roger sent the message to his mother and her reply came two days later. She would be very happy if Roger would come to visit her.

He was excited and went immediately to find Nell. They had come in from hunting and she was in their room changing her clothes. He came into their bedroom as her maid was stripping off her undertunic.

"My lord!" Nell said in surprise. She was wearing only her long white chemise shirt and her braids hung over her shoulders. She was so small that she would have looked like a child if it were not for the swell of her breasts under the thin linen.

"I received a missive from my mother," he said. He tried to keep the jubilation out of his voice. "She wants to see me."

Her face lit up. "Oh, Roger, that is wonderful." Impulsively she came across the room to hug him. The feel of her body against his was not childlike at all. He hugged her back, inhaling the scent of her hair. His whole body stirred with desire.

Finally she stepped away from him. Reluctantly he let her go.

She smiled up at him, her small face bright with happiness. She was beautiful when she looked like this. She was beautiful when she was grave also. "I am so happy for you," she said.

I don't know how much longer I can stand this, Roger thought desperately. *She doesn't understand what she is doing to me. I'm going to have to do something soon.*

He dragged his mind back to thoughts of his mother.

"I wonder what she will look like," he said. "I wonder what we will have to say to each other."

"To begin with, you can find out if it was your grandfather that kept you apart all these years."

Roger's eyes were drawn like magnets to the swell of Nell's breasts under her chemise. He swallowed.

"Do you know, I never wrote to her myself," he said. "It never occurred to me to do that. My grandfather was always so adamant that she didn't want to hear from me."

"She never wrote to you, either," Nell said.

"Maybe she did," Roger returned.

They looked at each other.

"Well, you will find out soon enough," Nell said. "When are you going to Cirencester?"

"I'll leave tomorrow," he said.

Roger was on the road at sunup the following morning, with an escort of five knights. They rode directly north, aiming for Cirencester, a city in Gloucestershire, but which had declared its allegiance to the king. It was a misty autumn day and the only sound made by the traveling party was the footfalls of their horses' hooves and the occasional jingling of the bridles.

Roger rode in silence. The rest of his knights respected his mood and didn't talk among themselves. Their usually good-natured lord had been troubled of late and they had learned to tread lightly. They traveled through the forest and past small villages and towns nestled in the hills that owed their allegiance to Roger. The mist gave an eerie atmosphere to their journey. A party of the enemy could be on them before anyone saw them, and the knights rode with more alert attention than was usual on such a journey.

They reached Cirencester in the afternoon. During the days of the Romans, Cirencester had been the second-largest city in the country, but it was most famous now for the wool that was sold there. The abbey had been recently built but the convent across town was older.

Roger gave his name to the convent portress, who proceeded to send to the order's superior. The prioress seated him in the reception room of her house and sent for Lady Cecily. Then she absented herself.

Roger's heart was thudding as he awaited the arrival of his mother. His thoughts were jumbled. *What shall I say to her? Suppose she blames me for not writing to her for all of these years? Suppose she doesn't like me?*

It seemed like an eternity until the door opened and a woman came in. She was wearing the brown habit of a Benedictine nun, but her hair was uncovered. It was the same golden color as his. Roger jumped to his feet.

"Roger?" she asked, her voice husky with emotion.

"Yes," he said. Then, tentatively added, "Mother?"

"Oh, my God." She raised her hands to her mouth. "I never thought I would see this day."

"My grandfather always told me that you didn't want to see me," Roger said.

"Didn't want to see you?" Her voice was incredulous.

"That is what he told me."

She held out her arms. "Come to me," she said.

He strode across the floor and went into her embrace. She held him tightly and he put his arms around her and held her back. Then she began to cry.

"Don't cry, Mother," he said awkwardly, although there was a pain in his chest and tears stung his own eyes. "It's all right."

She held him for a long minute, trying to control her sobs. Then she loosened her grip and stepped back. "Let me look at you." She gazed at him, the tears still running down her face.

Anyone who saw the two of them together would know instantly that they were mother and son. He had her hair and her eyes. His finely cut features were a masculine version of hers. It was uncanny, Roger thought. He had always known he looked nothing like his grandfather, but he hadn't expected this almost identical resemblance to his mother.

She gave a watery laugh. "No one would doubt that you are my son."

"No," he agreed shakily. "That is for certain."

"Why did you come to see me now, after all these years?" she asked.

"My grandfather is dead. I just thought I would write to you and see what you answered."

"Lord William is dead?"

"Yes."

She shook her head. "Somehow I thought that old man would live forever." She looked at Roger and smiled. "Come and sit down and tell me all about yourself." She led him toward a wooden bench that was pushed against the wall. They sat down side by side. She turned to him.

She looks young, Roger thought. *She must be almost forty, but she looks young.*

"Why would Grandfather want to keep us apart?" he said with a mixture of bewilderment and pain.

"Lord William hated me," she said bitterly. "He acted as if I seduced his son, when the truth was the other way around."

"For all these years, Grandfather led me to believe that my father was dead," Roger said. "I only learned a few weeks ago that he was alive."

She stared at him in amazement. "He told you Guy was dead?"

"Yes."

"Lord William thought he could control the whole world," Lady Cecily said in a hard voice. "And he did a fine job of doing it. He banished Guy to France and me to this convent. Apparently he managed to isolate you, as well."

Roger ran his fingers through his hair, dislodging a few strands, which fell down over his forehead. He pushed them back. "I don't understand why he wanted me to believe my father was dead."

"Who knows what went on in Lord William's mind? Guy was dead to him. I suppose he wanted him to be dead to you, as well."

Her voice was pleasantly husky. She was still a very

beautiful woman. Roger could see why his father had fallen in love with her.

"Have you ever heard from my father?" he asked.

"No. In all the years I have been in this convent I have heard from no one except one of my sisters."

She sounded deeply bitter. Roger said, "I always thought that you chose to leave me and come to the convent."

She laughed harshly. "Lord William clapped me in here as soon as he packed Guy off to France. Once you were born, and he had his heir, the two of us were just in his way."

"I'm sorry Mother," Roger said helplessly. "I'm so sorry." He reached for her hand. She gave it and clasped his tightly in return. "If you didn't want to be here why didn't you go home to your family?"

"My father is a vassal of Lord William's and I was just a younger daughter. They were happy to have Lord William pay the convent to accept me."

Roger bowed his head and said in a muffled voice. "I loved my grandfather. He was so good to me. It is hard to hear these things about him."

"He was furious when Guy had to marry me. He had plans for his son and Guy thwarted them by marrying beneath himself. All of your grandfather's energy was directed toward the dynasty of the de Roches. Guy spoiled things when he married me."

"Do you know why my grandfather banished him?" Roger asked.

"Guy drew his sword on Earl William in a moment of temper," Cecily said. "But he would never have used it! He would never have harmed his father."

"Did he put away the sword?"

"Yes, he did. There was no danger! There certainly was no cause to banish Guy for a moment's lapse of temper."

She shook her head as if to clear it and squeezed Roger's hand. "But tell me about yourself."

"Well…" Roger said. "I am married."

"You are? And who is the fortunate girl?"

"Eleanor de Bonvile, the only daughter of the Earl of Lincoln."

Cecily raised her perfectly arched eyebrows. "It seems as if Lord William was able to make a dynastic marriage for you where he failed with your father."

Roger stared at the tips of his boots. "When Nell's father dies, I am to inherit his earldom." He looked at his mother to see how she would take this news.

Lady Cecily smiled. "You will be a double earl then."

"Yes."

"Lord William must have been ecstatic." There was a note of scorn in her voice.

"Mother…" Roger said the word hesitantly.

Her eyes filled with tears. "*Mother*… How long I have waited to hear you say that word."

He swallowed. Then he managed to ask, "Have you heard that my father has returned to England?"

She went very still. "No."

"He came back with the empress. It was the news of his return that killed my grandfather."

She loosened her hand from his and put both hands to her face. "Guy is back," she said in a trembling voice.

"Yes. He escaped from Arundel Castle with the Earl of Gloucester and is presently in Bristol. It looks like the empress has promised him the earldom of Wiltshire for his support."

She lowered her hands. "I can't believe this," she said.

"It's true."

"What are you going to do?" she asked.

"I promised my grandfather on his deathbed that I would not let Guy have the earldom." Roger lifted his chin. "I will keep my promise. And I have the support of the king."

She turned to face him. "Don't fight with Guy, Roger! He is a formidable fighter. No one was ever able to stand against him."

"I am not so bad myself," Roger said in return.

"You can't match him. No one can."

"I don't plan to fight him, Mother. I just plan to hold what is mine."

"My God," she said. "Guy is back in England."

"You have never heard from him over the years?" Roger asked again.

"No. I told you. I have heard from no one except my sister. She was the one who told me that Guy was supporting himself at the tournaments in France."

"I never knew," Roger said wonderingly. "For all these years I never knew."

"Just be careful," his mother said. "Guy is not a man to be taken lightly."

"He has bound himself to the empress," Roger said, "and I do not think she has a prayer of wresting control of the country from Stephen."

"I don't know anything about that," Lady Cecily said.

Roger changed the subject. "Are you happy here, Mother? Or would you like to come back to Wilton with me? I would love to have you there."

Once more tears began to slide down his mother's face. "Oh, Roger, how kind of you to ask me that."

He blinked back the tears that had come into his own eyes. "I have neglected you for too long. If only I had thought to write to you!"

She patted his arm. "Don't castigate yourself. Your grandfather would probably have intercepted my return message."

"I meant what I said. I am prepared to take you back to Wilton immediately if that is what you want."

Lady Cecily gave him a trembling smile. "I think you should talk to your wife first."

"Nell will be happy to receive you. I know she will. She was the one who told me to write to you in the first place."

"Still, I will feel better if you consult her. All will go more smoothly if she expects me and is prepared to receive me, Roger."

He began to argue but she cut him off. "Believe me, this is the better way."

He sighed. "All right. If that is what you want."

"It is."

"I'm sorry, Mother," he said intensely. "I'm sorry I neglected you all these years. I'm sorry you had to stay in a place you didn't like."

She lifted her hand to caress his cheek. "It wasn't your fault. They have been kind to me here, but I have felt as if I was buried alive. I was not meant for the convent and I will be happy to get out. But I want you to ask your wife first."

"I will come and get you soon," he said.

She gave him a radiant smile. "I am so happy to see you, Roger."

"And I to see you," he replied.

He returned to Wilton with a full heart, anxious to tell Nell what had happened.

Fifteen

As Roger had expected, Nell was in favor of bringing Lady Cecily to Wilton.

"She was not happy in the convent?" she asked Roger.

"She said she felt as if she was buried alive."

They were in bed and it was the first chance they had had to talk privately since Roger had returned late in the afternoon.

Nell said, "She knew the world before she went in. That is the difference between us. The convent was all that I knew."

"I am learning some things about my grandfather I would rather not know," Roger said grimly.

Nell heard the pain in his voice. "Keep remembering that he loved you, Roger," she said. "Everything he did was for you."

He turned toward her. "My mother said that my father would never have used his sword on my grandfather."

"He should never have drawn it," Nell said. "Aside from being his father, Lord William was his liege lord. No matter how bad his temper was, he should never have so lost control of himself that he drew his sword. Can you imagine yourself doing such a thing?"

"No."

"Your grandfather was not wrong to banish him," Nell said earnestly. "It was not your fault, Roger. He earned what he got."

"Well, thank you for agreeing to take my mother, Nell. She will be very grateful."

"I will be glad to have her," Nell said honestly. Privately, she thought it would be wonderful to have a lady who would not be under Lady Mabel's thumb.

A little silence fell. Then Roger said, "Would you mind if I held you for a little, Nell? We won't do anything else but I would like to hold you."

Nell's heart began to thud. She was suddenly very conscious of her nakedness. "All right," she said breathlessly.

He reached out and touched her arm. "Come here to me."

She moved toward him, sliding across the sheets. She felt his arms come around her, then she was being pulled against him. He felt warm and hard and his arms held her firmly. Her cheek came to rest against his bare shoulder. She inhaled his scent, a scent that had grown familiar over the weeks. She felt his cheek against the top of her head. Slowly and cautiously she put her own arms around him.

"You smell so good," he said.

"So do you."

Her breasts were pressed against his chest. The skin of his back was smooth but she could feel the muscles under her fingers. He was very strong.

"This isn't so bad, is it?" he said.

"No."

"Relax. You don't need to be so stiff. I'm not going to do anything."

She tried to relax. He began to stroke her back. "How does that feel?"

"Nice."

She felt herself beginning to unwind. *This is all right,* she thought cautiously.

Then she became aware of something pressing into her abdomen. She stiffened again.

He continued to rub her back and once again she began to relax. He wasn't going to do anything; he was just going to hold her.

"Roger…" she said.

"Yes."

"Thank you for being so patient with me."

He said, "Let's see if we can get you used to me holding you and touching you. Then perhaps the next step won't seem so frightening."

She ran her hands up and down his back, feeling the hard muscles, thinking of the golden color of his skin. She said, "What does your mother look like?"

"She looks just like me," he said, a note of wonder

in his voice. "It's the most astonishing thing, Nell. My hair, my eyes...everything."

"How did you feel, meeting her?"

"I was nervous. Do you know, in my heart I always blamed her for leaving me? And now I find out that it was my grandfather's doing!"

"Try not to think too hardly of him," she urged again. "He loved you. He was so proud of you, Roger."

"Did he love *me* or did he just love having another heir?"

She could hear his heart beating against her cheek. She said, "You were everything his son wasn't. I'm sure he loved you."

"I hope so." He didn't sound certain.

They were quiet for a while. Roger's hand continued to move up and down her back. Nell felt herself relaxing into him. Her eyes began to close.

"All right?" he asked, his voice sounding husky.

She opened her eyes. "Yes."

"I'd like to kiss you."

Nell willingly raised her head and his mouth came down on hers. She kissed him back with her mouth closed. Then he deepened the kiss and she could feel him urging her to open her mouth. When she did, his tongue came into her.

At first she was startled and tried to pull away, but he held her close. After a moment the movement of his tongue began to rouse sensations she had never known before. Tentatively, her own tongue answered.

A slow liquid heat began to run through her body. His body felt hard and solid against her. She stopped thinking and gave herself up to the sweet sensations that were running through her. When he released her mouth, she felt a little shock of separation.

"This is what it's like to make love," he murmured in her ear.

"This was nice," she said a little breathlessly.

"I'm glad you liked it." He moved away from her. "Now I think it's time we both got some sleep."

Roger had a plan. He would seduce her slowly, going a little further each night until she was ready to accept all of him. Until she wanted him to make love to her. It would require great self-control on his part, but the end result would be worth it. Her response tonight had been very gratifying.

I can break down her barriers, he thought, as he punched his pillow into shape. *I just have to be patient.*

But his young male body didn't feel patient at all. In fact, it was screaming at him for release. Perhaps he shouldn't have stopped. Perhaps he should have just kept going on.

He turned back to his wife, to see if perhaps he could pick up where he had left off, but her soft breathing told him she was asleep.

Roger shut his eyes and resigned himself to a sleepless night.

The following day the household was at dinner when a messenger from the king sought admission to the castle. Roger unrolled the parchment and read what was written there. The color left his face.

"What is it?" Nell asked, concerned.

"The Sheriff of Gloucester has been raiding and pillaging royalist supporters in Gloucestershire and Hertfordshire, burning all the villages and towns within his reach. One of the towns he has raided is Cirencester."

"My dear God," Nell breathed.

"My mother," Roger began. He was very white.

"Surely he wouldn't touch the convent!"

"He raided the convent in Worcester. Why wouldn't he do the same at Cirencester?"

Nell's eyes were huge. "What are you going to do?"

"Take my knights and ride for Cirencester," Roger said grimly. He stood up and spoke to the room. "I want all knights to be ready to ride in a half an hour. Miles of Gloucester has raided Cirencester."

The sound of benches being pushed back ran through the room. The knights all made for the stairs to go down to the guardroom, where they slept and kept their armor. A group of squires followed to help them arm.

Roger also made for the stairs, his squire following him, Gawain on their heels. After a moment's hesitation, Nell followed, as well.

When she got to their room, Roger was putting on his mail leggings.

"Is there anything I can do?" she asked.

"Simon will take care of things while I am gone," he answered. "Don't worry, Nell."

"When did this happen?" she asked.

"Yesterday."

"Who is the Sheriff of Gloucester?"

"Miles of Gloucester is one of the empress's main supporters," he answered. "He is the best soldier she has. The messenger also wrote that Miles attacked and destroyed the part of Stephen's army that he left behind to besiege Wallingford."

"I thought the king himself was besieging Wallingford," Nell said.

"It seems that Stephen has a habit of not finishing what he starts," Roger said grimly. "He took part of his army to besiege other castles and the men he left behind at Wallingford were vulnerable. Miles took advantage of that."

Nell was silent.

"I should have insisted that she come home with me when I was there," Roger said. "Fool that I was, I left her there."

"You had no hint that she would be in danger," Nell said. "It wasn't your fault, Roger."

"It's amazing how nothing is ever my fault," he said bitterly.

"It was your mother's wish that you ask me first. You were simply abiding by her desire."

Roger said nothing. His squire fitted Roger's hauberk over his head, the iron rings jingling. He began to buckle the sides.

When the hauberk was finished, Roger put his mail hood up and let Richard fit his cone-shaped iron helmet over it. He left the nose guard up.

He looked so different in his armor, she thought. Very different from the man who had held her last night.

"Be careful," she pleaded.

"Pray that the convent is safe," he returned.

"I will," she promised. Then he was out the door.

Nell stayed at the window to watch the knights ride out. They all had their helmets on with the nose guards down making it impossible to recognize them. The red banner with its leopard insignia rippled in the breeze. Roger rode in front, behind the flag bearers, with the knights in a phalanx behind him.

Dear God, she prayed. *Please let Roger's mother be all right. And please keep Roger safe. Don't let this Miles of Gloucester still be around Cirencester. Thank you for listening to my prayer.*

Roger and his knights were a few miles outside of Cirencester when they ran into loose livestock. Sheep were wandering aimlessly along the roadway and in the woods they could see domestic pigs rooting for food. After the livestock came the refugees—men, women and children carrying their belongings on their backs, streaming along the road in search of safety.

The news Roger gathered from the fleeing residents was not encouraging. The attack against Cirencester had come the day before, early in the morning, with

Gloucester's troops breaking into the city on its south side. The soldiers had driven off all of the town's livestock, murdered and maimed its inhabitants, and set fire to the town.

"How about the convent?" Roger asked the man he was talking to. "Did they ravage the convent, too?"

"I don't know," came the reply. "The soldiers were drunk. They attacked the abbey. They could have attacked the convent, as well."

Roger and his men continued on, poised to fight if necessary, but they encountered no soldiers as they drew near the city.

The raiders must have finished their work, Roger thought. *Please God, let my mother be all right.*

When they entered Cirencester, they entered a devastated city. Fires raged on every street. Groups of citizens had organized to put them out, and Roger and his knights passed by lines of firefighters throwing water on the roaring flames. The women and children who had remained in the city helped to pass the buckets along. The wet smoldering ashes of many houses testified to the fact that the firefighters had had some success.

Roger and his men rode in silence through the streets of the maimed city until finally they reached the convent.

The first thing Roger saw was the empty gatehouse. *Not a good sign,* he thought grimly as he rode through the unattended gate and into the small Benedictine enclave where his mother resided.

There were fires here, as well. The sanctity of the convent had evidently not stopped the raiders. Nuns, dressed in smoke-stained habits, scurried about trying to put the fires out. They were helped by a number of men from the town.

Roger dismounted and, holding Bayard, pushed up his nose guard and went up to one of the nuns and asked if she knew aught of Cecily de Roche.

"I haven't seen her," the nun replied. "You had better speak to the prioress." She directed him to the church. Roger gave his horse to one of the knights and went on foot toward the small church that was part of the enclave. When he reached the church he took off his helmet and pushed down his hood before he went in.

Inside, the light was dim and it was a moment before Roger could discern the nun standing in the middle of the center aisle, her hands clasped at her breast. Before approaching her, Roger took time to look around the church.

The altar was bare. No gold candlesticks. No gold tabernacle. No gold chalices. He looked around the walls and saw that even the stations of the cross were gone.

Roger tightened his grip upon his helmet and moved slowly toward the solitary figure in the middle of the denuded church. She waited until he had reached her before she looked at him.

"Reverend Mother," he said. "Do you remember me? I am Roger de Roche. I have come about my mother."

The nun looked at him. Her face, framed by her

wimple, was smooth and pale. Her eyes looked dark. In the way of nuns, it was almost impossible to tell her age.

"Is she here?" he asked.

The nun's face never changed. "No."

His heart began to slam. "Was she taken by the raiders?" he managed to say steadily.

She shook her head infinitesimally. "Someone came for her before the raiders got here. He said he was her husband."

His heart felt like it was slamming against the walls of his chest. "Guy? Was it Guy de Roche?"

"That was the name she called him. We could hear the noise in the town and see the smoke. I asked him to protect us but he said he couldn't, that the soldiers were all drunk. But he took Lady Cecily away with him."

"By force?" he asked tensely.

"No. She was happy to see him. She went quite willingly. She was lucky, she got away before those animals attacked."

Happy to see him? Did she love him still, after all these years? Or perhaps she was just afraid of the soldiers.

"Where did he take her? Do you know?"

"No."

Roger clenched his fists to try to steady himself. He said, "I am so sorry, Mother. *Animals* is the proper name for them—attacking a convent."

"They were drunk and wild," the prioress said. "They took all of our sacred objects and they took some of our novices, those that were young and well favored." Her voice quivered. "They laughed at me when I protested."

Roger shuddered. At least his mother hadn't been captured and raped! It was evidently a good thing that his father had taken her away.

Roger pushed his hand through his uncovered hair. "I am so sorry, Reverend Mother. You have been through a terrible time. Is there aught I can do to help you?"

The nun drew in a long breath. "Thank you, but the worst has been done. With the help of these good townspeople we will put out the fires and start anew." For the briefest of moments she looked very old. "But nothing will ever be the same again."

Roger nodded soberly. "We will help you with the fires before we go."

"Thank you. Your help will be appreciated," the prioress replied.

Roger walked across the ravished church and out the door. Part of him was relieved that Cecily was safe but part of him felt like a small boy who has been separated from his mother for the first time.

I just found her, he thought, *and now she is gone again.*

He walked out into the courtyard and went to give his knights orders to help put out the fires.

Sixteen

Roger and his knights rode into Wilton late in the afternoon of the following day. Nell was with her ladies in their solar but when she heard that the men had returned she flew down the stairs, Gawain at her heels. Gawain had taken to staying with her when Roger wasn't around.

She knew the moment she saw his face that something was wrong. There was no woman with him.

"What happened?" she asked quietly.

His face wore a strained, remote look that she had never seen there before. They were standing together in front of the fireplace. Richard stood at a little distance, holding Roger's helmet. The rest of the knights and squires had gone down to the guardroom. Roger bent, his armor jangling, to pet the excited Gawain. When he straightened up he said, "The raiders fired and robbed the town but my father took my mother away before they got to the convent."

"Your father? *Guy?*"

"Yes. Apparently he was with the sheriff's raiding party. I have no idea where he has taken her." His voice was expressionless.

Nell's heart contracted. To think that he had finally found his mother only to have her snatched away like this…

"Did he kidnap her?" she asked.

"According to the convent's mother superior, she went with him willingly."

Nell was silent, digesting this piece of news.

The fireplace flickered, glinting off the mail armor Roger wore. He ran a hand through his matted-down hair. He seemed so…closed up…she thought. This must be excruciatingly painful for him.

"What happened in the town?" she asked softly.

"They fired it, took all that they could find—including women—and drove off all the livestock."

Nell crossed herself. "Those poor people," she said.

"We saw many people on the road, looking for a safe place to stay in case the raiders come back."

"Do you think they will?"

"No. They pretty much took what was there. The town has been ravaged, Nell. They even took away some young novices from the convent."

Nell's hand flew to her mouth. Her eyes enlarged. "Oh, my God. They took them from the *convent*? How could they do such a thing?"

"It's war, Nell. Terrible things happen in war. And the men were drunk. When men drink, they can do anything."

"Then perhaps it was a good thing that your father got your mother away."

He nodded, but the strained remote look was still on his face.

She put her hand on his arm. "Go upstairs with Richard and let him get you out of this armor. Shall I order something for you to eat?"

"No." He removed his arm from beneath her hand and signaled to Richard. "I'll see you at supper, Nell."

She watched with troubled eyes as he left the hall.

Roger was quiet as Richard took off his armor. The squire, who was accustomed to having a conversation with his lord, made a few comments, but the unusual monosyllabic replies told him that Roger didn't want to talk. So the room remained silent, except for the clinking of the armor. When it was all off, Richard said respectfully, "I'll leave you, my lord."

"Thank you," Roger replied, the first time he had strung two words together.

When his squire had left, Roger went over to the window, which was unshuttered to let the cool autumn air into the room. He was so tense that he felt as if he might shatter, and he gripped the window's ledge, as if to get a purchase on something solid.

What could it mean, this reunion of his father and mother? She had gone with her husband willingly, the prioress had said. Did she still love him after all these years?

It's a good thing she didn't wait for me to return. It was the safe thing to do—to go with my father.

He had so been looking forward to having his mother come home with him. To think she had loved him for all these years and he had never known... And now she was with his father. His father, who was claiming his earldom.

What is my father going to do? What can he do? None of my vassals will follow him if he declares himself against me.

He thought of the tour he had made this spring with his grandfather, of how Lord William had insisted that each vassal swear allegiance to Roger as his future lord. Roger had not thought very much about it at the time, but in retrospect it had a great deal of significance. Could Lord William have foreseen the return of his son? Was that his way of ensuring the loyalty of Wilton's vassals to Roger?

I wonder what my father is like. Has he changed from the rash young man who pulled his sword on his father? Does he know I am earl? Does he hate me for having what he thinks belongs to him?

Roger thought of the deathbed oath he swore to his grandfather. Even if his grandfather was not as perfect as Roger had always thought him to be, still an oath to a dying man was a sacred thing. He would keep his oath. He would hold his own against all opposition—even if the opponent should be his own father.

Part of him looked forward to sharing these feelings with Nell, but part of him dreaded getting into bed with her. She was one of the reasons he was feeling so tense, so wound up, so stressed. His deepest instinct was to plunge himself into the heart of her and instead he had to hold her tenderly and restrain his own gut-wrenching desire.

The scene at Cirencester, and the news that novices had been taken from the convent, had disturbed him profoundly. He had been thinking that he would consummate their marriage tonight, but he couldn't behave like those drunken raiders at Cirencester. He must wait until she was ready. She had to want to come to him. Otherwise he was no better than those animals.

But the thought of getting into bed with her tonight, and holding her chastely, was enough to make him shudder.

He made an abrupt decision and ran down the stairs to the Great Hall in search of his squire. To his relief, Nell was no longer there. He gave Richard orders to bring him a horse from the stable. "Not Bayard, he has just been put away. Bring me Patrick. I am going to go into town."

Richard's blue eyes widened at this sudden request. "Aye, my lord. Do you want me to come with you?"

"No. I'm going alone."

Richard's whole face showed his surprise, which he was careful not to voice. "I will go and get Patrick for you, my lord," he said and ran from the room.

Roger had only to wait a few minutes before Richard appeared leading a tall bay. Roger swung into his

YOUR PARTICIPATION IS REQUESTED!

Dear Reader,

Since you are a lover of fiction — we would like to get to know you!

Inside you will find a short Reader's Survey. Sharing your answers with us will help our editorial staff understand who you are and what activities you enjoy.

To thank you for your participation, we would like to send you 2 books and a gift — **ABSOLUTELY FREE!**

Enjoy your gifts with our appreciation,

Pam Powers

SEE INSIDE FOR READER'S SURVEY

What's Your Reading Pleasure...
ROMANCE? <u>OR</u> SUSPENSE?

Do you prefer spine-tingling page turners OR heart-stirring stories about love and relationships? Tell us which books you enjoy – and you'll get 2 FREE "ROMANCE" BOOKS or 2 FREE "SUSPENSE" BOOKS with no obligation to purchase anything.

Choose "ROMANCE" and get **2 FREE BOOKS** that will fuel your imagination with intensely moving stories about life, love and relationships.

FREE!

Choose "SUSPENSE" and you'll get **2 FREE BOOKS** that will thrill you with a spine-tingling blend of suspense and mystery.

FREE!

Whichever category you select, your 2 free books have a combined cover price of $11.98 or more in the U.S. and $13.98 or more in Canada.

And remember... just for accepting the Editor's Free Gift Offer, we'll send you 2 books and a gift, ABSOLUTELY FREE!

YOURS FREE! We'll send you a fabulous surprise gift absolutely FREE, just for trying "Romance" or "Suspense"!

® and ™ are trademarks owned and used by the trademark owner and/or its licensee.

Visit us online at
www.FreeBooksandGift.com

Offer limited to one per household and not valid to current subscribers of MIRA, Romance, Suspense or "The Best of the Best." All orders subject to approval. Books received may vary. Credit or debit balances in a customer's account(s) may be offset by any other outstanding balance owed by or to the customer.

YOUR READER'S SURVEY "THANK YOU" FREE GIFTS INCLUDE:

▶ 2 Romance OR 2 Suspense books

▶ A lovely surprise gift

PLEASE **FILL IN THE CIRCLES COMPLETELY TO RESPOND**

1) What type of fiction books do you enjoy reading? (Check all that apply)
○ Suspense/Thrillers　○ Action/Adventure　○ Modern-day Romances
○ Historical Romance　○ Humour　○ Science fiction

2) What attracted you most to the last fiction book you purchased on impulse?
○ The Title　○ The Cover　○ The Author　○ The Story

3) What is usually the greatest influencer when you <u>plan</u> to buy a book?
○ Advertising　○ Referral from a friend
○ Book Review　○ Like the author

4) Approximately how many fiction books do you read in a year?
○ 1 to 6　○ 7 to 19　○ 20 or more

5) How often do you access the internet?
○ Daily　○ Weekly　○ Monthly　○ Rarely or never

6) To which of the following age groups do you belong?
○ Under 18　○ 18 to 34　○ 35 to 64　○ over 65

YES! I have completed the Reader's Survey. Please send me the 2 FREE books and gift for which I qualify. I understand that I am under no obligation to purchase any books, as explained on the back and on the opposite page.

Check one:

	ROMANCE
	193 MDL D37C　393 MDL D37D

	SUSPENSE
	192 MDL D37E　392 MDL D37F

FIRST NAME　　　　　　　LAST NAME

ADDRESS

APT.#　　　CITY

STATE/PROV.　　ZIP/POSTAL CODE

▶ DETACH AND MAIL CARD TODAY!

(SUR-MI-05) © 1998 MIRA BOOKS

The Reader Service — Here's How It Works:

Accepting your 2 free books and gift places you under no obligation to buy anything. You may keep the books and gift and return the shipping statement marked "cancel." If you do not cancel, about a month later we'll send you 3 additional books and bill you just $4.99 each in the U.S., or $5.49 each in Canada, plus 25¢ shipping & handling per book and applicable taxes if any.* That's the complete price and — compared to cover prices starting from $5.99 each in the U.S. and $6.99 each in Canada — it's quite a bargain! You may cancel at any time, but if you choose to continue, every month we'll send you 3 more books, which you may either purchase at the discount price or return to us and cancel your subscription.

*Terms and prices subject to change without notice. Sales tax applicable in N.Y. Canadian residents will be charged applicable provincial taxes and GST.

If offer card is missing write to: The Reader Service, 3010 Walden Ave., P.O. Box 1867, Buffalo, NY 14240-1867

BUSINESS REPLY MAIL
FIRST-CLASS MAIL   PERMIT NO. 717-003   BUFFALO, NY

POSTAGE WILL BE PAID BY ADDRESSEE

THE READER SERVICE
3010 WALDEN AVE
PO BOX 1341
BUFFALO NY 14240-8571

NO POSTAGE
NECESSARY
IF MAILED
IN THE
UNITED STATES

high saddle, picked up the reins, and without another word rode off under the portcullis. The knights on guard duty watched him go.

The town of Wilton lay several miles away from the castle, along the River Avon. It had one main street that held most of the shops, which were really nothing more than open-fronted booths on the ground floor of the shopkeepers' residences. Streets of narrow, wooden residential buildings wound off the main street. Roger thought of what he had seen in Cirencester and feared that Wilton would go up like a torch if it was ever raided.

He rode down the main street, past the cloth merchants, past the fishmonger, past the shop that sold knives for pruning vines, sickles for cutting corn and spades for digging. He came to a stop in front of the silversmith's shop and dismounted. One of the boys who had been tossing a leather ball around in the street came to hold his horse.

A woman was behind the long table displaying the smith's wares. She was tall and strongly built, with long blond hair worn in two plaits over her shoulders. "Good afternoon, my lord," she greeted him. "Have you come to buy a gift for your new wife?"

"Good afternoon, Tordis," he replied. "Yes, I thought I would take a look at your wares."

She smiled. "I got some new things in yesterday from a peddler who had been in London. Let me show them to you."

Roger obediently bent his head and looked at the silver brooch that was being displayed for his benefit. It was very pretty.

"Perhaps your lady already has a silver brooch," Tordis said.

"My wife lived in a convent before we wed," Roger replied. "She has very little in the way of jewelry."

"Then perhaps she would like this piece."

"I'm sure she would."

"Shall I wrap it up for you?"

"Yes, please."

He stood in silence, watching Tordis as she wrapped the brooch in a piece of sheepskin. Her breasts were high and full under her blue tunic, and her waist, which was encircled by a leather belt, was small. She was a widow in her early thirties with no children. When her husband, who had been the silversmith, had died, Tordis had carried on his business by herself. Roger's patronage had helped her to establish herself among the mostly male-owned businesses in town.

Tordis placed the brooch in his hand, managing to touch his fingers with her own as she did so. Lust ratcheted through him.

"Would you like to come inside and see what else I got from the London peddler, my lord?" she asked softly.

"Yes," he replied, his face stark.

"Egon!" Tordis called to one of the boys who was still playing football. "Come and watch my shop while I show my lord some of the jewelry I have inside."

A boy detached himself from the group and came

into the silversmith's shop. "We will be about fifteen minutes," Tordis said. "I have several things I want to show to my lord. If a customer comes tell him I will be with him shortly."

"Yes, ma'am," the boy replied.

"Follow me, my lord," Tordis said.

Roger followed Tordis up the familiar set of narrow stairs and into the small solar on the second level. They crossed the solar and went into a room that opened directly off it. Roger closed the door behind him as he went in.

The room contained a bed covered with a blue wool blanket, two chests, a small table and a chair. The single small window was shuttered so the light in the room was dim.

Tordis began to take off her belt. "I assume you're not here for my wares," she said practically.

"No," he said. "But only if you want to, Tordis."

"Oh, I want to," she said. "It's been a long time since you last visited me, my lord. I've missed you."

"I'm married. I shouldn't be doing this…." But he was undressing even faster than she was.

"I own I was surprised to see you." She was down to her long white shirt and now she went over to the bed and pulled the covering down to expose the sheets underneath.

Roger followed her to the bed and they fell upon it together.

Her mouth was urgent under his, her fingers hard as she ran her hands up and down his arms. He tried to restrain himself. It was bad enough he was here; he didn't want to fall on her like a ravening animal.

But she was as hungry as he was. He caressed her breast and she arched upward toward him. She reached out and caught his rock-hard erection in her hand.

"Please, my lord," she whimpered. "Please."

"Are you ready?" he panted.

"Yes. Dear God, yes."

He poised himself over her, like an eagle ready to strike. Then he plunged into the wonderful wet warmth of her and she rose to meet him. He drove into her again, then again and again. He could feel her rippling all around him and he heard her cry out. His own climax came almost immediately and he groaned at the intensity of the sensation.

Afterward they lay wrapped in each other's arms.

"God, that was wonderful," Tordis said after a while. "It was never like that with my husband."

Through the haze of satisfaction that was gripping him, Roger felt a pang of guilt. At least Tordis was a widow; she wasn't committing adultery. The same could not be said for him.

Tordis said, "I told the boy fifteen minutes. The time must be almost up."

"Yes." He detached himself from her and got out of bed. He picked up his drawers and began to put them on as she reached for her clothes.

He said grimly, "I suppose the news that I have been visiting you will be all around town by suppertime."

"It's no one's business but ours," she replied placidly. "I never let gossip bother me."

Roger sighed. "I'm sorry, Tordis. I did mean it when I said goodbye before I was married."

"What's the matter?" she asked, her manner almost maternal. She was ten years older than he.

"She's a girl from the convent. She was afraid of me when first we wed. I am trying to go slowly, not to scare her. But it's been hell on me."

"What a good lad you are," Tordis said genuinely.

Roger wasn't feeling like a good lad. The pang of guilt he had felt before began to deepen.

What had he done?

He forced his mind to return to the woman he was with. "How about you? You still have no desire to wed again?"

"Absolutely not. I am my own mistress and I like that very much. I'm not about to let a man into my house and into my business, thank you very much."

"Women of the merchant class have it easier than women of the upper class," Roger said. "You can marry to please yourself. My wife was not given that opportunity."

"I must admit that I like my life the way it is," Tordis said complacently. "And your wife was lucky to marry a kind man like you."

Roger's sense of guilt deepened still further at her words. How could she call him kind? He had just betrayed Nell.

He thought of his present situation and how he must try to cover up what he had done.

When Roger rode out of Wilton some twenty minutes later, his body felt much better but his mind was a tangle of tormented thoughts. He had just betrayed his innocent wife with another woman. He thought of Nell's trusting blue eyes, and he felt terrible.

I should have been able to hold out, he thought. *It wouldn't have been much longer.*

He hadn't thought. He had come back from Cirencester and he had just got on his horse and ridden into town. It had been almost a mindless thing to do. He had needed sexual release and he had sought out his old mistress almost automatically.

What if Nell should find out?

He shuddered at the thought. Over the weeks of their short marriage, he had become deeply attached to Nell. She drew feelings of warm protectiveness from him. And now he had done something that would hurt her deeply if she should ever find out.

Everyone in town would know that he had been to visit Tordis. They would all suspect the reason.

No one would dare to say a word to Nell. There isn't a chance that she will find out.

As he rode toward the castle, he realized despairingly that his newly found peace of body wasn't worth his newly lost peace of mind.

Seventeen

Nell was delighted with the pretty silver brooch that Roger had brought her from Wilton and expressed a desire to go into the town herself to look around.

"I've never been shopping," she confided to Roger that night in bed. "You said we would be going to the king's Christmas Court this year and Lady Mabel says I need a fancier dress than anything I've got. Perhaps I could find some cloth in town. Could you take me?"

She couldn't see him in the dark but she sensed his hesitation. She said diffidently, "I don't like to bother you, but it wouldn't be much fun to go with any of my ladies."

"Of course I'll go with you," he finally said. "I am hunting in the morning but we can go after dinner."

"Thank you, Roger."

They were lying side by side, close together but not touching. Nell waited for him to make a move and when he didn't she said shyly, "Aren't you going to hold me tonight?"

"Of course I am," he said. "Come here."

She turned to him and felt his arms come around her. She nestled against him and inhaled his scent, a clean, slightly musky smell.

"Look up, Nell," he said.

This time she gave herself up to his kiss. She didn't think at all, just felt the pressure of his mouth on her mouth, the slide of his tongue along her tongue. She was lost in a haze of purely physical sensation. He bent her head back and she encircled his neck with her arms. Her breasts were pressed against the hard wall of his chest.

"Nell," he whispered against her lips. "How I have longed for you."

She made a little mewing sound in return.

He moved his lips from hers and covered her face with kisses. Then his mouth moved lower, to her throat, then to her breasts. At first she was startled, then she found herself arching her back, offering her nipples to him. When he took one of them in his mouth, a strange tide of sensation flooded between her legs.

All thinking stopped as he continued to kiss and caress her. She didn't come back to herself until he touched her between her legs. Then she jumped.

"Hush," he murmured. "It's all right, sweeting. It's all right. Just relax and enjoy this. It will be fine."

His finger was inside her, moving back and forth, and the sensation it was calling up was shocking in its intensity. Instinctively, she spread her legs wider, to give him better access. The sensation was building and building and she was arching upward, her fists clenched, when all of a sudden the sensation shattered into a cataclysm of feeling, causing her body to spasm again and again with the intensity of what he had done to her.

"All right," she barely heard him mutter. "Now be strong, Nell. This might hurt you a little. Bend your knees."

She did as he asked and he poised himself above her. Then, almost before she knew what was happening, he was inside of her. He thrust once, hard, and involuntarily Nell cried out.

"I'm sorry," Roger said. "Just hold on for a few more moments, all right?"

She forced herself to remain quietly beneath him as he drove in and out of her. Then he gave a little cry of his own and fell forward, his arms around her.

He was still inside her and it still hurt. She squeezed herself together down there and felt him give way a little.

"Am I hurting you?" he panted.

"Yes," she managed to say.

He withdrew and Nell let out her breath. His face was buried in her shoulder and he was breathing as if he had been running.

They stayed like that for a short while. Then she lifted her hand and gently ran her fingers through his hair. She could feel his heart hammering against her ribs.

It was done, she thought with wonder. This big thing

that had loomed over her marriage from the beginning was done.

It had hurt, but the strange thing was she didn't feel resentful or embarrassed at all. She wasn't quite sure what had happened to her when he had touched her down there, but it had been amazing. She had never imagined anything like it.

His heart continued to slam and she asked a little worriedly, "Are you all right, Roger?"

"Yes." He lifted his head to look down at her. His golden hair swung forward around his face. "I'm sorry if I hurt you, but it is always hard the first time for a woman."

"How do you know that?"

He hesitated. He was still breathing hard. "A woman once told me that. She said it is because the virginal barrier must be broken. Once that is done, there is no longer any pain. In fact, there is very great pleasure."

He levered himself off her, settled beside her, picked up her hand and pressed a kiss into her palm. "You were wonderful," he said.

She turned her face to give him a smile. "It was very nice up until the end."

"Good. And it will be even nicer the next time. You have my word on that."

Her dark blue eyes regarded him gravely. "You have been so good to me, so patient," she said. "Thank you, Roger."

He reached out and drew her into the shelter of his

arm. She nestled her cheek against his shoulder. She felt his lips touch her hair.

"Go to sleep, Nell," he said softly.

She felt relaxed and oddly fulfilled. His skin under her cheek was smooth and warm. She closed her eyes and inhaled the scent of him.

"Good night," she whispered.

"Good night, sweeting."

Long after Nell had fallen asleep, Roger lay awake, his physical satisfaction overlaid by feelings of guilt and regret. If only he had not gone to see Tordis this afternoon! If only he had restrained himself one more day!

Nell had been so sweet tonight, so yielding. It had been worth the long wait, to have her give herself to him as trustingly as that. He felt badly that he had had to hurt her, but at least he had given her joy first. He felt fiercely protective of her. She had never known any man but him. He would take care of her always.

He loved her.

He loved her and on the very day that he had first made love to her, he had betrayed her with Tordis.

Roger lay still; he didn't want to disturb Nell. It was so sweet to have her sleeping in his arms. But his mind was restless.

She'll never find out, he assured himself. *I will just have to live with the guilt. The important thing is that Nell never find out.*

The following afternoon, Nell and Roger, accompanied by Roger's squire, rode into the town of Wilton.

They left their horses with Richard at the top of the main street, the Strait, and walked down the shop-lined road, with Nell looking at all the wares with a childlike delight.

The boot maker's shop, the weaver's shop, the glover's shop, the vintner's, the master carpenter's, the potter's, all drew Nell's attention as she passed by. She admired a cradle in the master carpenter's shop, and blushed when the guildsman said, "Perhaps you'll have use for that one of these days, my lady." Roger bought her a pair of black leather gloves at the glover's—the only ones in the store that were small enough to fit her.

The street was quite busy and Nell commented on this to Roger, who laughed. "Everyone's come out to get a glimpse of my new wife. You'll be the topic of conversation in most households this evening."

Nell particularly wanted to see the silversmith in order to thank the merchant for selling Roger the beautiful brooch that she was so delighted with. Roger told her several times that it was unnecessary, but she insisted, so the two of them entered the shop together and Roger greeted the tall, statuesque blond woman behind the table that displayed the smith's wares.

"Nell, this is Tordis Martenson. She is the owner of this shop." Roger's voice sounded stiff.

"I am pleased to make your acquaintance," Nell said courteously. "I was very taken with the silver brooch that you sold to my husband."

Nell saw the woman flash a quick look at Roger before she answered. "I am glad you liked it, my lady."

Nell looked around. "Do you run this shop all by yourself?" she asked curiously.

"Yes. It belonged to my husband and I learned the craft from him. When he died I had the skills to be able to take over."

"And the townsfolk supported you?" Nell asked.

"Yes. They all knew me and they knew I had been doing all the work of the shop while my husband was ill. The town guild allowed me to join with no dissent."

"That speaks well for the town guild," Nell said gravely.

"The people of Wilton are good people."

"That is so," Roger agreed.

"Did you make the brooch my lord gave me?" Nell asked.

Once again there was that quick flick of the eyes to Roger. "No. I bought that brooch from a peddler who had been in London. I am glad that you liked it, my lady."

Nell nodded. There seemed to be a little current of awareness between Tordis and Roger that puzzled Nell and made her uneasy.

"May I look at your wares?" she asked. "Everything is so pretty—it is a pleasure just to see them."

"Thank you, my lady. You are welcome to look for as long as you like."

"We don't want to be too long," Roger said. "We have to be home before supper."

Nell looked surprised. "There is plenty of time until supper, my lord."

A small boy came into the shop carrying a pair of leather shoes. "Here are the shoes you bought from my father," he told Tordis. He was an adorable child, with straight black hair and big brown eyes.

"Thank you, John," Tordis replied. She beckoned the boy forward and took the low boots from his hand. "How is your mother?"

"She's still sick," the child replied. "I think my father is worried."

Tordis frowned.

Nell said quietly, "How is she ill? I know a little bit about healing. Perhaps I could help."

The little boy looked up at her earnestly. "She has a fever, my lady."

"I can give her something for fever, if you think your father wouldn't mind."

The little boy bounced on his toes. "I'm sure he would be happy, my lady. Can I go and tell him?"

"I will come to see him myself," Nell said.

"I'll come with you," Roger said.

They walked back up the street to the boot maker's shop and entered into the booth, which had a strong smell of leather. The boot maker was a broad, dark-haired man and he greeted Roger. "It is good to see you in town, my lord."

"Thank you, Walter. This is my wife, Lady Eleanor. She has heard that your wife is ill and has come to offer one of her medications."

Walter Hovis swung his dark eyes to Nell. "Do you think you have something that might help her, my lady?"

"I was apprentice to our herb woman in the convent," Nell explained, "and I have a number of her medicines back at the castle. I'm sure I have something that will relieve her."

"If you wouldn't mind coming upstairs, my lady, you will be able to see for yourself how ill she is, " the boot maker said gratefully.

"I'll wait here for you," Roger said.

Nell nodded and followed Walter Hovis into the house and up a narrow flight of wooden stairs. The master bedroom opened off a small solar and Nell went right up to the side of the bed.

"I hear you are ill," she said gently to the woman lying there. "I am Lady Eleanor de Roche and I have some knowledge of healing herbs I would be glad to share with you."

Heavy brown eyes looked up at Nell. The woman in the bed was as pale as the linen she was lying on. "I am so hot, my lady," she said. "I feel like I'm burning up."

Nell reached out and put a hand on her forehead. "Are you coughing?"

"Yes. And my chest hurts."

"I think I have something that will help you, but I have to go back to the castle to get it." She smiled reassuringly at the woman. "We'll soon have you feeling better."

"Thank you, my lady. This is so kind of you...."

"Not at all," Nell said. She looked at the boot maker, who was standing on the other side of the bed. "I'll be back soon with the medicine."

"Thank you, my lady!"

Nell nodded and went down the stairs by herself. When she was back in the shop, she told Roger what she was going to do.

"Is she really that sick?" he asked.

"She has a high fever—too high for an adult. And there is some congestion in the chest. I can give her a draught of borage and other herbs that Sister Helen had very good luck with. It's certainly worth trying."

"Well, let's collect our horses from Richard, then, and be on our way."

As soon as she returned to the castle, Nell went into the pantry to brew a concoction of borage and other fever-quenching herbs. Roger went with her and watched her at work as she measured the ingredients carefully.

"What will you mix them with?" he asked.

"A little wine, to make them go down more easily." She poured some wine into the herbs and stirred the mixture briskly.

"If it is ready, I'll have Richard take it into the boot makers," Roger said.

Nell swung around to look at him in surprise. "I am going to take it myself."

His level golden brows drew together. "That's not necessary. I don't want you exposing yourself to sickness if you don't have to."

"But I want to go, Roger."

"It isn't necessary," he repeated. "Richard is perfectly capable of delivering the medicine."

"It may not be necessary, but I still want to go. This is important to me."

"Nell," he said reasonably, "it is good of you to want to help a sick woman, but be sensible. Why expose yourself to contagion if you don't have to?"

Nell set her jaw stubbornly. "A healer can't worry about exposure to contagion. This is my medication and I want to watch my patient drink it and I want to tell her husband what to do if the fever breaks during the night. I think this is the work that God has sent me out in the world to do, Roger. Please don't try to stop me."

His frown deepened. "It just doesn't seem reasonable to me."

"I am going," she said with fierce determination.

There was a long silence. Nell's dark blue eyes glittered with resolve. Roger had never seen her like this before.

"All right," he said reluctantly. "If you are so determined, I won't try to stand in your way. But I still think you can heal by sending the medication in with Richard."

Nell gave him a radiant smile. "Thank you, Roger."

"I will send Richard to escort you."

"Thank you," she said again.

Nell rode out on her second trip of the day to the town escorted by Roger's squire, who was carrying the bottle of Nell's precious medication. When they reached the boot maker's shop, Richard went in with Nell, who told Walter Hovis that the medicine would go down better if it were heated up. She followed the proprietor to the kitchen, which was on the ground floor of the house, and watched while he heated it. Then they took it upstairs. The boot maker supported his wife while Nell got her to slowly drink the medicine. Then she was laid back down again.

"The fever may break sometime during the night," Nell told Walter. "If she starts to sweat profusely, don't worry. It's a good sign. Just replace any wet bedclothes, make sure she is warm and dry, and let her sleep. She should be feeling much better in the morning."

"Thank you, my lady," the boot maker said gratefully. "You have been very kind."

"It is my pleasure to try to help," Nell returned gravely. "I will come by tomorrow to see how things are going."

Nell went downstairs, where Richard awaited her, and the two of them rode back to the castle.

Eighteen

Nell arrived back at the castle just in time to sit down to supper. As she washed her hands in the basin provided by the servants, she told Roger about her second visit to the boot maker's house.

Lady Mabel, who was sitting on the other side of Nell, beside Father Ralph, eavesdropped on the conversation and gave her opinion that Nell had been foolish to enter the same room as the sick woman.

Roger, who agreed with Lady Mabel, forebore to comment.

"I am an herb woman, Lady Mabel," Nell said evenly. "My job is to help people who are sick. I can't help them if I can't see them."

"It's one thing to doctor the folk in the castle, but quite another to be running around the town doctoring merchants," Lady Mabel said disdainfully. "You are a countess, my lady, not some peasant herb woman."

Nell said forcefully, "I am a child of God, and so are the merchant class children of God. God makes no distinction between classes. To Him all are important. My herbs are for the benefit of all humanity, Lady Mabel. In God's view, Mistress Hovis is fully as important as you are."

Roger had to smother a smile. *Good for you, Nell,* he thought.

"That's ridiculous," Lady Mabel snapped.

"It is not ridiculous at all," Father Ralph said diffidently. "In fact, it is very good theology."

Nell gave the priest a radiant smile.

She is so beautiful when she smiles, Roger thought. He thought of the upcoming night and felt his manhood stir. He hoped the day would go by quickly.

After supper was over, Nell invited one of the knights to sing for them and a group of knights gathered with Nell, Roger and Nell's ladies around the fireplace. Thomas had a clear, true tenor voice and the song he sang was a chanson of chivalry and romance. Nell listened to the story of a knight's devotion to his lady and watched the firelight flicker on Roger's hair.

Just sitting there in his chair, he dominated the room. It was not the first time she had had this thought. Even though Thomas was singing, still the focal center of the room was Roger. He wasn't the tallest man present, or the most massive, but there was something about him that always made one aware of his presence.

It isn't just that he's the earl, Nell thought. *It's something in him. Mother Superior had that quality, too. You just sense that this person is the leader.*

Thomas struck the last note on his lute and smiled. Everyone applauded.

"Let's do a roundelay song," Roger suggested. "How about 'The Knight Rode Through the Forest'?"

Everyone agreed.

Roger quickly divided the group up into three separate singing sections and then said, "Give us the note, Thomas."

Nell didn't know the song so she sat and listened as the rest of them sang lustily. Roger had a strong, clear voice and he joined in with as much vigor as the rest of the group as they sang about the hapless knight who rode through a thick forest only to be beset by an onslaught of troubles at his journey's end. The more troubles that were piled on the knight, the more enthusiastically the group sang. Nell smiled listening to them.

They remained at the fireside singing until it was bedtime. Then the knights went off to the guardroom below, the ladies went to the bedrooms that they shared off the ladies' solar, and Roger and Nell went to their own apartment in the south tower.

The chanson this evening had caught Nell's imagination, with its emphasis on the devoted love between the knight and his lady. *That's like Roger and me,* she thought. For the first time in their marriage, she felt as if she were fully his wife.

A little to her surprise, she found she was actively looking forward to going to bed with him tonight. The picture her mother had painted for her had turned out to be very different from what she had experienced. And Roger had said it wouldn't hurt anymore.

She went up first and was in bed behind the curtains when Roger came in with his squire. She listened to the two males as they conversed while Roger was being undressed. They were talking about the morning's hunt. Nell thought that Roger had the most pleasing voice of any man she had ever known. It wasn't a baritone and it wasn't a tenor; it was just in the middle—very clear, very flexible, not at all loud. It was the kind of voice that could give orders easily and pleasantly. He had stepped into his grandfather's shoes without a single hitch.

Her heart began to hammer as she heard Richard leave the room. She didn't hear Roger crossing the floor—he had the gift of moving silently—but she was ready when the curtain opened on his side of the bed. He was wearing his wool bed robe, which was belted at the waist.

"You sound as if you had a good hunt this morning," she said a little breathlessly.

"Yes, it was exciting."

His hair glowed golden in the light of the candle. He got into bed without closing the curtains and reached for her.

Nell moved into his arms, lifting her face for his kiss. As his mouth covered hers, she closed her eyes, ready to slip into the world of pure sensation that she had discovered with him last night.

Her tongue answered readily to his and her right hand went up to caress the back of his neck. It felt so strong. He was a slender man and his strength was always a surprise to her. He kissed her until she was dizzy from it.

Their bodies were pressed together and she could feel the hardness of his erection. It was amazing, she thought hazily, how frightened she had once been of that part of his body.

He lifted his mouth away from hers and rained a series of kisses along her cheekbone to her ear. Then he kissed her throat and she raised her chin to give him better access.

"You are so beautiful, Nell," he murmured. "Everything about you is perfect."

She, who had been raised never to think of her body, felt a rush of pride that he should feel that way. "I think you're beautiful, too," she said.

He laid her on her back and began kissing his way toward her breast. "Men aren't beautiful," he said.

You are. But she didn't say it. He had taken her nipple into his mouth and suddenly she was incapable of saying anything. She slid her hands into his hair and closed her eyes more tightly. His tongue flicked back and forth across her nipple and then he began to suck on it. As he sucked, deep within her loins she felt the sweet surge of sensation, like the powerful surge of water beginning to rise. Involuntarily, she arched up toward him.

Roger, she thought. *Oh, Roger.*

His hands, which had been stroking her, began to move lower on her body. When his finger went into her she gasped. It began to move and she quivered, totally intent on the sensation he was creating. The tension ratcheted higher and higher. Nell was aware of nothing in the world, not the enveloping curtains, not the candle that lit Roger's hair to gold. All she was aware of was this unbelievable need in her loins. She lifted her hips, urging Roger on.

"All right," she heard him mutter through the mist, "I'm coming in, Nell."

She opened her legs to let him come between and lifted her legs to encircle his waist. Then he was thrusting into her need, driving in and out, in and out, and the tension went higher until she thought she would scream, when suddenly the explosion came. Her whole body spasmed and she clung to him as her only anchor in a vortex of overwhelming sensation. As if from a long distance, she heard him cry out.

Afterward they lay together, wrapped in each other's arms.

"When my mother told me about it, it sounded so horrible," Nell murmured, her cheek against his shoulder. "Who could imagine that such a thing could be so wonderful?"

His lips were buried in her hair. "I'm glad you think it's wonderful. It's wonderful for me, too."

"God was so good to give me you for a husband. I was so mad at Him for letting me be taken away from the convent, and now I can't imagine my life without you."

"God was good to me, also," Roger said. She felt him kiss the top of her head. "I love you, Nell."

"And I love you," she returned fervently. Roger held her tenderly and once more his mind went back to his recent encounter with Tordis. *I don't deserve to have this happiness with Nell,* he thought. *Dear Lord, please forgive me for what I did. I will never do anything like that again. And please don't ever let Nell find out.*

They both had a hard time waking up the following morning and they almost missed mass. Later, at breakfast, Nell told Roger she wanted to go into Wilton town to see how the boot maker's wife was doing.

He looked as if he might object, then shook his head. "All right. I'll send Thomas with you."

"I don't need a knight to go with me," Nell protested. "One of the squires will be fine."

"I'll send Thomas," Roger reiterated. "We're practicing horsemanship drills this morning and Thomas is one of my best horseman. He doesn't need to do drills. He can go with you."

Nell bowed to the inevitable. "All right. Thank you very much. I'd like to leave within the next half hour."

"He'll be ready."

The first thing Nell did when she and Thomas rode

away from the giant walls of Wilton Castle was apologize for pulling him away from his duties.

"It is an honor to accompany you, my lady," he protested in reply. "I spend my whole life with men. It is a pleasure to have some time in company with a woman."

Nell thought of this statement as they rode across the open field that surrounded Wilton. It *was* a relentlessly masculine world, the world of knights. A world of armories, of hunts, of manly sports. Perhaps, soon, of war. Boys were plucked away from their mothers and their sisters at the tender age of eight and thrust into this male domain, where they were subject to a new and strange lord, who was responsible for educating them as page and squire so that they could eventually attain the exalted title of knight.

"Do you like being a knight, Thomas?" she asked as they passed by the farmland that lay between the castle and the village. Cows grazed to the left of the road and on the right was a flock of sheep.

He gave her a look of such blue-eyed astonishment that it was almost comical. She might have asked him if he liked to breathe. "Yes, my lady. Of course I like being a knight."

"Where were you born?" she asked.

"In Foxley, my lady," he replied. "My father is the castellan there."

"Did you like it when you first came to Wilton?"

He was silent for a minute, his freckled face thoughtful. Then he said, "I missed my mother, of course, but I had the other lads to keep me company."

I wish I had some company, Nell thought a little sadly. *I will have to ask Roger if he has had any luck in getting some younger ladies for Wilton.*

"How old are you, Thomas?" she asked next.

"Twenty-two, my lady."

"That is the same age as my lord."

"Aye."

"Do you plan to spend your life at Wilton, as one of the household guard?"

"If my lord will have me," came the simple reply. "It is a good position for me, my lady. My father was only a castellan, he was not the owner of our keep. It was a coup for our house when the old lord took me. And then, instead of sending me out into the world when I was dubbed knight, he elected to keep me on as part of the castle guard. I consider myself very lucky."

"Perhaps he kept you for your singing voice," Nell said teasingly.

Thomas grinned. "You are not the first person to say that, my lady."

The houses of the town came into view. "The fair will be starting next week," Thomas said. "That should wake the town up a bit."

"A fair? What fair is that?" Nell asked.

"St. Michael's Fair," Thomas replied. "It's the fair granted by the king to the earls of Wiltshire. It's not one of the big fairs, it's rather a small thing, in fact. That's why we have it in November. All the big fairs get the spring and summer dates. But it brings income to the earl and it's a chance for all the neighborhood to buy goods they wouldn't ordinarily get a chance to purchase."

"A fair," Nell said. "That sounds like fun. My lord never mentioned it to me."

"It probably just slipped his mind. As I said, it is not a great thing. But the local people enjoy it."

"How does it bring income to the earl?"

"Everyone who sets up a stall must pay a fee to the earl. And every barge that ties up on the river must pay a fee, as well."

They had entered the town and were proceeding side by side down the Strait. When they reached the boot maker's shop, Nell dismounted and Thomas held the horses as she went inside.

Walter Hovis was thrilled to see her. "My lady!" he cried. "All went just as you said it would. My wife began to sweat sometime early in the morning. She soaked through all of her coverings! We kept watch on her and when she had stopped sweating, we wrapped her up warmly and she slept deeply and this morning the fever is gone!"

Nell smiled radiantly. "I am so glad, Master Hovis. Often it is thus, although not always."

"Would you care to come upstairs so she can thank you herself? We are keeping her in bed for the day even though she says she feels well enough to get up."

"No harm in being careful," Nell said. "I would be delighted to say hello to Mistress Hovis."

Nell spent perhaps ten minutes with the boot maker and his wife, and when she left the house she was feeling very good. *Thank you, God, for letting me help these people. Let me always be as good a judge of an illness as I was this time and give your blessing to my medicaments. Thank you for helping me find my way.*

Thomas was waiting with the horses when she went out into the street. "From the look on your face, I must conclude that the boot maker's wife is better," he said.

"Yes, the fever broke last night."

"It seems you know what you are doing, my lady. You doctored a few coughs at the castle and now you have cured a fever. Once the word goes out about what you can do, you will be busier than you can believe."

"If I can help someone, then I will," Nell said simply.

A tall, blond woman stepped out into the street a few yards down the road from them. "Oh, there is Mistress Martenson," Nell said. At that moment, the woman turned toward them and Nell waved. After a moment's hesitation, the silversmith waved back.

"I don't think you should have anything to do with her, my lady," Thomas said a little harshly.

Nell turned to him in surprise. "But why? Surely you don't hold it against her that she is a woman doing a man's job?"

"It's not that. It's just...I don't think she is a fit person for you to associate with."

"Don't be ridiculous," Nell said. "My lord was the one who introduced us."

"*My lord* introduced you?" Thomas said incredulously.

"Yes. I told him I wanted to meet the person who had sold him that pretty silver brooch he gave me."

Thomas digested this piece of information in silence.

"So you see, it is perfectly all right for me to know Mistress Martenson."

"Yes, my lady," Thomas said evenly.

"I'm ready to go home," Nell said.

"Yes, my lady," Thomas repeated, and they turned their horses back up the Strait.

When Nell asked, Roger told her that he had indeed found four younger women for her and two of them arrived a few days later. Juliana was twenty and Mary was nineteen, both the daughters of two of Roger's vassal. Both girls were one of several daughters and their fathers had been more than happy to provide them to the earl as companions for his wife.

Nell was so happy to see some girls her own age. The elderly ladies of Wilton had banded with Lady Mabel against her, and the silent, and not so silent, wall of their disapproval had been very difficult to bear. Roger had been her only real companion, but he was busy with his knights and had only limited time to give to her. She had often felt lonely.

The two girls were pretty enough and seemed enthusiastic about being at Wilton. They both hunted and hawked and were conversant with all the niceties of life in a lord's household. Nell took them on a tour of the castle and then showed them around the bailey. All of the knights that they passed seemed very interested in the new arrivals.

"It's so big, my lady," Juliana said when they returned to the ladies' solar after the tour. "Why, I believe you could fit ten of my father's castles into Wilton!"

"Yes," Mary agreed. "I have never seen so large a castle."

Lady Mabel said haughtily, "Wilton is one of the premier castles in the kingdom. Of course it is nothing like the places you came from."

The girls exchanged a look.

Nell said gently, "I'm sure you didn't mean to be rude, Lady Mabel. I'm quite sure that Lady Juliana and Lady Mary come from very nice homes."

Lady Mabel glared at Nell.

One of the other women said pleasantly, "Most castles pale in comparison to Wilton."

"That is so," Nell agreed. "Even my father's castle of Bardney is not as big."

"Can you girls sew?" Lady Mabel demanded.

"Yes, my lady," the two newcomers chorused.

"Good. We are embroidering new shirts and extra hands will be a help."

"Do you know many songs?" Nell asked.

"I know all the usual songs, my lady," Juliana replied with a little surprise.

Mary agreed.

Nell smiled happily. "Good. Then you can teach them to me so I can join in when we sing in the evening."

Lady Mabel pinched her lips together.

"What songs don't you know, my lady?" Juliana asked.

"I don't know any songs," Nell replied. "I lived in a convent until I married and all I know are hymns."

Juliana and Mary looked at each other. "We will be glad to teach you," they said with smiles.

"And can you teach me to dance, as well?"

Juliana laughed. "Yes."

"We don't dance at Wilton," Lady Mabel said stiffly.

"We will now that we have some young women here," Nell said pleasantly.

One of the younger ladies, who was in her forties, said, "It will be fun to dance again."

Lady Mabel's small, plump body quivered, but she had nothing to say.

Nineteen

"I am thinking of entering Wilton under cover of the St. Michael's Fair and having a meeting with my son." Guy de Roche paced the floor back in the empress's stronghold in Bristol.

Lady Cecily stared at her husband in horror. "Are you mad, Guy? Why would you try to do a thing like that?"

"I think a talk between the two of us might be profitable. From what you tell me, he was very happy to meet his mother. Why should he not be as pleased to meet his long-lost father?"

The two were talking in the privacy of their bedroom after Guy's return from raiding in Hertfordshire with Miles of Gloucester. A goodly amount of territory had gone over to the empress as a result of these excursions.

"You will be courting danger by going to Wilton," Lady Cecily said now. "What if Roger should take you prisoner?"

Guy's brilliant blue eyes glittered. "That wouldn't look good for him, taking his own father prisoner."

She hesitated. "You can't be sure, Guy. Plus you will be putting Roger in a difficult position."

Guy raised a reckless eyebrow. "I think I'll chance it."

She watched him pace up and down. He was always in motion, rarely still. "But *why*?" she asked. " What is the point in talking to Roger?"

Guy threw her an impatient look. "I want to be the Earl of Wiltshire," he said shortly. "I can do it the slow way, by waiting for the empress to best Stephen—if she can. Or I can do it the fast way, by convincing my son to give way to me and take his natural place as my heir."

He reached the wall at the end of their bedroom, turned and came back toward her again. Cecily rubbed her hands together, as if they were cold. "But I told you what Roger told me. Lord William made him swear a deathbed oath not to let you become the Earl of Wiltshire. Roger said that he meant to uphold that oath."

Guy waved his hand dismissively. He stopped by the window and turned to her. "That was before Roger had a chance to talk to me. My father treated me outrageously! I am the Earl of Wiltshire by right of birth. If Roger has any sense of justice, he will realize that. Besides, didn't you say he was in line to become the Earl of Lincoln? How greedy can the little brat be?"

"He's not a brat, Guy!" Cecily said indignantly. "He's a fine young man. He wanted to make up for everything that his grandfather had taken away from me."

He started pacing again. "Fine, then let him feel the same way about me."

Cecily watched him in silence. Finally she said, "You haven't changed at all. You still think there is only one way of looking at things, and that is your way."

"There is little to be lost in going to see the boy. In fact, why don't you come with me?" He raised his eyebrows in inquiry.

She stared at him. "You can't be serious!"

"Perfectly. In fact, the more I think of it the more I like the idea. We'll be a cozy family. You said Roger wanted you to go and live at Wilton. Well, we can offer him his mama back if he accepts his papa, too."

"That's not fair," Cecily said.

Guy's eyes flashed. "Fair? What my father did to me wasn't fair! He took my birthright from me and gave it to my son. If there's any justice in the world, my son will give it back to me."

"He won't, Guy," Cecily insisted softly. "He told me he would abide by the promise he made to Lord William. I don't think it's a good idea to go to Wilton to see Roger."

Guy took a step toward her. "I'm going. And if you're any kind of a wife, you'll come with me."

Cecily looked away from his burning eyes. "It's too long a ride for me."

"We'll hire a barge. It will be a good disguise. There are plenty of barges tying up along the river during the fair. We'll pretend to be traders."

Cecily bit her lip. "I don't think you're being fair to him, Guy," she repeated. "He was raised to be the Earl of Wiltshire...."

"What do you think *I* was?" His fury flared out at her and she pressed her back against the wall, as if to get away from him. "For twenty years I lived in exile, waiting for that old man to die. Now at last he has and my own son stands in my way! I can make him see how unfair it is, I *know* I can. Come with me, Cecily, and lend your voice to mine. How can he stand against the two of us?"

She hesitated and he went over to her. "Sweetheart." He picked up her hand and lifted it to his lips. "Do this for me. We've been apart for so long. I'm so happy to have you back again."

"Are you, Guy?" There was a catch in her voice.

"You know I am." His voice had deepened. "One of the things I hold most deeply against my father is that he separated me from you." His tall, strong body bent over her. His piercing eyes looked directly into hers. "Come with me to see our son, Cecily," he whispered. And he bent to find her mouth.

Nell was thrilled by the thought of the fair. She didn't care that it was a small fair—to one who had never been to any fair, the prospect of some of the wider world coming to Wilton was exciting.

The merchants started arriving in by cart on Monday night, setting up their wares in the part of town that was usually the livestock market, getting ready to open for business Tuesday morning. Some merchants came by water, tying up their barges along the town wharves. Folk poured in from the countryside to shop, taking up all the rooms at the local inns.

Roger had explained to Nell that fair days were generally not good business days for the Wilton merchants, whose everyday wares palled in comparison to the new offerings of the fair vendors. In fact, the merchants and their families usually joined the crowds of shoppers and stocked up on the luxury items so temptingly for sale.

Nell and the four young girls who had joined her circle of ladies were anxious to go shopping, and Roger assigned two knights to escort them, along with two squires to hold their purchases. He smiled with amusement as he watched them ride off toward town. Nell's cheeks were quite pink with excitement and he wished for a moment that he was escorting her himself. But Bayard had come up lame yesterday and Roger was going to poultice his foot—a delicate procedure he would not allocate to any of the grooms.

He spent the morning in the stable with his horse, then returned to the Great Hall for dinner, which was much emptier than usual as half the castle had gone in to the fair. He was talking to Simon when one of the knights who had been at the fair came into the hall. He hurried over to Roger.

"My lord. I have a message for you."

Roger reached out and took the folded parchment. He

opened it and read, *Roger. I am here in Wilton. Will you come to the barge that is drawn up before the town dock? It is painted blue. I will be waiting for you. Mother.*

The blood drained from Roger's face. *Mother? In Wilton? On a barge?* Roger's mind was in a whirl. It didn't make sense. He addressed the knight, who was still standing before him. "Where did you get this message?"

"The message was given to Adelard when he collected the docking fee from the barge, my lord. He passed it on to me to deliver to you."

"I see," Roger said.

"Is everything all right, my lord?" Simon asked.

"Yes." Roger made a quick decision not to tell Simon about the message. He would go into Wilton and see for himself what this was all about.

The streets of Wilton were clogged with people. Food vendors had set up their wares along the Strait and hungry shoppers were sampling the offerings as Roger steered his horse down the street. A number of the diners were folk from the castle, but Roger rode with his eyes focused straight ahead. His mind was set on what he was going to find on the barge.

Finally he came out along the river and there was an array of barges of all sizes, shapes and colors drawn up along the dock. He looked for a blue one and found it resting several boats down from where he was standing.

Roger looked around the empty riverfront for someone to hold his horse. A young man was coming along the quay, carrying a plate of food. "You," Roger called as the man came closer to him. "It's worth a gold piece to me to have you hold my horse while I pay a visit to one of these barges."

The young man promptly put his plate of food on the ground and came over to take Patrick's reins. "Done, my lord," he said cheerfully.

Roger advanced toward the blue barge, riding serenely at its docking. It looked deserted. Then a woman came out of the cabin onto the deck.

"Roger!" she called.

"Mother!" He was aboard in an instant and had her in his arms. She hugged him back tightly. "It really is you!"

"Yes, it really is." She pulled back a little. "Let me look at you."

He gazed into her face. "I was so worried about you! I rode to Cirencester as soon as I heard of the raid, but when I got there the prioress said that my father had taken you away."

"He came and rescued me before the soldiers got to the convent." A line came between her fine straight brows. "How bad was it, Roger?"

"It was very bad," he said grimly. His hands were still on her shoulders. "The soldiers were drunk. They burned the town and the convent and took away all of the sacred things from the church." He hesitated, then added, "They also took some of the novices."

"Oh, no!"

"It's a good thing you got away, Mother," he said soberly. "You are still a beautiful woman. God knows what could have happened to you."

He could feel her shiver.

"But what are you doing here?" he asked. "And how did you get here? This barge…"

She stepped away from him and drew herself up. His hands fell to his sides. She said a little breathlessly, "I did not come alone. Roger, there is someone with me that I want you to meet."

He stared at her with a mixture of bewilderment and alarm. She couldn't mean… Roger felt his heart begin to hammer in his chest.

A compact, strong-looking man of his own height appeared on deck. He wore a blue tunic and a blue mantel and the first thing Roger noticed about him was his blue eyes.

"So," he said. "I finally get to meet my son."

Roger's world wheeled. Instinctively, he turned to his mother.

"This is your father, Roger," she said. She was very pale. "He has come all the way from Bristol just to see you."

Roger turned back to the blue-eyed man. "You are all your mother," Guy said. "It hardly looks as if I had any doing with you at all."

Roger's mouth was dry and his heart was still hammering. He glanced around the empty waterfront and managed to say, "What are you doing here?"

"I have come to talk to you," Guy said evenly.

Roger fought to get his thoughts under control. "You are the empress's man. You are mad to come into Wilton like this."

Guy smiled. "No one knows I'm here except you. Are you going to arrest me, Roger? Your own father?"

Roger didn't answer, instead he looked at Guy, taking him in. His father had dark hair, with no sign of gray, and in his mouth and nose Roger detected a resemblance to his grandfather. But the most noticeable thing about the man, besides those blue eyes, was the sense of coiled energy that he projected.

This is my father, Roger thought. The whole situation felt unreal. They were waiting for him to reply. "Perhaps you had better tell me why you're here," he finally said.

"What a greeting!" Guy threw up his hands. "We meet for the first time, father and son, and this is the best welcome you can give me?"

The sun glinted on the water of the Avon and the barge shifted a little under Roger's feet. He said as steadily as he could, "Did you expect an embrace? You came to England to oppose me. At least that is what I have heard."

Guy shrugged. "I came to England the only way I could get back here. Can you blame me for that?"

Roger didn't reply.

A man walking along the embankment toward one of the barges cast a curious look at them as he went past.

Guy said abruptly, "I understand that he told you I was dead."

Roger drew a deep breath. "Yes."

"So you never knew about my banishment? You never knew that my father exiled me from my home, from my patrimony, from my rightful place in the world? You never knew that you were supplanting me?"

There was a long pause. A gull circled overhead. Finally Roger said, "No. I never knew."

"When did you find out about me?"

The boat rolled underfoot. "When I heard you had come to England with the empress and the Earl of Gloucester." He hesitated, then said starkly, "The news killed my grandfather. He had a heart seizure when he heard."

"Did he?" Guy looked pleased. "God, there's some justice in the world, at any rate."

Roger stared at him in disbelief. He set his jaw. "Why did you come here?" he asked, his voice hard.

"I came to ask you to give way to me," Guy said.

It took a moment for Roger to digest that statement. Then he asked in amazement, "You're serious?"

Guy's brilliant eyes flashed with anger. "I am perfectly serious. I am the legitimate Earl of Wiltshire. Now that my father is dead I have come to claim my rightful place. Surely you can see the injustice that was done to me. As a son you have an obligation to give way before me. I am the rightful earl, not you."

Roger said flatly, "You are the empress's man."

"I will be happy to pledge my allegiance to Stephen if he will recognize me as the earl."

This is unbelievable, Roger thought. He looked at his mother. Her face was unreadable. He turned back to the man who was his father. "Stephen has already recognized *me* as the Earl of Wiltshire."

Guy waved his hand. "The king's concern is to have a strong, loyal supporter in charge of Wiltshire. He will recognize me if you will step aside."

The sun beat down strongly on Roger's head. He kept his eyes on his father's face and said levelly, "But I have no intention of stepping aside."

A dark flush suffused Guy's face. He took a step closer to Roger. "I have the right!"

Roger said evenly, "My grandfather had the right to name his successor, and he chose to entrust his earldom of Wilton to me. I have been confirmed by the king. All of Wiltshire's vassals have sworn allegiance to me. I am the earl and I will not relinquish that honor to you or to any other man."

Guy turned his intense blue eyes to his wife. "Cecily, tell him. Tell him that I was wronged."

His mother took a step forward. "It's true, Roger. He was wronged. Lord William should never have sent him away like that. He betrayed his son."

Roger felt a pulse start to hammer in his temple. "Perhaps my grandfather felt that his son had betrayed him," he said calmly.

"That's not true!" Guy shouted.

The more Guy argued, the more clearly Roger was thinking. "My grandfather was a just man. I lived with him all my life and I know that. He dealt well and fairly with all his dependents. I cannot imagine him dealing unjustly with his only son."

Guy fixed Roger with an intense gaze. "Listen to me," he said. "You are my son and I am commanding you. Give me my rightful place and I will recognize you as my heir."

Roger could feel the full force of his father's character bearing down on him. It was a powerful personality, exuding a kind of magnetic energy that was immensely compelling. "Give over to me, Roger, and your mother and I will come back to Wilton. We will be a family for the first time, the way we should have been for all these years. You will not lack for reverence under my watch, I promise you that."

"No," Roger said. His stomach was churning but he remained calm and his gaze did not waver. "I will not give over to you."

"You little weasel," Guy said viciously.

"Guy, don't lose your temper," his mother pleaded.

Guy paced once back and forth across the deck. Then he swung around to face Roger again. "I hear you are in line to become the Earl of Lincoln. Why can't you settle for that and leave the earldom of Wiltshire to me?"

"You don't understand," Roger said. He looked to his mother. "My grandfather entrusted the earldom to me. It was the very last thing he said to me before he died." His eyes swung back to his father. "It was his choice to make, his earldom to leave as he chose. I will not go against him. I will do as he wished me to do. I will not give up the earldom to you."

"I am not a good enemy to make, Roger," Guy said menacingly. "Think carefully. Isn't it better that we should all be friends, you and me and your mother?"

"My mother is welcome to come to Wilton whenever she wishes. She will always have an honored place in my household."

"My wife stays with me!" Guy roared.

Cecily put a hand on his arm, as if to restrain him. "Roger, we could all be together if you could find it in your heart to give way to your father," she said hopefully.

Roger's stomach tensed into a knot. "I can't do that, Mother. I can't go back on the promise I made to my grandfather."

She nodded sadly. "Then I will stay with your father. He is my husband. We have been separated for so long...."

"I understand," Roger said in a low voice.

Guy's head was lowered like that of a charging bull and his eyes were slits of glittering blue. "I will have the earldom. It is mine and I will have it. My advice to you is to watch your back."

Roger said in a hard voice, "Leave this place. It is only out of respect for who you are that I am letting you leave. But do not return."

He looked at his mother. "I meant what I said, Mother. Should you ever change your mind..."

"She won't!" Guy shouted.

She smiled painfully. "Thank you, Roger. Thank you, my son."

He went to the edge of the barge and jumped lightly onto the dock. Without once looking back he went over to the man who was holding his horse, handed him a coin, leaped into the saddle and rode away.

Twenty

Roger stopped Patrick once he was out of sight of the waterfront and dismounted. He was shaking so badly he didn't think he could stay in the saddle.

The confrontation with his father had shaken him to his core. He had not been immune to his father's cries of injustice, or to the intense power of his personality, but he had held steady. He had been true to his grandfather. He held onto Patrick's bridle with shaking fingers and tried desperately to regain his composure.

His father had said he was willing to change sides in order to get what he wanted. Well, in that he was no different from dozens of other nobles, who were all waiting to see which side would benefit them most. Roger supposed he couldn't fault Guy for his lack of allegiance.

It doesn't matter what anybody else does, Roger told himself. *What matters is that I am honorable and true to my vows as a knight. I pledged my loyalty to Stephen,*

*and I will keep that pledge. I pledged to my grandfather
that I would not let my father become the earl and I will
keep that pledge.*

Guy must have done some terrible things to cause his
grandfather to act as he did. It was true what he had said
to Guy, his grandfather had been a just master to all his
dependents. Roger had never seen him act in an unrea-
sonable way toward any of his knights or his vassals.
The provocation must have been huge to cause him to
put aside his only son.

*But God—to face his father like that! To have to
stand against him!*

Roger's upbringing had been remarkably untroubled.
He had been smart and extraordinarily athletic from the
time he was a child, the apple of his grandfather's eye.
His education had been one of his grandfather's chief
preoccupations. He had learned his skills from the finest knights, imported by the earl for just that purpose.
He had never been to war, but he had learned all about
warfare from men who had; never participated in a real
tournament, yet he could knock down a man much heav-
ier than himself in the lists. His horsemanship skills
were legendary among his men. He had been created by
his grandfather to be the perfect knight, the perfect
leader, the perfect Earl of Wiltshire.

Never before had his birthright been challenged. And
by a father who had been so suddenly resurrected from
the grave!

I need to talk to Nell about this, he thought.

It was a comfort to feel that he had someone he could confide in. That was something that had been missing from his life until he had met her. His grandfather had always made sure that there was a distance between Roger and the knights who served under him. Even when he was a boy he had not really had a friend. He was always apart. And his grandfather had been so much older that he was scarcely a confidant.

There was something about Nell, a sense of understanding, that drew him to confide in her. She was not someone who took the world lightly. You could be sure that whatever you told her would be seriously considered. And she had her own sort of wisdom. It came from growing up close to God, he thought.

The shivering was slowing down and he took a few deep, long breaths. The people passing him while he stood there eyed him curiously, but fortunately none of the knights from the castle had happened by. He put his foot in the stirrup and swung back into the saddle.

Nell and the girls returned from the fair loaded with packages and in high good humor. Nell was particularly pleased with a gown she had bought that she thought would look very nice at the king's Christmas Court. The castle tailor would have to make some alterations to fit her smaller figure, but the dark blue samite matched her eyes and the girls even made her order some new matching slippers from Walter Hovis.

Even the older ladies had gone to the fair, and the

ladies' solar was lively as everyone showed their purchases and told about their plans to go back on the morrow and maybe pick up one or two more things.

The talk at supper was all about the fair, as well. Roger was quiet but Nell supposed that was because he had not accompanied them and so had nothing to contribute. She asked him about his horse and he said that Bayard was doing better, so she smiled at him and turned to talk to Lady Mabel, who had found some wall hangings she actually wanted Nell to go look at tomorrow.

They gathered round the fire to sing after supper, and Thomas showed off the new lute he had bought at the fair. It had a fine sound, and for the first time Nell was able to join in on some of the songs she had been learning from the girls.

Finally it was time to go to bed. The page brought Gawain in from his last walk of the night and he followed Nell and Roger up the stairs to their bedroom.

"Lady Mabel asked me today when we were going to move into the earl's apartment," Nell said as Roger got into the bed beside her. "I told her that we were very comfortable here."

"I've thought about that," Roger said.

"Is the earl's apartment very different from this?"

"The rooms are bigger. It's finer, there's no disguising that. I suppose I just wasn't ready to make the move so soon after my grandfather died."

"We can continue to stay here if you like. It's perfectly comfortable."

"No. Lady Mabel is right. I am the earl and I should be using the earl's apartment. We'll move whenever it's convenient for you, Nell."

"All right. I'll see about it," Nell said.

He didn't move toward her, just sat upright against his pillows, as if he had something more to say. Nell waited, but Roger remained oddly silent.

"Are you sure Bayard is all right?" Nell said. "You've been very quiet tonight, Roger."

"It isn't Bayard," he replied finally. "I got a note from my mother today. She came to Wilton by barge and she asked to see me."

Nell turned to stare at him in surprise. With the curtains open and the candle burning, she was able to see him clearly. He was still staring straight ahead, his profile rigid. "Your mother? Here in Wilton?"

"Yes. Needless to say, I went immediately."

More silence.

"And was it she?" Nell pressed.

"Yes." The line of his mouth looked grim. "She had my father with her, Nell."

"Your father!" She was stunned. "He was on a barge? In Wilton? Today?"

He shot her a sideways look. "That's right."

"Dear heaven," Nell exclaimed. "But why, Roger? Why would he come here? Wasn't it dangerous for him?"

"He said he trusted me not to give him up."

Nell reached out and took his hand. His fingers curled tightly around hers. "What happened?" she asked quietly.

"He asked me to give over my title as Earl of Wiltshire to him. He claims he was treated unjustly by my grandfather and that it is his right to be earl. He offered to name me as his heir."

Nell tightened her own hold on his hand and said nothing.

Finally he turned to look at her. "He really expected me to do it, Nell. He kept talking about my duty as his son, and his wrongful exile by my grandfather. He said he would swear his allegiance to the king if Stephen would recognize him as the earl. Even my mother said that he had not deserved to be banished. She was on his side, Nell."

She could hear the repressed anguish in his voice. "Roger," she said, "you know how your grandfather was with you. Why would he have been a different man with his only son? He would have wanted to be proud of Guy, to have trained him to be his successor as he trained you. Most earls have several sons, he had only Guy. Can you imagine what it must have cost for him to have done what he did? The provocation must have been enormous. He had to have been convinced that Guy would be a disaster as the earl."

Roger reached out and put an arm around her. She nestled against him. "Thank you," he said. He rested his cheek against her hair. "I needed to hear that."

"It's true. You are your grandfather's heir and you are right to hold to that. He was the one who knew you both and he was the one to make the decision. The very fact that he made you swear that oath on his deathbed tells you how vital he felt it was that Guy not be allowed to have the earldom."

"You're right." His voice was muffled by her hair.

"What was he like?" she asked curiously.

"He looks like my grandfather, but his eyes are a different color blue. They are so bright, Nell! And they change all the time."

"Does he look old?"

"Not at all. He looks like a man in his prime. There is a sense of energy about him. As if he scarcely ever stands still."

"What did he say when you refused to give way to him?"

"He told me he was a bad enemy to make."

She thought about this, her cheek pressed against his shoulder. "He can't do anything to hurt you, Roger. The empress does not have the strength to attack Wiltshire."

"That is true. He knows that, I'm sure. That is why he made the attempt to sway me. The chances of his taking Wiltshire otherwise are next to nothing."

Nell turned her face and pressed her lips against his shoulder in a quick hard kiss. "This is so hard for you. It isn't a natural thing, to have to oppose your father."

She could feel him let out a long breath. "It is hard. I wish he had stayed in France." His voice tensed. "I wish I had never found out that he was alive."

"I know."

She thought a little longer. "Roger, you don't think

he would try to go to Stephen behind your back? To get the king to name him earl instead of you?"

"Stephen would never do that." Roger was positive. "The king is an honorable man."

"I don't suppose Guy can afford to alienate the empress, either," Nell said. "If she found out that he had tried to switch sides, she would scarcely continue to support him. Then he would have nothing."

"The king would never betray his word to me and give the earldom to Guy," Roger said.

Nell nodded, her cheek brushing up and down against his bare skin.

"How was your mother?"

"That is the hardest part of all of this," he said. "We were robbed of each other for all those years, and now we are apart again. I told her she was welcome to come and live here at Wilton, but she said she would rather stay with my father." His voice sounded constricted. "I suppose she must love him still."

Nell didn't reply and silence fell. The only sound in the room was Gawain, snuffling a little on his bed in the corner.

Then Roger said in a different voice, "The hell with my father—let's concentrate on us."

"That's all right with me," Nell said, and lifted her face for his kiss.

Twenty-One

Several weeks passed. The weather turned colder and news came that Stephen had arranged a truce with the empress for the holy season. The result of the previous season of raiding was that the empress had taken over the west and Brian fitz Count was still holding out at Wallingford. Stephen had taken a few castles, which had subsequently fallen again to the empress, and the king's sum total of success was zero. Yet Stephen had control of the great bulk of the kingdom while the empress was largely confined to the west.

At Wilton, the castle went about its business. Roger made several visits to vassals who were near to him and Nell remained at home, more and more comfortable in her role as lady of the manor. She visited the kitchen every day to confer with the cook and check that all was well there, and she was even more meticulous than Lady Mabel about the dirty rushes in the

Great Hall being swept up and replaced. The knights loved her. She had thought that some of them were looking shabby and was having the tailor make new tunics for them. She spent time every day in private conversation with Father Ralph, reading the bible and talking about spiritual matters. The younger girls were all avid horsewomen and they all went out hunting several times a week.

Nell was happy.

The one cloud on the blue sky of her life was the continued opposition of Lady Mabel. Nell had been called to town on two other occasions to doctor the sick, and Lady Mabel did not think this was an appropriate way for the wife of the Earl of Wiltshire to comport herself. Also, the other older ladies were becoming more reconciled to Nell and were beginning to look to her for leadership, which Lady Mabel resented. She also did not like the new young girls who had come to the castle, and she blamed Nell for bringing them. They were too loud, she complained, too boisterous, and they paid no reverence at all to her opinions.

The culmination of this resentment came to a head one afternoon when Nell and Lady Mabel found themselves alone together in the ladies' solar. Nell smiled companionably as she came in. "All alone, Lady Mabel? Where is everyone else?"

"They will be here shortly," the woman returned.

The window was shuttered against the cold and the charcoal brazier in the center of the room was glowing.

The chairs were grouped in a large circle around the brazier and baskets full of sewing were heaped on the chests along the wall. Two hangings adorned the walls, paintings of different views of the River Avon.

Lady Mabel fixed her eyes on the silver brooch that held together the blue mantle over Nell's tunic and a sour look came over her face.

"How can you stand to wear that brooch?" she asked.

Nell looked at her in surprise. "Why not? It was a gift from my lord."

"Some gift," Lady Mabel muttered.

Nell frowned. "What are you talking about?"

"It came from Tordis Martenson, didn't it? That should be answer enough."

Nell walked slowly over to her chair and sat down across from Lady Mabel. She needed to put her feet on a footstool as they did not reach the ground. A flutter of apprehension tightened her stomach. She remembered Thomas's comment about Tordis Martenson. "What is it you are saying, Lady Mabel?" she asked steadily.

Lady Mabel's chin jutted into the air. "Lord Roger had an affair with Tordis Martenson. All in the castle knew about it. It started after her husband died and went on for about a year."

An affair? Nell struggled to understand. Her convent upbringing had taught her nothing about affairs. "What do you mean?" she asked plainly.

Lady Mabel gave her a scornful look. "They were

lovers, that's what I mean. They were lovers right up to the time that he married you."

Nell felt a tightness in her chest. Suddenly it was hard to breathe. The thought of Roger with that tall blond woman…

"Why are you telling me this?" she demanded of Lady Mabel.

"I just hate to see you make a fool of yourself, that's all," Lady Mabel replied. "All do know why he gave you that brooch. And to see you flaunt it… I just thought you ought to know, that's all."

Nell's small fists clenched. "What do you mean, all do know why he gave me the brooch?" she asked, her voice sounding a little breathless.

"I'm saying that it wasn't just before you got married that they were lovers. He went into Wilton to see her and came home with that brooch for you. I suppose he had to have *some* excuse for his visit. But I have felt badly for you, parading that brooch around the castle, not knowing what a fool it was making you look," she finished smugly.

Nell sat staring with horror at Lady Mabel's satisfied face.

It can't be true, she thought. *She is making it up to upset me.*

But it was true that Thomas had warned her that Tordis Martenson was not a person she ought to know.

Lovers? she thought. Then, frantically, *I have to get out of here. I can't bear to look at Lady Mabel one more minute.*

She stood up. She didn't look at Lady Mabel. "The ladies can sew without me today," she said. She had almost made it to the door when two of the older women came in.

"My lady!" one of them said, getting a glimpse of her face. "Is everything all right?"

"Yes," Nell said with as much control as she could manage. "I will see you at supper."

They stood aside to let her pass. She went down the staircase to the Great Hall, which was almost empty in the middle of the afternoon. A few servants were replacing some of the flambeaux on the wall and another was fixing one of the trestle tables that were used for eating. Nell crossed the hall in silence and went up the spiral stair that led to the earl's apartment.

Everything was quiet. Nell went over to the window in the solar and opened the shutter. The window looked over the river, which came close beneath the castle on one of its sides, acting as another wall. She drew a deep, long breath of fresh air, as if she had been breathing foul air for the last fifteen minutes. She stood there for a long time, clutching her mantle around her. Then she went over to her chair and sat down. She began to tremble.

That vicious, vicious woman. Everything she said could be a lie. She hates me, Nell thought. *She must hate me, to tell me such a tale.*

Her hand went up to touch her brooch, then she jerked it away, as if it had been burned.

Roger and Tordis Martenson. It would be hard enough to imagine them together if it had happened before they were married. But if he had been with her since...

A picture came into her mind, of Roger doing to Tordis Martenson the things he did to her, and her stomach twisted.

Why would he do such a thing? I thought he was the perfect knight. I thought he was an honorable man. I thought he cared about me.

I have to ask him. I have to find out if this is true. If it is true...if it is true...I don't know what I will do.

A breeze blew in the open window, chilling her. She huddled in her cloak. Then, suddenly, she ripped the brooch away from its fastening and hurled it across the room.

If it's true, she thought, *then nothing will ever be the same again.*

Roger came in late in the afternoon after holding exercises for his knights. The servants were setting up the trestle tables as he passed through the Great Hall and he ran lightly up the stairs to the earl's apartment, followed by his squire and his dog.

The apartment was empty.

Nell must have dressed already, he thought. He and Richard moved through the solar and into his dressing room, where Richard got him out of his armor and into clean clothes for the evening meal. He sat on a chair while Richard cross-gartered his hose, then thrust his feet into the low slippers that were the standard costume for around the castle.

He talked casually with Richard as he dressed, discussing the tactics they had practiced today on the big field in front of the castle. With simple pleasure he looked forward to his meal and to seeing his wife. They would be leaving in two days time for the king's Christmas Court, which was to be held this year at Salisbury. The Bishop of Salisbury had died recently, and Stephen was appropriating both his palace and his treasure for the crown.

Nell had been scandalized when she had learned of Stephen's actions, but Roger had explained the long-standing feud between the two. "The Bishop of Salisbury was one of old King Henry's chief ministers and even though he was ostensibly pledged to King Stephen he secretly supported the empress. Before the empress landed, Stephen arrested him and seized his castles and a good bit of his treasure. He had become a very powerful man under King Henry. Stephen eventually released him and let him resume his duties as bishop, but he never regained the position of power he had held under Henry. Now that he is dead, the king is taking over whatever treasure the bishop had left. I believe it was considerable."

It's hard for Nell to understand the imperatives of power, Roger thought as he wound a belt around his waist. *She is so good and simple herself that she is shocked when people don't act the way she thinks they should. And of course she has a reverence for the religious—it's the way she was raised, after all.*

He finished dressing and dismissed his squire so Richard could go and get himself ready for dinner. He sat for a few moments in his high carved chair in the solar, waiting until it was time to go downstairs, and in his mind he went over the exercises he had conducted today and the areas he had seen that could use improvement.

His mind drifted to his father. *I wonder what he is doing. He wouldn't dare try to attack Wiltshire. I can't imagine Robert of Gloucester being fool enough to accede to that kind of request. They would be crushed.*

And the thought that came to his mind every time he thought of his father. What could he have done that was so terrible that his grandfather had banished him? It couldn't have just been that his father drew his sword. There had to be more to it than that.

There was no answer to that question and he roused himself from his reverie. Time to go down to supper, to Nell. He smiled with anticipation as he went out the door.

At supper Roger had a conversation with Simon about the possibility of buying new horses for the castle guard and it wasn't until halfway through the meal that he did more than exchange greetings with Nell. When he turned to ask her about her day, for the first time he realized that something was wrong.

She talked mainly in monosyllables and she wouldn't meet his eyes. After persevering for a few minutes, he finally lowered his voice and asked, "Are you all right, Nell? Did something happen today to upset you?"

She shot him a quick dark blue glance, then looked away again. "We'll talk about it later, when we're alone," she said.

It's that damn Lady Mabel, he thought. He thought things had gotten better once the younger women had come. He looked down at the table of young women who were sitting at the front of the hall. They were talking and laughing with the knights who were seated with them. They certainly weren't acting as if anything had gone wrong.

Nell has handled Lady Mabel very well, he thought. *Surely she wouldn't let the old harridan upset her like this.*

For Nell was terribly upset. That became clearer to Roger as the evening progressed. After supper the company gathered around the fire in the Great Hall while the tables were cleared and there was a great deal of jesting and laughing among the knights and the girls.

Usually Roger and Nell joined in these entertainments but tonight Nell bowed out, saying she was not feeling very well.

Perhaps that's what's wrong, Roger thought. *Perhaps she has a headache or a stomachache.*

"Perhaps you ought to take one of your own remedies and go to bed," he said to her. "You are looking a little peaked."

She nodded. For some reason she still wasn't meeting his eyes. "I would like to talk to you, Roger. Will you come upstairs with me?"

"Surely," he said and followed her up the stairs to their apartment. She stopped in the solar and turned to him. He looked at her by the light of the candle that was burning on the table.

"Are you sure you're all right?" he asked. "You don't look well."

"I am not ill."

He sat down in the earl's chair and gestured for her to take her chair beside him. "Then what is wrong? You have not been yourself all night."

"I learned something today that has upset me," she said flatly. "I wanted to ask you if it was true."

He searched her face. She looked very pale in the dim light of the candle. "What can have upset you, sweeting? Was it something Lady Mabel said? Surely you have learned how to deal with her by now."

"Actually, it *was* something Lady Mabel said." For the first time all evening her eyes met his. "It was something very ugly."

An alarm sounded in his brain. Surely it couldn't be? He asked in a slightly unsteady voice, "What is it, Nell?"

"Lady Mabel told me that you and Tordis Martenson were lovers." She looked away from him.

Roger felt fury sweep through him. *Damn that woman!* He looked at his wife's averted face and struggled to say something. "Why would she have told you such a thing?"

"Because she wanted to hurt me, of course. But I need to know the truth, Roger. I can't be the only one in the castle not knowing the truth."

Roger thought frantically for a minute, trying to decide what to say. When he finally spoke he chose his words with great care. "Nell, what was between me and Tordis happened before I ever met you. It has nothing to do with you and me. It has nothing to do with what is between us."

Nell was silent, her head bent, eyes staring at the blue wool of her dress. He hurried to explain further. "Men and women often have these kinds of arrangements," he said. "Tordis was a widow and I was unmarried. We hurt nobody. It was just a convenient arrangement that suited us both. I broke it off when I married you."

"Did you?"

The words were a whisper and he had to strain to hear them.

"Yes," he said strongly. "I did break it off. You are my wife, Nell, and I love you. Surely you must know that."

"Then you didn't go to see her again after we were married? You didn't buy me that brooch to have an excuse for going there? Lady Mabel says that you did. She says that everyone knows that you did. Everyone, that is, except me."

Roger was panicked. If Lady Mabel were in the room at that moment, he would gladly have strangled her. How could he explain this to Nell? How could he make her understand that his encounter with Tordis had meant nothing to him?

Should he deny it?

But he looked at his wife and knew that he couldn't lie to her. *I can make her understand,* he thought desperately. *Tordis means nothing to me. Surely I can make her understand that.*

"It happened once, Nell," he said desperately. "You and I had been sleeping together in the same bed for weeks and physically I was so frustrated. You don't understand how hard it is for a man. I would hold your naked body, then have to turn away and try to go to sleep. I was going mad. I went to Tordis to relieve my bodily frustration, that's all. It had nothing to do with how I felt about you."

"We were married!" Nell cried. "You committed adultery."

Roger flushed. "We were married but we weren't physically intimate. You were grateful to me for giving you that time to grow accustomed to me. I just don't think you understand how hard that time was on me," he pleaded. "I had a wife who lay beside me in bed every night, but I couldn't touch her. You don't understand men, Nell. We're not like you. We have needs that must be met."

"Do all men go to another woman if their wives can't satisfy their needs? What if I should get sick? Would you go back to Tordis then?"

"Of course not!"

"From what you have just been saying, you would," she said accusingly.

She had backed him into a corner. "Well, I wouldn't," he insisted. "Now that we are properly married I swear I will stay faithful to you, Nell. I don't need to go to another woman. You give me all that I need or want."

"I am convenient for you," she said. "I am right there in your bed. You don't have to go into town to see me."

"No!" he said strongly. "That's not it at all, Nell. You are my wife. I love you."

"How could you love me, Roger?" she demanded. "Everyone knows how you came by the brooch, that you went to see Tordis and came home with it as an excuse for visiting her. And you gave that brooch to me! And you let me wear it! How could you love me and humiliate me like that?"

He had never given a thought to the damn brooch. "That wasn't how I meant it," he said weakly.

"But that's what you did. I thought you were a different kind of person than that. I thought you loved me."

"I do love you! Nell, I tell you everything...."

"You didn't tell me that you committed adultery." She squeezed her eyes shut. "I don't want to talk anymore," she said. "My heart is too sore."

"Nell... You have a right to be angry, but truly I never meant to do you any harm!"

"Well, you did," she replied. "I trusted you and you betrayed me. That's not something I can easily forget."

He sat there staring at her ivory profile. He didn't know what else he could say.

She stood up. "I am going to bed," she said. "I can't go downstairs tonight and face all of those people."

He watched helplessly as she walked away from him. The thing that he had dreaded had happened. Nell had found out about Tordis.

I could wring Lady Mabel's neck, he thought.

But he couldn't blame it all on Lady Mabel. He was the one who had cheated on his wife; he was the one who had committed adultery.

That damn brooch, he thought again. He had given it to her because it was pretty and because he thought she would like it. Now she saw it as the token of his deception, which, he supposed, it was.

He had acted thoughtlessly, let the needs of his body push him into doing something he knew was wrong, and now he was paying the price.

And Nell was paying the price, as well.

Twenty-Two

The next few days Nell was occupied with packing for the visit to Stephen's Christmas Court. Part of her didn't want to go; the very idea of the festivities of Christmas made her feel ill. On the other hand, she liked the idea of getting away from Wilton Castle and all the eyes that were upon her there.

She was profoundly upset. Her whole image of Roger and of their marriage had received a terrible shock. All of her new, deep sexual feelings toward him had been drained from her, as if a brimming cup inside her had suddenly been emptied.

He had betrayed her. She couldn't think of it any other way. And the fact that it had been a public betrayal made things even worse. She felt as if she could no longer hold up her head around the castle, as if her life was one long public humiliation.

He kept trying to explain things to her, but she

couldn't listen. Her mind was too filled with what she saw as a scalding betrayal of her trust, of the sanctity of their marriage.

They left for Salisbury early on December twenty-third, a cold overcast day with a low sky that threatened snow. Five knights attended them, as well as Roger's squire and one of Nell's new ladies, Juliana, who had come along to act as Nell's maid. They stayed overnight at the castle of one of Roger's vassals and arrived in Salisbury early on the afternoon of the twenty-fourth.

The bishop's palace, where the king was staying, was a large, elegant edifice built upon spacious grounds. Stone columns stood at the entrance to the property and an expanse of open lawn fronted the long stone building. Roger and Nell were greeted at the door by William Martel, Stephen's steward, and shown upstairs to their room.

When they came back downstairs to the main hall they found it full of people, most of them finely dressed in fur-trimmed robes.

"I wonder if my mother and father are coming," Nell said to Roger as she looked at the roomful of strangers.

"We shall soon find out," Roger said in reply.

A man approached them. "Lord Roger," he said. "I have been looking for you. I have a few questions for you, if you don't mind."

Roger turned to Nell. "May I introduce my wife," he said. "Nell, this is the Earl of Hertford."

"I am pleased to meet you, my lord," Nell said.

"Would you excuse us for a few moments, my lady?" the man said. "I have a need to speak to your husband."

"Of course," Nell said and stood by herself as the two men moved away.

She felt very alone in the middle of the big room. It was high-ceilinged and had a gallery running along one of the walls. Splendid needlework tapestries hung on the walls. It was quite the grandest room Nell had ever been in.

"All alone, my lady?" a man's voice said. "How unchivalrous of your husband to leave you thus."

Nell turned to see a young man with black hair and large brown eyes regarding her. She smiled. "He had to talk to someone," she explained.

"I am William de Vere," the young man introduced himself. "My father is the king's constable. I saw you come in. You must be the new Countess of Wiltshire."

"That is right," Nell said.

"And your father is the Earl of Lincoln."

"Yes. Do you know if he is coming to the Christmas Court, my lord?"

The young man shook his head. "He's not coming—he's ill."

Nell frowned, concerned. "I didn't know that." She hoped it was not serious.

"We heard only a few days ago. I'm sure he'll be all right. This winter season brings on many annoying ills, doesn't it?"

"Yes," Nell agreed, feeling relieved. "It certainly does."

"Why don't you let me take you around and introduce you to some people?" William said. "A beautiful lady like yourself should be made known."

"Thank you, that would be kind," Nell said, a little embarrassed by the compliment.

William de Vere seemed to know everyone and Nell was introduced to a large number of men and women whose names she meticulously committed to memory. She kept glancing to see where Roger was. She might be angry with him, but he was the only familiar person in this roomful of grand strangers.

"Where is the king?" she asked William de Vere as they stood in a circle near the fireplace with a group of men and women.

"He is meeting with his ministers," one of the men replied. "We'll see him at supper."

At this point Roger came over to join them and Nell moved close to him. She didn't speak unless she was spoken to, but when she was addressed she answered with a quiet dignity. William de Vere gave her an encouraging smile every now and then and she thought that he was a very nice young man.

The next day was Christmas and the highlight of the celebration was to be the feast that was served at midday. They started the day with mass and after breakfast Nell joined a group of men and women who were taking a walk around the palace gardens. Roger was elsewhere and William de Vere once more gravitated to

Nell's side, engaging her in conversation. Nell was grateful for his attention.

The palace hall was being set up for dinner as the garden party went back inside and everyone went to their rooms to put on their finery. Nell went upstairs and found Roger there before her. He was alone; neither Richard nor Juliana had arrived yet to help them dress.

"I have a gift for you," Roger said as she came into the room.

Nell had had very few presents in her life and normally she would have been delighted. Now all she could think of was the brooch. "That is kind of you, my lord," she said stiffly.

He went to the chest in the corner, picked up something and brought it back to her. He handed it to her and Nell's mouth opened in surprise.

It was a blue velvet mantle lined with rich dark fur.

"That should help to keep you warm," he said.

"Oh," she breathed. "It's beautiful." She stroked her hand over the fur. She looked at Roger. "When did you get this?"

"I got it at the fair. I have been saving it to give to you for Christmas."

She felt a lump in her throat. How happy she would have been with this present a few weeks ago! Now all she could do was force a smile.

"I've never had anything so splendid in my life."

"You're my wife," he said. "You should have splendid things."

She folded it and laid it on the bed. "I don't have anything for you. I made you some new shirts, but they are
at home. I didn't think to bring them."

He came to her and took her hands into his. "There's
only one thing I want from you for Christmas, Nell," he
said. "And that is your forgiveness."

She let him hold her hands but didn't return his clasp.
God would want her to forgive, she thought. And it was
Christ's birthday. He was able to forgive anything. She
should try to do the same.

But she couldn't forget. She had given her whole
self to him and he had betrayed her. She felt that nothing would ever be the same between them again.

She looked up. The sun slanted in the window and
picked up the brightness in his hair. He was looking at
her so earnestly, his eyes more darkly gold than usual.
She felt as if a knife twisted in her heart.

"Please, Nell," he said.

"I will try," she said in a low voice.

"Really?" His smile was blinding. He took her in his
arms. "I'll make it up to you, sweeting, I promise. I'll
be the best husband any woman ever had. I'll never
even look at another woman. I don't *want* to look at another woman. You are all the woman I will ever want or
need. I love you."

She stood there, feeling his warmth and strength
against her, and she closed her eyes. He said he loved
her. Surely that should be enough.

But deep inside there was still that pain that wouldn't

go away, no matter what she said or how she tried to feel.

If they hadn't been so close, she wouldn't be feeling this way. It was losing something that had become the very core of her life that was so painful.

He bent his head and kissed her long and deep. She tried to return his kiss but her heart wasn't in it.

"I can't do without you," he said. "You have become the very heart of me."

She should have been so happy to hear those words. But somehow she was not.

The trust that she had felt in him had been broken and she didn't think it could ever be repaired.

The Christmas feast was like nothing Nell had ever experienced. The hall was decorated with a splendid array of greens and the amount of food served was enormous. Nell sat at the high table with Roger, the king, and several other earls and their wives. The first course consisted of five meat dishes and vegetables; the second included two fish and six birds; the third consisted of three meat and two fruit; then came the custard and egg dishes, then nuts, cheese, comfits, sugar candy, raisins and dates. Each course was announced with a fanfare of trumpets, and entertainment was provided between the courses.

There were acrobats, tumblers, jugglers, conjurors and dancers, but the singer was the entertainer that struck Nell the most. He was from Aquitaine and he sang songs that Nell had never heard before—songs of love between a knight and his lady.

The songs had been written by the Duke of Aquitaine himself and they were undisguisedly carnal. The knight wooed his lady with single-minded determination and the lady bestowed her love freely and willingly.

What scandalized Nell was that the knight and his lady were not married. In fact, the lady was married to someone else—the lord of the manor.

The rest of the company seemed charmed by the songs. Nell looked at Roger and he had a smile on his face as he listened to the liquid vowels of southern France pouring out of the singer's mouth.

When he had finished, the audience clapped and shouted its approval.

Is this how things are done in great households? Nell thought in horror.

She said to Roger, "I have never heard songs like that. We certainly don't sing them at home."

"It's something new," he replied. "They say that there is a cult of what they call courtly love in the south, created by William of Aquitaine. This particular singer is actually from his court. We don't get many entertainers from that part of the world. They prefer the mildness of their own climes."

"But he is singing about adultery, Roger," she said in a low voice.

A little color came into his face. "It's just a pretty song, Nell. No one in England takes it seriously."

Nell did not reply.

After the dinner was over the tables were taken up and there was dancing. William de Vere came to Nell's side and took her hand as they formed a large circle. Roger was holding her other hand. As the song started and the circle began to move, William smiled at Nell. He was such a nice young man, she thought, and she smiled back.

Roger's hand tightened on hers and she looked to him inquiringly.

"Don't take that courtly love business too much to heart," he said to her in a low voice.

She stared at him in amazement. Then, suddenly, she was angry. It was all right for him to commit adultery with another woman, but she wasn't allowed to smile at a pleasant young man.

"Don't worry, *I* take my marriage vows seriously," she said to him, her voice as low as his had been.

He scowled.

Then the ladies had to form an inner circle away from the men and she moved away from him.

They danced for most of the afternoon and then it was time for supper. William de Vere kept close to Nell the whole time, and she didn't discourage him.

"I told you to keep away from de Vere and you deliberately courted his attentions all evening long," Roger said as they got into bed together that night.

"He is a nice young man and I was polite to him," Nell replied innocently. "Just because you are inclined to stray doesn't mean you should put that inclination on me."

"Good God," Roger exploded. "I thought we had put that behind us! Haven't I groveled enough, Nell? I made a mistake. I admitted it and I begged your forgiveness—which I thought you had given me. Evidently I was mistaken. Are you going to hold Tordis over my head for the rest of our married life?"

He was making it sound as if their estrangement was her fault.

"It is you who are making a rift between us now," she said angrily. "Just because I was nice to William de Vere doesn't mean that I'm unfaithful."

"You were more than just nice to him. You were flirting with him."

Nell was incensed. "I have never flirted in my life! I wouldn't even know how to flirt."

"Every woman is born knowing how to flirt. You were acting as if he was the most interesting person in the room tonight."

In her heart Nell knew that she had used William de Vere to give Roger a taste of his own medicine. But it made her angry to have Roger accuse her of doing just that. Roger was the one at fault in their relationship, not her.

"You sound ridiculous," she said coldly. "I don't know anyone here and William has been friendly to me and I appreciate that. That's all that's involved here."

Silence.

Then Roger said wearily, "I'm tired of being at odds with you, Nell. I miss you. I miss my best friend. Can't we put all this behind us and start again?"

Something inside Nell responded strongly to these particular words. She, too, missed the way things had been. She too missed her friend.

"I'd like to," she said in a quiet voice. "It's just…you hurt me bitterly, Roger, and I'm having a hard time forgiving you. I never thought of myself as an unforgiving person, but this is hard."

"I don't know what else I can say to you to convince you of how sorry I am. It was a moment of thoughtless stupidity on my part. But I don't think I should have to pay for it for the rest of my married life, Nell. Can't I just promise you that it will never happen again and let us forget it?"

Let it go, she told herself. *Take him back and let it go. It is what God would want you to do.*

"All right," she said finally.

"Thank you," he said with great relief. He reached out. "Let me hold you. I have missed holding you so much."

She turned to him and as his arms went around her she said in a small voice, "I have missed you, too."

His arms tightened and he bent his head to kiss her. The touch of his lips lit a fire inside of her and she responded strongly, winding her arms around his neck and opening her mouth to his.

They clung, their bodies pressed together, their kiss deep and powerful and erotic. Nell felt the surge of passion, dormant for so long, rise within her loins. She wanted him.

Their mouths separated and his lips trailed kisses down her neck and shoulders.

She could feel the hardness of his erection pressing against her. She reached down to touch him.

He needed no further urging, but laid her back upon the mattress and within a moment he was inside of her. She took him in deeply, lifting her legs to encircle his waist.

He felt so good as he moved back and forth inside her, softening the responsive flesh until she had reached the height of readiness. Her mouth opened in a silent cry as he plunged once more, and then the orgasm exploded, rippling all through her, down her legs and up her back, so powerful, so intense that she actually cried out loud with the violence of the sensation.

Her cry was echoed almost immediately by Roger and they clung together in the throes of mutual passion, two bodies made one by the act of love. Afterward they lay together, recovering.

"Nell," Roger said, his voice husky. "I love you. Only you. There's no one else but you in my heart."

"I love you, too," Nell said.

And she did.

Finally, she thought she could let Tordis go.

Twenty-Three

The following morning the entire company, including the king, went hunting. It was a beautiful sight, Nell thought, as she sat her mare next to Roger and Bayard— the men and women in their colorful clothes, the eager dogs, the huntsmen and dog handlers, the glossy horses. Then the horn sounded in a series of one-pitch notes, the signal for the greyhounds that a deer had been found. The hounds took off, followed by the horses and the chase was on.

Nell rode next to Roger, the sound of many hooves thundering in her ears, the cold December wind whipping around her. Part of her was always a little frightened by the speed—she was still new to riding—but part of her exulted in the excitement. The hunting field flowed over the rough terrain as the greyhounds ahead chased the stag to bring it to bay.

It was dinnertime when the hunting party arrived back

at the bishop's palace. Nell and Roger were heading toward the stairs to go up to their room to change clothes when they were intercepted by the king's steward.

"A messenger came for Lady Eleanor while you were out hunting, my lord," he said. "It is from the Earl of Lincoln."

Roger frowned. "Is everything all right?"

"I don't know, my lord. I will have someone bring the message to your room."

"What can it be?" Nell said as they climbed the stairs together. "The steward said the message was for me, not you."

"We'll know soon enough," Roger returned.

They had been in their room ten minutes when a page arrived with a scroll of paper in his hand. Nell took it, unrolled it and read it in silence. Then she looked at Roger.

"It is from my mother. Evidently my father is very ill. She asks that I come to Bardney and help care for him."

Roger held out his hand for the scroll and Nell gave it to him. He read it and then looked at her. "It doesn't sound good."

"My mother knows that I studied the healing arts at the convent. I will have to go, Roger. I don't know if I can help, but I have to try."

"Of course you have to go. The king will understand."

"Can I leave this afternoon? My mother sounds as if it's urgent."

"We'll leave immediately. I'll let our knights know."

"Are you coming with me?"

"Of course I'm coming with you. I wouldn't let you make such a long trip by yourself." He went to the door. "Get our things packed up. I'll go to inform the king."

They rode out of Salisbury while the court was at dinner, heading north and east to Lincoln and the castle of Bardney, where the Earl of Lincoln was lying gravely ill. It was a long ride, but Nell was much more accustomed to the saddle than she had been when she had left Bardney after her wedding, and when they stopped at an inn for the night she wasn't sore at all.

They reached Bardney early on the twenty-eighth of December, a day of gray skies and biting winds. Nell and Roger had only to wait a few minutes in the Great Hall before Nell's mother came rushing to greet them.

"Nell!" Lady Alice enveloped her daughter in a hug. "How good of you to come so quickly."

"I came as fast as I could," Nell replied, hugging her mother back.

"Roger." Lady Alice exchanged the kiss of peace with her son-in-law. "Thank you for bringing Nell to me. I'm sorry I had to pull you away from the king's Christmas Court."

"The king sends his good wishes to Earl Raoul," Roger said.

"How is he, Mother?" Nell asked anxiously.

"Oh, Nell, I fear that he is very ill indeed," Lady Alice

said, her voice quivering slightly. "He has a terrible cough and when he coughs he spits up blood."

Dear Lord, Nell thought. *He's dying.*

She looked into her mother's face and could see that Lady Alice was exhausted. "How long has he been coughing up blood?" she asked quietly.

"For a few weeks. He's had the cough for longer than that."

"Is he in pain?"

"Yes."

Nell looked at Roger. His golden eyes were grave. She pressed her lips together. "Mama," she said gently, "coughing up blood is not good."

"I know," Lady Alice said starkly. "I suppose I was hoping that you would know something that would help."

"I can help to make him comfortable. I will have to get some poppy juice from Sister Helen. That will help with the pain. But once the lungs start bleeding, I don't know of anything that can stop them."

Lady Alice closed her eyes.

"I'm sorry, Mama."

Lady Alice opened her eyes and focused on Nell. "He is so angry, Nell. I think he knows that he is dying and he's angry with God. Father Clement has tried to talk to him, but to no avail." Lady Alice touched Nell's arm. "I fear for his soul. I think that is the true reason why I called you home. I was hoping you could talk to him. You were in the convent for so long. Perhaps you can find the right words to say to him."

She wants me to talk to my father? I don't even know him. How can I find the words that will bring him to God?

Lady Alice was looking at Nell so hopefully.

"Mama… how can I reach my father when his own priest has failed?"

"You are his daughter, Nell. You share his blood."

But I feel no connection to my father. He is the man who gave me away. He gave me away twice, once to the convent and once to Roger. He never cared about me. How can my mother think I might help him?

But she couldn't say these things to her mother. They were too hurtful.

"Have *you* spoken to him?" she asked Lady Alice.

Her mother shrugged. "Oh, Raoul never listens to me."

If he doesn't listen to you, Mama, then why should he listen to me?

"Will you try, Nell?" she pleaded.

Nell sighed. "I will try."

Raoul de Bonvile was sitting in his solar by the glowing brazier when Nell and Roger went to greet him. Nell was shocked by her father's appearance. He had lost a great deal of weight and the bones in his face were prominent.

"Father," she said softly. She went to kiss his cheek. His skin was cold under her lips and it felt very dry.

"What are you doing here?" he asked. He looked at Roger. His dark blue eyes were sunken into their sockets. "I thought you were at Stephen's Christmas Court."

"We were," Nell replied. "Mama asked me to come and visit you. I know of a potion that will make you more comfortable."

"Will it cure me?" Earl Raoul asked harshly.

"It will help with the cough and relieve your pain," Nell said.

"But it won't make me better."

"We can give it a chance," Nell said firmly.

"Don't humor me," the earl said angrily. "I'm dying, aren't I?"

"Coughing up blood is not a good sign, but miracles have happened," Nell replied.

"Miracles may have happened, but not for me." The earl's voice was deeply bitter. "First my son and daughter were cut down in their prime and now it's me. I may not be young, but I can tell you this—I'm too young to die."

Nell and Roger exchanged glances. Neither of them spoke.

The earl said, "You will be the Earl of Lincoln sooner than you expected, Roger."

"I am in no hurry, my lord," Roger said. "Let Nell treat this illness of yours. As she said, miracles have happened."

All of a sudden, Lord Raoul began to cough. It was a deep, wrenching cough and he held a cloth up to his mouth to muffle it. The cloth came away with a red stain on it.

"See that," he said. "It will take a miracle to save me now."

"Where do you hurt, Father?" Nell asked.

"Everywhere. Even my bones hurt."

"Would you be more comfortable in bed?"

"I'll be in bed soon enough. I want to stay upright for as long as I can."

"I'll send to Sister Helen for her poppy-juice potion. It will help you to feel better."

The earl nodded. His eyes went to Roger. "I'm glad that you're here. I can go over things with you, help you to orient yourself to the earldom."

Roger looked uncomfortable and shot a quick glance at Nell. She nodded. Clearly her father understood his condition. There was no point in trying to pretend that things were other than what they were.

"Your advice would be very helpful to me," Roger said soberly.

The earl gestured. "Pull a chair close to me so I don't have to talk so loudly."

Once more Roger glanced at Nell.

"Do as he says," she said gently. "I will see about getting the poppy juice from Sister Helen."

"Send our knights," Roger said.

Nell nodded. "I will return soon, Father," she said and left the room, closing the solar door quietly behind her.

As she went down the stairs, Nell thought about what she was going to do. Then she found her mother and told her that she would take Roger's knights and go to St. Cecelia's herself to collect the medicine she needed.

"There's no need for you to go," Lady Alice protested. "Can't the knights go alone?"

"I am only a few hours away from Sister Helen and I am going to go and visit her," Nell said. "I have missed her badly."

"Did you ask Roger?"

"Roger is busy with my father."

"Nell, you can't just take Roger's knights and ride away. They won't go with you without his permission."

Nell scowled. Her mother was right. "Very well, then I will go and tell him what I am going to do."

"Don't tell him, Nell, *ask* him," her mother said. "Men don't like to be told."

Nell stuck her chin in the air. "I am going to go to see Sister Helen if I have to go alone," she said determinedly. She headed toward the stairs and Lady Alice hurried after her.

Roger and Earl Raoul were sitting close together and Earl Raoul was talking when Nell came back into the room, Lady Alice behind her. Both men looked at her in surprise.

"What do you want?" Earl Raoul asked his daughter.

Nell said to Roger, "I am going to ride to St. Cecelia's with the knights to get my father's medicine. I have this chance to see Sister Helen and I am not going to miss it."

Roger frowned. "The roads…"

"I will be perfectly safe. No one will be foolish enough to attack a party of five armed knights."

Earl Raoul said in his new, hoarse-sounding voice, "It is not necessary for you to go, Nell."

"I want to go," Nell said. "I *need* to go."

"Your needs are not the question," her father said in annoyance. "The roads aren't safe."

"I got here without any trouble, and we came all the way from Salisbury," Nell retorted.

Earl Raoul scowled but before he could reply, Roger said, "Are you truly set on this? You have just made a long ride—you must be tired."

"I'm fine. I feel energetic just at the thought of seeing Sister Helen. Please don't stop me from doing this, Roger. It is very important to me."

"You will do as your husband says," Earl Raoul snapped.

There was a long pause. Then Roger said slowly, "All right. Send Thomas to see me and I will give him his orders. It will be best if you remain overnight at the convent so that you are not returning home in the dark."

Nell gave her husband a radiant smile. "Thank you, Roger. I'll find Thomas right away."

As she was leaving, she heard the earl say, "You are going to spoil that chit, Roger."

"Sister Helen was like a mother to Nell," Roger replied. "I won't stand in the way of their reunion."

Nell's mother followed her out of the room. "You have a kind husband," she said as they walked down the stairs together.

"Yes," Nell replied a little distractedly. She was

thinking of what she would say to Thomas. "Roger is very kind."

"I'm glad," Lady Alice said. "I'm glad the marriage has worked out so well."

They arrived in the Great Hall and Nell sent a page running to find Thomas and the rest of the Wilton knights.

Twenty-Four

Sister Helen was in the herb garden shed when Nell walked in and found her. It was a moment before the nun recognized her former protégé, who was wearing the fur-lined mantle that Roger had given her for Christmas. Then, "Nell!" she cried, and held out her arms.

Nell ran to embrace her mentor and for a long moment the two women stood, hugging each other and blinking back tears. Then Sister Helen held Nell away from her. "Let me look at you."

Nell smiled into her gray-blue eyes.

"You look wonderful!" Sister Helen said. "So grown up!"

Nell laughed. "And you look just the same as always. Oh, Sister, I have missed you!"

"And I have missed you."

The two women laughed and blinked back more tears.

"But what brings you here?" Sister Helen asked. "Surely you haven't come all the way from Wiltshire?"

Nell shook her head. "I have come from Bardney. My father is very ill and I have need of your poppy juice. He is in pain."

Some of the glow left Sister Helen's face. "I am sorry to hear that. What is the problem?"

"He is coughing blood. And he says that even his bones hurt."

Sister Helen looked grave. "That is not good, Nell."

"I know. My mother sent for me in hopes that there was something I could do for him, but I'm afraid that all I can do is make his going easier."

Sister Helen nodded. "I will give you the poppy juice. It will help to ease him."

"Thank you."

"Now, tell me about yourself," Sister Helen said. "What kind of a life are you leading? How do you spend your days? Tell me everything."

The two women sat on the bench that was pulled close to the charcoal brazier on this winter day and Nell began to talk.

In a little while she was telling Sister Helen about the summons from her mother that had brought her to Bardney.

"My mother is worried about the state of my father's soul, as well as his body, Sister," she confided. "He is angry with God for all the things that he thinks God has taken away from him. I can't imagine why she thought

I could be of spiritual assistance. I scarcely know my father."

"Who knows what instruments God may use to reach a human soul?" Sister Helen asked. "Don't dismiss your mother's idea out of hand, Nell. Perhaps you are the one whom God has chosen to deliver your father from his anger."

"I don't think so," Nell said. Her hand nervously stroked the fur on her cloak. "Truthfully, I don't even think my father likes me very much. He has scarcely ever spoken a kind word to me."

Sister Helen was sitting upright on the backless bench, her spine perfectly straight. "Still, you are his daughter," she said. "You have a special tie to him that no one else has."

Nell bent her head and said in a low voice, "Truthfully, *I* don't like *him* very much, Sister Helen. He forced me into a marriage I didn't want. True, it has turned out happily, but that was not his concern. He didn't care if I was happy or if I was miserable. He only cared about his own worldly concerns—he didn't care about me at all."

"It sounds to me as if there is a father *and* a daughter who both need some healing," Sister Helen said gently.

Nell still looked downward. "I will do for him what I would do for any soul who was ill like he is. But my mother's idea of me talking to him—he wouldn't listen to me, Sister. I would be wasting my breath."

Sister Helen shook her head. "Never say that, Nell!

We never know how the most careless of our words may affect others. I will pray that God will open your father's heart and take away his anger. And I will pray for you, that you will find the connection with your father that you have long missed."

Nell lifted her face and turned to Sister Helen. "Thank you, Sister," she said softly. "Your prayers are always much appreciated. And needed, as well."

Sister Helen stood up. "Come, it is almost time for supper. The other nuns will be so happy to see you."

Nell stood up and followed Sister Helen out of the cozy shed and into the cold December afternoon.

Nell spent the rest of the evening renewing old friendships and that night she went to bed in the tiny room that had belonged to her for all of the years she had spent in the convent.

It was a strange feeling, walking into the room with its narrow bed and single crucifix upon the wall. She knelt by the bed and bowed her head to say her night prayers.

Dear Lord, thank you for your many blessings to me. I thank you especially for my wonderful husband. Please give me the grace to be a good wife to him and a good chatelaine to his people. Give me the patience to be kind to Lady Mabel. Help me to make her my friend and not my enemy.

Especially, dear Lord, help me with my father. If it is at all possible, let me cure him. But if this is not possible, then let him be reconciled to you. Don't let him pass

*out of this life with anger in his heart. Help him to give
himself to you, to achieve your peace, the peace that
passeth all understanding.*

*And help me, dear Lord, to put aside my own anger
at my father. Help me to put aside my injuries and love
him the way I should, the way Christ loved us even
after all the terrible offenses we had committed
against you.*

She raised her head a little and looked around the familiar room.

*If I had been able to change my father's heart about
my marriage, I would be a nun by now. If I had a choice,
would I change things? Would I give up Roger to come
back to the convent and resume my old life?*

No. The answer was quick and positive. She would
not give up Roger to return to the convent. He was part
of her now; to give him up would be like an amputation.
She would be a shell of a person without him, he was
so deeply entwined in her being.

I have forgiven him, she thought with dawning wonderment. *I have truly forgiven him.*

She lowered her head into her hands and was quiet for
a while just listening to the silence and letting her heart
be open to God. Then the thought came into her mind.

I must also forgive my father.

That would be harder to do, she thought. Roger had
been truly sorry that he had hurt her. Her father had no
such idea in his head.

Still, I must do it. Jesus forgave the men who cruci-

fied him. Surely I can forgive my father, who gave me in marriage to the man that I love more than anything else in this world.

Perhaps, if I forgive him, my father will be able to forgive God.

She gathered her thoughts. *Dear Lord, help me to do this. Help me to forgive my father and help me to help him during this, the most important time of his life. I ask you this through Christ our Lord. Amen.*

She was chilly when she got into bed, but her heart was warm. Coming here to the convent had helped her to see things clearly. Now she knew what she had to do.

The poppy juice did help with Earl Raoul's pain and he was able to come downstairs to the Great Hall for several days in a row. But then a relapse forced him to take to his bed.

Nell increased the dose of poppy juice, which made him more comfortable but he was no longer able to get up. He dozed a great deal, which was partly due to the medicinal drink. Nell and her mother took turns sitting with him. Father Clement sat with him, as well, but the earl showed no signs of wanting to reconcile himself to God and the church.

Nell was with him one cold January afternoon when the earl's eyes opened.

"Nell?" he said.

She had been sitting by his bed and now she stood up to come and stand close to him. "Yes, Father. I'm here."

"It appears that I'm still here, too," he said with hard irony.

She looked down into his face. It was all bone, the wasted flesh pressed against the underlying skeleton. "Are you in much pain?" she asked.

He moved his head slightly on the pillow. "It's bearable. I don't want any more of that stuff you've been giving me. It makes me sleep. I'll be sleeping soon enough. I want to be awake for the time that I have left."

Nell hesitated. Then she said, "Father, you will soon be facing the greatest journey that any of us human souls must face. I think you should prepare for it."

He scowled. "I'm not ready for it," he said. "That's the problem."

"Then it is time to rectify that."

There was a long pause. Then the earl whispered, "I don't know if I can."

Nell sent up a brief prayer. *Please, God, give me the right words to say.* She took a deep breath. "Every one of us must die, Father. Sooner or later it comes to us all. And the few years we spend on this earth are but nothing in comparison to eternity. I know you feel that God has taken years away from you, but it's really just the opposite, Father. He has given you more years to spend with Him in heaven. And the same was true for Geoffrey and Sybilla. They died too soon to accrue earthly honors, but what are earthly honors to God? They achieved perfect happiness with Him. If they were offered a choice, they wouldn't come back to earth. Not even to be an earl or a countess. They are where they were meant to be since the day they were born. They are with God."

The earl had closed his eyes halfway through her speech and now he opened them again. "Do you truly believe that, Nell?"

"Yes, I do," she replied earnestly.

Lord Raoul slowly clenched and unclenched his fist. "It is hard to let go," he said.

"You worked hard all your life to be a good earl," Nell said. "Now that part of your life is over. Now it is time to fix your mind on other things."

He began to cough. Nell handed him a cloth. When the coughing fit was over, he said, "I was angry with God for taking away my son and my daughter."

"I know," Nell said. "But you will be reunited with them soon, Father. And there will be no more pain and no more anger. Only joy."

His sunken eyes searched hers. Then he said in a low voice, "I want to believe that, Nell."

"Look deep into your heart and you will believe. God will give you the faith that you need, Father. All you have to do is ask for it."

After a brief silence, the earl spoke. "Send me Father Clement and I will make my confession."

Nell's heart leaped with joy. She stood up. "I will, Father."

"And Nell…"

"Yes, Father?"

"You're a good girl. A good daughter."

"Thank you, Father."

"Roger is kind to you?"

"Yes, Father. I love him very much."

He nodded. "That is good."

She smiled at him. "I will go for Father Clement." And she left the room.

Lady Alice was thrilled when she learned that her husband was being reconciled to God.

"Thank you, Nell," she said to her daughter. "Thank you for reaching him."

"It was God working through me, Mama," Nell said. "I only said the words that came into my head. I truly think that this was the work of God. Father was ready and I happened to be there."

The two women were standing apart from the group of knights and ladies who were gathered in front of the fire, waiting to sit down to supper. The servants were bustling around the hall and no one was paying much attention to Lady Alice and Nell.

"I believe everything in life happens for a purpose," Lady Alice said. "None of those years you spent at St. Cecelia's was wasted. It was because of them that you were able to help your father today."

Nell had never once thought of her years in the convent as wasted, but she held her tongue and did not correct her mother.

"How much longer do you think he has?" Lady Alice asked.

"A few days. Perhaps a few weeks. No more than that."

Lady Alice's hand came up to shade her eyes. "I hope it's not too long, Nell. It is so painful seeing him like this."

"I know," Nell said softly.

Lady Alice gave her a trembling smile. "I'm so glad that you're here, my daughter."

Nell reached out to take her mother into her arms. "I'm glad I'm here, too, Mama."

The two women clung together briefly, then Lady Alice took out a square of linen and blew her nose.

Father Clement came down the stairs and joined the group by the fireplace. When he caught Lady Alice and Nell looking at him, he sent them both a reassuring smile.

"Father has made his confession," Nell said.

"Thanks be to God," Lady Alice said.

The horn blew announcing dinner and the two women moved to the high table to find their seats.

Twenty-Five

Earl Raoul died in the early days of January and was buried with his son and daughter in Lincoln Cathedral. Stephen was still at Salisbury, so Roger and Nell stopped to see the king on their return trip to Wilton.

The king invested Roger with the title Earl of Lincoln, thus instantly making him the single most powerful man in the country outside of the king himself.

"I never expected these honors to come upon me at so young an age," Roger confided to Nell as they lay in bed in the bishop's palace of Salisbury that night. "Especially not your father's title. He was a relatively young man." He reached over and picked up her hand. "It is a huge responsibility."

She squeezed his fingers. "You are up to it."

"I was trained for it," he said. "I hope I can live up to my grandfather's expectations."

"You will."

"I think I will spend a week or so at Wilton and then return to Bardney. I need to have all your father's vassals swear allegiance to me."

Nell nodded. "That is wise."

Silence fell as they lay there comfortably, hand in hand. Then Nell said, "My mother and her ladies will be able to remain at Bardney, won't they Roger?"

"Of course." He turned to look at her. "Bardney will still be their home."

"What would have happened to them if the king had chosen someone else to be the earl?" Nell asked.

He frowned a little. "I don't know. Perhaps they would have had to go back to their families."

"I think it's terrible, the way women are treated like chattel," Nell said indignantly. "That a woman could lose the home that had been hers her entire life, just because the earldom changes from one man to another."

"Men are in the same situation," Roger said. "They grow up in one household and when they are finally made knight they must go out into the world alone and find a place for themselves. That is the way of the upper classes, Nell. If you want stability in your home life, you would be better off being born to a tradesman."

Nell sighed.

Roger said, "The king has given me a job."

"What is that?"

"The Bishop of Winchester—Stephen's brother—is convening a conference in Bath to discuss the terms of a peace. Robert of Gloucester has agreed to represent the empress and Stephen is sending his wife, Queen Maud, to represent him. He wants me to go with her."

"A peace conference?" Nell echoed.

"Yes. Bishop Henry hopes for a negotiated settlement."

Nell's brow puckered. "Why would either side agree to that?"

"Well, we are at a stalemate right now," Roger explained. "The empress has consolidated her holdings, but her loyal territory is restricted to the west and to Wallingford. To be successful she needs to seek new allies and to increase the territories that are under her power—something she has failed to do thus far.

"As for the king—he must realize that it is going to be extremely difficult to capture the empress's main bases at Bristol, Gloucester and Wallingford. They can hold out forever if they want to. We could be in for years and years of siege warfare. If the church can come up with a way for the country to avoid that fate, then it is worth exploring."

"And the king chose you to go with the queen?"

"Yes."

"Why you?"

"Because I hold the most land in the kingdom, I suppose."

"And who is moderating this conference?"

"The Bishop of Winchester and the Archbishop of Canterbury."

"Well, it sounds like a good idea," Nell said. "When is the conference starting?"

"Soon, I believe. Bishop Henry is organizing it."

"It would be wonderful to see this war ended," Nell said. "I hope the bishops can work some magic."

"I think it is going to have to be magic," Roger said grimly. "But it is certainly worth a try. Now, enough talk of politics. How are you feeling?"

For the last week, Nell had been nauseated in the mornings. Why this was happening was a mystery to her. She had mentioned it to Roger but not to her mother, who she felt had enough to bear with her father's death. She said now, "I felt sick this morning but now I feel fine. I can't understand it. I wonder if my stomach is sensitive to something that I'm eating at breakfast?"

"You're not eating anything that you haven't always eaten."

"That's true."

"You're the herb woman," Roger said. "Can't you cure yourself?"

"Most stomach problems are not like this," she said. "This goes away as the day progresses. I can eat my dinner and my supper with no problem."

"That is odd," Roger said.

"Yes. If it doesn't stop I'll write to Sister Helen and ask her about it."

"But you feel fine now?"

"Yes."

He smiled. "That's good." He reached out and pulled her into his arms.

She chuckled into his shoulder. "I should have known why you were so concerned with my health."

"I am always concerned with your health, love. But I confess that it is convenient that your nausea has confined itself to the morning."

Nell put her arms around his neck and snuggled her face into his shoulder. "Can I come with you to the conference?"

"If you're feeling well enough," Roger murmured into her hair.

"I've never seen Bath."

"Neither have I."

Nell said, "I love you, Roger."

"Oh, Nell. You are so sweet. And so good. I am such a lucky man." He bent his head, his lips came down on hers, and she gave herself up to the bonfire of desire that had ignited inside of her.

In the great castle at Bristol, Guy de Roche was talking with the empress's half brother and champion, Robert, Earl of Gloucester. News had just arrived of the death of the Earl of Lincoln.

"I would like to accompany you to the peace conference, my lord," Guy said.

Gloucester was a medium-sized, dark man with deep-set brown eyes. He smiled faintly and leaned back in his carved chair. The two men were alone in Gloucester's private solar, with Guy standing in front of the earl. Gloucester said, "You are hardly the most peaceable of men, Guy. What interests you in this conference?"

"Given his new position, I'm sure my son will be

there, my lord." Guy struggled to keep his voice mild. "I haven't seen him since he was an infant and, even though we are political opponents, I own I would like to meet him."

Gloucester thought for a moment. "Yes, I suppose I can understand that."

Guy's blue eyes glinted. "I would just make up one of your party, my lord. I would not expect to contribute anything to the conference."

Gloucester stretched his legs in front of him. "I don't have great hopes of this conference, Guy, and neither does the empress, but it is worth a try. We have more to gain from a settlement than Stephen does."

"Yes, my lord," Guy said.

Gloucester thought for a moment. Then he said, "All right. If you wish to accompany me, you may come. I have sons. I can understand a man's natural desire to see his own blood."

Guy hid a triumphant smile. "Thank you, my lord."

He let the smile bloom as he left the solar and went down the tower steps. *Now,* he thought, *Roger Double-Earl, we will see if I can make you sorry that you rejected my proposal. Perhaps you will be seeing your blessed grandfather sooner than you ever thought you would.*

Roger and Nell arrived back at Wilton on the afternoon of a bright, cold, sunny day. The first thing that Roger noticed as he came into the Great Hall was that Gawain was not there to greet him.

"Where is Gawain?" he asked one of the squires who was in the hall.

"He has not been well, my lord," the boy said. "He's barely dragging himself around. We've had to carry him out to the bailey and back."

Roger's heart clenched. Gawain was an old dog. Was this it? He said, "Where is he now? He should be in front of the warm fire."

"He is in your apartment, my lord. We have kept the brazier going for him."

Roger nodded, turned to Nell, "I'm going upstairs." He strode across the floor and ran lightly up the stairs to the earl's apartment.

Gawain was in the solar, lying on a fur blanket next to the brazier. He lifted his head when Roger came in and made a small whimpering sound.

"Gawain." Roger went to kneel next to his dog. "How are you doing, fellow? Not feeling too well, eh?"

The dog's tail thumped on the ground but he made no attempt to get up.

Roger stroked his head. "As soon as I turn my back, you go and get sick."

The dog looked up at him, his brown eyes a little cloudy.

"Are you in pain, fellow? Perhaps we'll get some of that poppy juice of Nell's to help you."

"How is he?" It was Nell, coming in the door.

"He hasn't gotten up," Roger replied.

Nell went over to the dog and knelt down next to him

on the opposite side to Roger. He was still stroking Gawain's head.

"What is wrong?" she asked.

"He's old. I think he is just wearing out. This happened with the dog I had when I was a boy. There's nothing anyone can do."

Roger blinked back tears. He bent and kissed Gawain's head.

Nell said, "I'm so sorry, Roger. I know how much you love him."

He nodded, unable to reply.

A little silence fell as they both petted the dog, whose eyes remained fixed on Roger.

"What should we do?" Nell asked at last.

"Wait," Roger said. "That's all that we can do."

Nell nodded.

"Could you give him some of your poppy juice, Nell?" Roger asked hopefully. "I hate to think of him in pain."

"I could…but I don't really know the dose, Roger. Too much of the juice can kill."

"He's dying anyway. I'd rather he died in comfort than in pain."

Nell hesitated, then nodded. "I'll give him a quarter of the amount that I was giving my father. How does that sound?"

"Good. Thank you, Nell."

"Do you want me to get it now?"

"Yes. And bring some bread. Gawain loves bread. We'll soak the bread in poppy juice and give it to him that way."

Left alone once more with his dog, Roger lay down next to him. "You're such a good dog, Gawain," he said. His voice broke. "I am going to miss you so much."

Gawain inched his head closer to Roger.

"Go soon," Roger whispered. "Don't linger, fellow. I don't want you to suffer."

They were still like that, lying side by side, when Nell returned with the medicine. They gave it to the dog and watched beside him as it took effect and his eyes closed.

"He seems to be breathing normally," Nell said.

Roger nodded.

They sat for a while longer. Then Roger said, "You don't have to stay here, Nell. I'm sure you have things to do. Gawain is just going to sleep."

"Yes, I think he's all right. I don't think I gave him too much of the medicine." She stood up. "I do have some things to do...."

"Go ahead," he said. "I'm going to stay here for a while longer."

"All right." She bent and left a kiss on the top of Roger's head. "Call me if you need me."

He nodded.

Nell went out and left him alone with his sleeping dog.

Roger got up off the floor and went to sit in his chair, the chair that had belonged for so many years to his grandfather.

He had gotten Gawain when he was nine years old. The dog had been with him for all his growing-up years. He remembered how he had found the lost and starving puppy in the streets of Wilton and how he had brought him home lying across the saddle in front of him. His grandfather hadn't wanted to keep the mongrel, but Roger had begged. He had felt a connection to Gawain from the first moment that their eyes had met.

"Oh, Gawain," he said now in a low voice. "It is so hard to say goodbye."

He sat there as the sun went down and the room gradually turned dark. Nell came back in, carrying a candle.

"You must get ready for supper, Roger," she said softly.

He nodded and got to his feet.

Nell came over and bent over Gawain. "He's still sleeping," she said. "Do you want me to have one of the pages sit with him while we're at supper?"

"Yes," Roger said. He didn't want his dog to be alone.

Nell sent for the page and Roger changed out of his riding clothes and into clothes fitting for supper. He sat in his chair at the high table but he ate hardly anything. He was grateful that Nell didn't press food on him. As soon as dinner was over, he went back upstairs to sit with Gawain.

It took Gawain two more days to die. Roger had a grave dug in the bailey and Nell laid Gawain's sleeping blanket in it. "So he won't have to lie on the cold hard ground," she said to Roger.

Roger only nodded. Tears were too close to the surface for him to chance speech.

"Come away," Nell said to him after Gawain had

been lowered to lie on his blanket. "You don't need to stay to see him covered up with dirt. It's best to say goodbye now."

Roger couldn't reply, but allowed her to walk him away from the grave and back to the castle.

They sat together in front of the fire in the Great Hall and Roger said, "I feel as if I just buried my childhood. Simon said I should get another dog, but I would feel as if I was betraying Gawain if I took a new dog now. There can never be another Gawain."

"You are still too sore from losing Gawain to think of another dog," Nell agreed. "One day there will be a dog for you, Roger, but not right now."

She reached over and took his hand. "He loved you so much," she said.

"I know." His voice was thick with emotion. His hand tightened around hers.

Thank God for Nell, he thought. *She understands the way no one else ever could. She isn't going to try to force a new dog down my throat.*

"You had a special relationship with Gawain," Nell said. "It will always be a part of you, Roger. Gawain will never die because he will always live in your heart."

"He will," Roger said after a while.

Nell's hand was warm in his. It was a comfort just to have her near, to have the warmth of her love and understanding.

"Thank you for being here, Nell," he whispered.

She squeezed his hand in answer.

Twenty-Six

Nell had been wondering how she should deal with Lady Mabel. Should she just ignore the fact that Lady Mabel had hurt her so bitterly or should she confront the woman? She didn't want to discuss her problem with Roger—the less said between the two of them about his infidelity, she thought, the better.

She lay awake for a long time on the night of her return home, thinking about her course of action. She still hadn't decided upon what to do when she fell asleep, but when she awoke in the morning, the solution was clear in her head.

After breakfast she asked Lady Mabel to attend her in the earl's apartment. The two women went to the solar and turned to face each other, rather like two jousters without horses or swords. Nell looked steadily into Lady Mabel's eyes, and said, "You don't like me, Lady Mabel, and it has finally become clear to me that you would do anything to hurt me. I think it would be best for the two of us if you and Sir Simon relocated to Bardney Castle. I believe my mother is more equipped to deal with you than I am. And I think you would be happier if the lady of the castle was an older woman."

All of the color left Lady Mabel's plump face. "You can't mean that!"

Nell's eyes never wavered. "I do. You did a terrible thing to me, Lady Mabel, and you did it because you knew it would hurt me. I can't live with a woman who feels that way about me."

Color flared back into Lady Mabel's cheeks. "I did it because I couldn't bear to see you being humiliated!"

"We both know that's not true. You did it to drive a wedge between me and my lord. And you were successful for a time. But now that we are reconciled I am able to see more clearly what your motive must have been. And the sight is painful."

"I never meant to hurt you," Lady Mabel said nervously. Her hand went to the veil that she wore over her gray-blond hair. "I told you for your own good."

Nell shook her head. "No, you told me because you don't like me. You have never liked me. I have tried to be nice to you and you have paid me back with disloyalty and pain. I think it would be better if you and Sir Simon went to Bardney."

"Lord Roger will never agree to moving Simon," Lady Mabel countered.

"Lord Roger will agree because he wants you out of

his sight. Do you know how angry he was when I told him what you had told me?"

"Dear God," Lady Mabel said. She took a step closer to Nell. "Don't send us away, my lady. It would kill Simon to have to leave Wilton."

"You should have thought of that before you meddled in my life," Nell said.

"I only wanted to do you good…."

"Stop saying that!" Nell said angrily. "We both know it's not true."

There was a long pause. Then Lady Mabel spoke in a low voice. "It was hard for me, having so young a woman running the household I had come to think of as mine."

"I understand that. But you should never have interfered between my husband and me."

"I know." Lady Mabel's voice went even lower. "I knew that the minute you left the room. The look on your face! But I could not take the words back."

There was another pause, then Nell said, "Do you think you can accept me as the Lady of Wilton now?"

"Yes, my lady!" The words came swiftly, eagerly. "I have learned my lesson, I promise you. I have been berating myself all these past weeks for telling you such a thing."

"You will stop trying to turn the other ladies against me?"

"Yes."

"You will stop criticizing and questioning every move that I make?"

"Yes!"

"Are you sure that you can do this, Lady Mabel? Because I will not live in the poisoned atmosphere you create any longer."

"I am sure, my lady. I was very wrong to do as I did, and I am sorry. From now on, I will be a supporter, not a criticizer."

Nell looked for a long time into the other woman's pale blue eyes. "Very well, then, you may remain at Wilton. But if I find you are not living up to your end of our agreement…"

"I will honor our agreement, my lady. I swear it."

Nell nodded, as if satisfied. "Good," she said. "You are free to go, Lady Mabel. I look forward to seeing you later in the day."

Lady Mabel dipped in a little curtsy. "Thank you, my lady. Thank you very much for giving me this second chance."

After Lady Mabel had left the room, Nell sat down in her chair, pulled her cloak around her and smiled.

Her threat had worked.

The weather turned very cold, too cold for hunting over iron-hard ground, and the Great Hall was more filled with people than usual during the course of the day.

Nell continued to be sick in the morning. She wrote a letter to Sister Helen in the convent asking for an explanation but before Sister Helen had time to reply, a diagnosis came from another source altogether.

Lady Mabel sat next to Nell at mealtime every day and she noticed that Nell wasn't eating her breakfast. A week after her conversation with Nell in the solar, she asked Nell if she was feeling well. Nell replied that she felt fine, but she just wasn't hungry. When she gave this excuse for several days in a row, Lady Mabel asked to speak to her alone.

After breakfast, Nell and Lady Mabel went up the stairs to the earl's apartment, Nell wondering what on earth Lady Mabel had to say to her. In public the two women had gotten along very well since Nell had threatened Lady Mabel with expulsion. Lady Mabel had smiled and been pleasant both to Nell and the younger ladies. So Nell had no idea what the other woman wanted to say to her as they walked into the cold solar.

Nell was not feeling very well and she went to sit in her chair, waving Lady Mabel to sit, as well. The older woman said softly, "Lady Eleanor, for how long have you been feeling ill in the mornings?"

"For a few weeks, I think," Nell said.

"Do you know that nausea in the morning is a powerful sign that you are with child?" Lady Mabel asked.

Nell's eyes enlarged. "No," she said in a low voice. "I did not know that."

"I had a feeling you might be ignorant of the reason for your illness. After all, you grew up in a convent. I wish your mother was here to tell you this, but she is not. So I thought that I should."

Nell said huskily, "I never thought of that explanation."

"Have you had your flow? A cessation of that is also a sign of pregnancy."

"No," Nell said. "But sometimes I'm irregular, so I didn't think that anything was amiss."

Lady Mabel gave her a smile, a real smile, not the painful one that Nell had seen so often in the past. "Nothing is amiss, my dear. These are signs of something very right. You are going to have a baby."

Nell felt a joyful bubble swelling her heart. At one time the thought of having a baby had frightened her, but now…

"How happy my lord will be!" she said to Lady Mabel.

"I am sure he will be," Lady Mabel agreed. "As will be everyone in the castle."

Nell laughed. "Do you know, I wrote a letter to Sister Helen at the convent describing my nausea and asking her what it might mean."

Lady Mabel smiled warmly. "Convents are not the best places to learn about bearing children," she said.

Nell laughed again. "I certainly didn't learn anything. Sister Helen never did any midwifery."

"Do you know how to calculate when the babe will be born?" Lady Mabel asked. "Go back to the time of your last missed flow and count forward eight and a half months. The baby will be born then."

Nell counted in her head. "September, I think," she said.

"That is a good month," Lady Mabel said. "My son was born in September and he was a very happy child."

"Your son is the castellan of one of my lord's castles, isn't that so?" Nell asked.

"He is," Lady Mabel replied proudly.

"Do you ever get to see him?"

"He usually comes to Wilton to see us. But he hasn't been in a while, because of the war."

"This wretched war," Nell said. "I hope the bishop's peace conference is successful. It is hard bringing a baby into a world that is so filled with strife and pain."

"Don't think like that," Lady Mabel advised. "Just think of the miracle of life you are carrying, and of how joyful your husband will be."

Nell smiled radiantly. "Thank you for telling me this, Lady Mabel. I feel so stupid for not knowing myself."

"The circumstances of your upbringing account for that, I think."

Nell laughed again. "My lord has been as mystified as I about my morning nausea. How surprised he will be to learn the cause."

"You must take care of yourself, my lady," Lady Mabel cautioned. "The babe you carry is the heir to both Wiltshire and Lincoln."

Nell sobered. "I am sorry that my father did not live to see his grandchild—the fruition of his dynastic dream."

"It is a shame," Lady Mabel agreed.

"Will I be sick the whole time I am pregnant?" Nell asked.

"The morning nausea usually lasts but a few months."

Nell sighed. "That sounds like a long time to be sick."

"You are being sick for a happy reason. Think of all those poor souls who suffer for no reason at all."

"You are right, Lady Mabel," Nell said. "I must concentrate on my good news and look upon my nausea as a blessing."

Lady Mabel nodded her agreement.

"Don't say anything to anyone until I have told my lord," Nell said.

"I will hold my tongue, Lady Eleanor. It is up to you to disclose your news, not me."

"Thank you," Nell said. Her face broke into its radiant smile once again. "And thank you for telling me, Lady Mabel. It was the work of a friend to do so."

Lady Mabel smiled back. "God bless you, Lady Eleanor, and God bless the child you are carrying."

The two ladies left the solar feeling very happy with each other.

Nell waited to talk to Roger until they were in bed that night. They had a fur blanket on the bed in this cold weather, and Nell cuddled down under it waiting for Roger to join her. He got in swiftly, not wanting to expose his bare skin to the cold air longer than was necessary. She waited until he had the cover pulled up to his ears before she said, "I have found out the reason for my morning sickness."

He turned on his side to face her. "Oh, did you hear from Sister Helen?"

"No, it was actually Lady Mabel who enlightened me."

"Well, what is it? It's nothing serious, I hope."

"It's good news. Roger, I am going to have a baby."

It was dark behind the bed curtains and Nell wished she could see his face.

"A baby?" he said. "That's what the sickness is all about?"

"Yes."

"Oh, Nell," he said. "Oh, Nell. That is wonderful news."

"I thought you would be pleased."

"Pleased? I'm ecstatic." He reached out. "Come here to me."

She scooted over into his arms.

"Is Lady Mabel sure?" he asked.

"Yes. I am also late with my flow. Apparently that is another sign."

He held her close. His body felt so nice and warm against hers. She cuddled her cheek against his neck.

"Do you know when?" he asked.

"Around September, I think."

"A baby," he repeated in an amazed tone. "I'm going to be a father."

"Yes. And I'm going to be a mother."

"You will be a wonderful mother," he said.

"And you will be a wonderful father."

His voice hardened a little. "One thing is sure, I will always be there for my son."

"What if we have a girl?"

She could hear the smile in his voice. "Then I will be there for my daughter."

"I felt so stupid when Lady Mabel told me, but she was so nice, Roger. She said it was understandable that I wouldn't recognize the signs, that it was because I was raised in a convent. I really think her heart has changed toward me."

"I think you're a saint for putting up with Lady Mabel," Roger said, the hard note back in his voice.

"I played a trick on her," Nell confessed. "I told her that I was sending her and Sir Simon to Bardney to live with my mother. She was so frightened that she promised she would be my friend. I didn't really mean to ask you to do it, Roger. I just used it as a threat."

Roger chuckled. "You're learning guile, love."

She closed her eyes and inhaled his scent. "Oh, dear, am I?"

"It's a good thing. To live in the world you have to learn the weapons of the world. You were so innocent when first you came to Wilton, but you have grown up a lot in the last few months, Nell. And now you are going to be a mother."

"A mother…" she repeated wonderingly.

Roger kissed her hair. She said warningly, "Roger, it is freezing in this room. If you take these covers off of me…"

"I promise I'll maneuver under them," he said.

"Well, in that case…"

"Kiss me," he said, and she obliged.

Twenty-Seven

At the end of January, Roger received word from the king that the peace conference called by Bishop Henry was due to start. Stephen asked Roger to ride to Bath, where he would be joined by Queen Maud, who would act as the king's agent during the conference.

Roger made ready to leave immediately.

Nell clung a little as she was saying goodbye to him in the Great Hall. At the last moment it had been decided that it would be better for her to remain at Wilton and not make the ride in the cold winter weather.

"Everything will be fine," he promised, holding her close for a moment before letting her go. "If we're really lucky, we will settle this war and then we can all go back to leading our normal lives."

"I hope you do," she replied a little shakily.

He smiled at her and said more loudly, "I leave my castle and its occupants in your capable hands, my lady."

She replied in the same tone, "With Sir Simon at my side, all will be well, my lord."

Roger motioned to the four knights and Richard, who were accompanying him, and they all strode across the hall, their armor clinking as they went. Their horses were waiting for them just outside the castle door and they all vaulted into the saddle in the maneuver they practiced assiduously during their daily drills. They rode out through the great portcullis gate, over the moat and onto the cleared field that surrounded Wilton. The men posted on the castle battlements watched them go.

The day was relatively pleasant and Roger held his face up to the sun and enjoyed its mild winter warmth. "A good day for a long ride," he said to Thomas, who was riding next to him.

"Aye, my lord. It has been so cold of late, a little moderation feels good."

When they reached the main roadway, they turned west. The city of Bath lay within the empress's territory, but it yet held out for the king.

The ride was uneventful, through the winterscapes of barren pastureland and bare woodland, and they reached Bath as the light was fading and the day was growing more chill.

They entered through the walls of Bath by the east gate and made for the abbey, which took up a great space in the center of the tiny Roman city. The porter at the gatehouse directed them to the abbey guest hall and said he would send for grooms to take their horses. Roger and his men rode across the great court to the building that had been pointed out as the guest hall and dismounted. Richard took Bayard from Roger, who then went to the door of the guest hall and went inside.

A rotund, round-faced brother wearing a brown robe was in the vestibule waiting for him. As Roger was shown to his room, he told the brother that he had four knights and a squire with him and the brother assured him that they would be looked after.

"Is the queen here yet?" Roger asked.

"Aye, my lord. She arrived a few hours ago."

"Will you tell her I am here?"

"Aye, my lord."

The brother left Roger alone in the cold room and he went to the window to open the shutters and look out.

The window was at the side of the house and looked out over a hedge-lined alley to the house next door. Roger closed the shutters again, took off his helmet and pushed back his metal coif. He rubbed his scalp a little, as if to get the circulation going, and walked around the room to stretch his legs after the long ride. It was not long before Richard appeared with the saddlebag holding Roger's clothes.

Another brother knocked on the door to tell him that he and the queen were to dine at the abbot's house in half an hour's time.

"I will need some warm water to wash up with," Roger said.

"I will bring you some immediately, my lord," the brother told him.

In half an hour's time, Roger was meticulously attired in a blue tunic, fresh hose and clean white shirt. His hair was brushed to a dark golden sheen.

The abbot's house was the building next door so he had not far to go. He knocked on the door and was admitted into a plain, unadorned room with only a few chairs along the wall for furniture. Men were standing about and a blond woman of about forty was sitting in one of the chairs talking to the Bishop of Winchester and another man. She was Queen Maud.

Before he went to pay his respects, Roger glanced quickly around the room to see whom the other people present were. His roving gaze was caught and held by a pair of familiar blue eyes. Roger felt his heart drop into his stomach. He had not expected this. It was his father.

Guy smiled as their eyes met. It was not a friendly look.

Roger's heart began to hammer. *Damn it,* he thought. *How the hell did he manage to come here?*

With a great effort, he kept his face blank, pulled his eyes away from that taunting blue stare and started toward the queen. She watched him as he approached.

"Your Grace," he said as he went down on one knee. "I hope your journey was not too difficult."

"Not at all," she said. "I am glad to see you, my lord of Wiltshire and Lincoln." She raised her voice slightly when she said his title. Roger wondered if that was for the benefit of his father.

"It is an honor to be here, Your Grace," Roger replied.

"Have you met the Earl of Gloucester?" Maud asked.

"No, I have not, Your Grace."

Maud turned to the man standing next to the bishop. "My lord of Gloucester, will you let me introduce the Earl of Wiltshire and Lincoln? Like me, he is here on the king's behalf."

A compact man of middle height with dark brown hair and brown eyes looked at Roger. His face was very stern. "My lord of Lincoln," he said, nodding his head to Roger. "As you must know, the empress has recognized your father as the true lord of Wiltshire."

The queen said with an edge to her voice, "The true lord of Wiltshire is the one who has been named thus by the king. And that is Earl Roger."

"Perhaps this is a matter for negotiation," Gloucester suggested.

Before the queen could answer, the abbot entered the room. "All is prepared for dinner," he announced. "If you would just follow me into the dining room."

The queen stood up and gave her arm to Roger. The men fell back and let her go first. Once in the dining room, the abbot went to the head of the table.

"Your Grace," he said, "will you sit here?"

He indicated the seat to his right. The queen moved to accept it. She was followed by the Bishop of Winchester. Then came Roger.

The seat to the abbot's left was occupied by the Earl of Gloucester and seated next to him was the Archbishop of Canterbury. Next, and directly across from Roger, was Guy.

Damn, Roger thought again. He glanced at his father's face. Guy looked sober, but the intense blue eyes that met Roger's held a look of violence.

The abbot fed his guests well and the conversation around the table studiously avoided the topic that had brought these great ones together this winter day in Bath. Roger held up his share of the talk, but throughout the entire meal he felt his father's burning eyes upon him.

He was excruciatingly uncomfortable.

When the meal finally broke up, he was relieved to see that the Earl of Gloucester and Guy were not staying at the abbey guest hall. Instead the Bishop of Bath had graciously put one of his houses at their disposal.

Roger watched somberly as Gloucester and Guy mounted up and their two horses headed across the great court in the direction of the gate.

The queen was standing next to Roger and she said, "We had no idea that he would bring your father with him, my lord. I don't know what he can mean by it."

"My father is determined to wrest the earldom from me, Your Grace," Roger said. He turned to her. "I cannot let that happen. I swore a solemn oath to my grandfather on his deathbed that I would never allow Guy to have the earldom."

The queen's attractive face was grave. "Does the king know about this oath?"

"I never told him, my lady. It didn't seem necessary. The king recognized me as earl right away."

The queen smiled at him. "The king knows you are loyal, Lord Roger. And he knows of your prowess as a knight. We are fortunate to have you in our camp."

"Thank you, my lady."

The queen retired to bed and Roger went up to his own room, where Richard was waiting to undress him.

He had made a long ride that day and should have been tired, but once he got into bed his mind wouldn't let him sleep. He missed Nell to talk to. He always felt better after he had talked things over with her.

Why had Gloucester brought his father to this meeting?

What did Guy hope to gain from this conference, aside from Roger's discomfiture?

And deep down there was always the buried, scarcely acknowledged wish that things were different, that somehow, he and his father could be friends.

The conference convened at ten o'clock the following morning in the abbot's dining room.

The Bishop of Winchester took the seat at one end of the table and the Archbishop of Canterbury sat at the opposite. Robert of Gloucester and Guy sat on one side of the table and the queen and Roger sat facing them. The day began with both sides presenting their differing views of the present state of the country.

The Earl of Gloucester declared that the empress was the sole surviving child of the late king and as such had the right to the sovereignty of England. In fact, while the late king was still alive, all of the earls and barons had sworn their allegiance to Mathilda. When King Henry died, Stephen had snatched the monarchy while Mathilda was in Normandy, having himself anointed as king and collecting feudal oaths from all the earls and barons who had previously sworn loyalty to the empress. Stephen was an upstart with no claim to the throne, he finished. If feudal law was followed, the throne should go to Mathilda.

Queen Maud had a different view. The death of the late king's only legitimate son had left the monarchy of England wide open. The earls and barons, who did not want a woman on the throne of England, had been forced by King Henry to swear their allegiance to Mathilda. Specifically, they did not want Geoffrey Plantagenet, who was Mathilda's husband, having aught to do with England. Stephen was as much a grandchild of the Conqueror as Mathilda was. And he was a strong leader, Maud argued, a leader committed to England. The empress's interests lay primarily in Anjou and Normandy, where her husband was so busy waging war that he could not even be bothered to visit England. The earls and barons had sworn their allegiance to Stephen because they thought he was the man who could best lead England. And Stephen had been crowned and anointed king. He *was* the king, and the empress should yield before him.

There was nothing new in these presentations and as

Roger listened, his eyes on the face of the speaker, he was aware of his father's eyes on him. The blue gaze seemed to bore into him and it was with great difficulty that he kept his attention on what was being said.

After the queen had finished, Stephen's brother, Henry, the bishop of Winchester, talked about the civil war and how disruptive it was to the land. Next the Archbishop of Canterbury spoke of all the little people who were being damaged by the war. "And this is only the beginning," the archbishop warned. "We could be in for years more of this kind of fighting if the war is not stopped now."

"The king is all for putting an end to the war, Archbishop," the queen pointed out. "He was not the one who started it. It was the empress who landed in a peaceful country and opened attack."

Robert of Gloucester said in a measured voice, "The Empress Mathilda is the rightful sovereign of England. She was named thus by her father, the late King Henry, and was sworn allegiance to by all of the lords of England. She has returned only to claim what is rightfully hers."

This is an impossible standoff, Roger thought. *Neither side is going to give up its claim to the throne. What do the bishops think they can accomplish here?*

Then the Bishop of Winchester said what he had called the conference to say. "Perhaps we can resolve this situation if we move into the next generation. Would the Empress Mathilda be willing to recognize Stephen as king if Stephen promised to allow her son, Henry, to succeed him?"

Roger looked at the queen. She and Stephen had one son, Eustace, who was fifteen years old. Such a solution would cut him out of the monarchy.

The queen's lips compressed into a straight line. She said nothing.

After a little silence, the Earl of Gloucester said slowly, "We would be willing to discuss such a solution."

Roger looked at his father. A solution such as this held two possibilities for Guy. If Stephen should die and Henry inherited, the likelihood was that the new king would disinherit Roger and install Guy as Earl of Wiltshire. On the other hand, if Stephen should live a long life, Guy could be dead before he was able to inherit.

Guy was looking at his hands, which were clasped tightly upon the table, and for the first time Roger couldn't see his eyes.

The queen said crisply, "The king and I are not willing to disinherit our son."

"We will find a good marriage for Eustace," the archbishop said. "I'm certain we can marry him to one of the princesses of France."

"Eustace is the heir to the throne of England," the queen said firmly. Her jaw was set in a stubborn line. "I am not giving his birthright away to someone else."

"Why don't we think about this?" Bishop Henry said. "Think about it and pray about it and we will meet again this afternoon."

Robert of Gloucester agreed and after a moment, the

queen agreed, as well. As Roger followed the queen out, he found his way blocked for a moment by Guy.

"You think you've won," Guy said through his teeth. His eyes glittered feverishly. "Well, you haven't. This is your last chance. You're the Earl of Lincoln now. Give over the lordship of Wiltshire to me. Otherwise I can't account for what may happen."

Roger tried to feel some connection with Guy, but there was none. There was only a stranger, threatening him.

"I will never give Wiltshire to you," Roger said steadily. "I am my grandfather's heir and so it will always remain."

"Then be damned to you," Guy said violently, turned on his heel and stalked away.

Twenty-Eight

Roger decided to take a walk through the town to clear his mind and to see the old Roman baths so he could tell Nell about them. There were a number of people gathered in the great court of the abbey as he walked toward the gatehouse. He paid little attention to them, however, as he turned over in his mind what he had heard at the conference.

The solution the bishops had posed had some merit, he supposed, trying to be open-minded. The empress's son was about the same age as Eustace and, from what Roger had heard, he was a likely lad. However, Roger doubted that the king would agree to put his own son aside.

Roger thought of Nell. *If I have a son I will want him to succeed me, he thought.*

However, this was probably the one possible solution to the civil war. The empress was not going to just go away, and Stephen was not going to divide his kingdom by ceding the west to her. It was name Henry of Anjou as heir or nothing.

It is not a solution that would benefit the de Roches, though, Roger thought grimly. *Once he is king, Henry will doubtless reward his own followers at the expense of Stephen's adherents.*

It was easy to say that Stephen was not an old man, that his successor would not take the throne for a long time. *But look at Nell's father. He was not an old man and he died. And Stephen would be a target for assassins. If the king agrees to the bishop's proposal, Henry could be king in a year. Or sooner.*

If that should happen, then Guy would undoubtedly be made the Earl of Wiltshire.

Roger frowned, deep in thought as he walked down the Westgate in the direction of the Roman baths. He never noticed the hole in the walkway until he had tripped and fallen to his knees, just as he heard something whiz over his head. There was the sound of *thwack* and an arrow buried itself in the wall of the building just beyond him. Instinctively, Roger dropped flat on the ground.

A woman screamed as the other people on the street hurried for cover. Some followed Roger's example and dropped prone to the ground.

Someone cried, "Get that archer!"

There came the sound of running footsteps, then silence.

Nothing happened. Cautiously, Roger lifted his head.

Still nothing happened. Slowly he got to his knees and then to his feet. He went to pull the arrow out of the building wall. It was an ordinary arrow. There was nothing about it to tell him who might have shot it.

The street began to stir as people got up and other people came out of the shops where they had taken shelter.

"What lunatic was shooting arrows on this street?" an angry elderly man asked.

No one knew.

"Whoever it was seems to have got away," a woman said.

"I think they were shooting at you, my lord," another man said. "If you hadn't fallen you would have been hit."

Roger brushed off the knees of his hose. One knee had a tear in it. "Did anyone see who it was?"

A young man came to join them. "I think it came from one of the upstairs windows, my lord, but it is hard to say which one it was."

Roger drew a deep breath. "Well, we must be grateful that no one was hurt."

The people around him murmured their agreement, then, slowly, went on their way. Roger hesitated about continuing on to the baths, wondering if it wouldn't be smarter for him to return to the abbey.

If I hadn't tripped, I would be dead by now.

The arrow had come from an upstairs window.

He remembered Guy's last words to him. *Give over*

the lordship of Wilton to me. Otherwise I can't account for what may happen. Could it have been his father?

His mind shied away from the thought that his father might have tried to kill him.

But who was it, then? Who else would my death benefit?

Perhaps it is someone who desires the earldom of Lincoln. There are a number of people who fit that description—the Earl of Chester and William of Roumare, his half brother, for example.

He grasped at this thought. Someone like the Earl of Chester could have hired an assassin to kill him so that the earldom would be open again.

But Guy's words kept echoing again and again through his mind. *Otherwise I can't account for what may happen.* A shiver ran down Roger's spine.

However he looked at this incident, the fact of the matter was that someone wanted him dead. That arrow had been aimed straight at him. A lucky fall had saved his life. He turned back toward the abbey. Clearly it wasn't safe for him to wander by himself around the streets of Bath.

Roger arrived at the abbey in time to receive a summons from the queen to attend her in the abbot's reception room. When he presented himself he found that the queen was alone, seated in the carved chair that obviously belonged to the abbot.

"Come in, my lord of Wiltshire," she said, and gestured him to the chair that was placed next to hers.

Roger sat down.

"We never should have come here," the queen said. Her face was somber. "I knew it, but the king is always swayed by his brother. He can't say no to Bishop Henry."

"It was a worthy ambition, trying to end the war," Roger said diplomatically.

"We have nothing we can give up," the queen said. "We control the great part of the country. Why should we give up aught when it is clear that the empress and Gloucester are trapped in the west? We can take Bristol and Gloucester. It will be a long, hard struggle, but eventually we will take them. We have nothing to gain from this conference at all."

Roger couldn't disagree with the queen's cold, hard reasoning. In many ways, he thought, she saw things more clearly than her husband.

"It is just that the idea of peace is so tempting," he said. "Perhaps the king felt he had to try."

"This offer the bishops have made. Why should we disinherit my son in favor of hers? We won't do it, my lord. It would be disloyal to all our lords to name Henry the heir. How many earls would find themselves put out of office, succeeded by friends of the Angevins? You, for instance. The moment Henry became king he would name your father Earl of Wiltshire."

"That thought has crossed my mind," Roger said wryly.

"This proposal is impossible. And now we will look bad because we turned it down and they accepted it. Of course they will accept it! It gives them everything they want. The empress does not want England for herself— she wants it for her son. She will be content to live in Normandy and Anjou with her husband."

"I cannot disagree with what you have said, Your Grace," Roger said. "There would be a complete up- heaval amongst the nobility of England should Henry become king."

"We can win this war," the queen said. "They do not have the numbers to beat us."

"I agree, Your Grace. Outside of the west, and Wal- lingford, they have nothing."

"It is not that I don't feel badly for the little people," the queen said. "I understand that they are suffering from this war. But I cannot just give away England!"

"All of your adherents will support your decision," Roger said firmly. "There is no one who expects you to turn over the kingdom to Henry of Anjou."

The queen nodded. "I wish we had never come."

"We can leave tomorrow morning," Roger said. "There is no point in lingering. Obviously we have noth- ing to discuss."

"You are right," the queen said. "Why don't we plan to do just that?"

The afternoon session of the peace conference was short and to the point. The bishops proposed that the church be allowed to draw up a peace treaty, which the two opposing sides would then be obligated to accept.

The Earl of Gloucester, speaking for the empress, agreed to abide by whatever the church decided. The queen refused.

To the regret of the bishops, the conference was dissolved.

"I want to speak to you," Guy said to Roger as the parties were walking out the door.

"I don't believe we have anything to say to each other," Roger said.

"I have something to say to you," Guy returned. "Come in here with me a moment." Guy pushed open a door and for the second time that day Roger found himself in the abbot's reception room.

They stood next to the closed door and looked at each other. Roger's heart began to beat faster. Could his father really have tried to kill him?

Guy said, "Don't fool yourself that you are safe, Roger. You will have to leave the thick walls of Wilton sometime. And so will that wife of yours."

It took a moment for Guy's words to register. Then Roger answered in a hard voice, "Are you threatening me?"

"Some threats are empty," Guy replied. For the first time his eyes were not glittering; instead they looked very cold. In some ways the coldness was more frightening than the feverish glitter. "My threats are not empty. I want what is mine and I will get it, one way or another. So be warned."

"Did you shoot that arrow at me?" Roger demanded.

Guy stared at him. "What arrow?" he asked.

"I think you know," Roger said grimly. He stared back into his father's cold eyes, refusing to be intimidated. "I wonder what my mother will think if she learns you tried to kill me?"

Guy's mouth tightened. "My wife will think as I tell her to think."

There was a moment's silence. Steps went by in the hallway outside the room. Then Roger said evenly, "Now it is your turn to listen to me. Stephen is the king of this country, and for as long as he is king, I will be the Earl of Wiltshire. You can't frighten me into giving you my earldom, so you might as well stop trying." His narrowed golden eyes were fully as cold as Guy's. "I never want to see or speak to you again."

He turned and began to walk away.

"You may never see me, but I'll be there," Guy said as Roger walked out the door.

Twenty-Nine

Roger was glad to get home. He sat at supper between Nell and Simon and told both of them what had happened at the conference. "It was a waste of time," he concluded. "Stephen never should have accepted the invitation. He had nothing to gain and everything to lose."

Nell was mournful. "I confess, I was hoping for a miracle," she said. "So now this war will just go on and on."

"I'm afraid so, sweeting, " Roger said. "But in the end, I am confident that Stephen will win."

Roger had decided not to say anything to Nell about the arrow; he didn't want to worry her. But that night, as they lay in bed together after making love, it just came out. It seemed he couldn't keep anything from her.

She was shocked and frightened that he had come so close to death. Then she asked, "Do you think it was your father?"

"Yes," Roger said. "I do. He as much as told me that he wanted me dead."

Nell was lying with her head propped against his shoulder and his arm was around her, holding her against his side. "It is terrible to think that a father would try to kill his own son," she said in a hushed voice. "What a horrible man he must be, Roger."

"He is utterly ruthless," Roger replied. "I am beginning to understand why my grandfather banished him. A man like that would be a terrible earl for Wiltshire."

She shivered and he held her closer. "Thank God you tripped! God was looking out for you, Roger," she said soberly.

"Yes, I think he was."

Nell turned so that her body was pressing into his. She put both arms around him. "Stay home," she said in a muffled voice. "If you stay home you will be safe from him. There is no way he can penetrate into Wilton."

He ran a caressing hand down her back. "I can't hide at Wilton forever, but for the time being I think I can promise that I'll be here."

It seemed a reasonable enough promise to make, but worldly events soon intervened to make Roger rescind his word. Ten days later, he received a missive from the king that Rannulf of Chester and William of Roumare had captured Lincoln Castle.

"What?" Sir Simon was disbelieving. "How could

that have happened? Lincoln is one of the great castles in the realm. Did the garrison just surrender?"

They were sitting in the Great Hall. It was after dinner and Roger and Simon had been playing chess when the king's messenger had been admitted. A number of the other knights were playing dice, but all the games stopped when the king's messenger came in.

One of the pages, who had become close to Nell, heard what Roger said and slipped away upstairs to the lady's solar to fetch her.

"According to the king, they were very clever," Roger said, glancing down once more at the message. "They waited until most of the garrison was in the town and then they sent their wives in to visit the castellan's wife. No one suspected a thing when Rannulf strolled in, unarmed, to collect his wife. But—the men he had with him had arms concealed under their cloaks. Once they were safely inside they overwhelmed the remaining castle guard and took control of the castle."

At this point, Nell came running down the stairs. "What is this about Lincoln Castle falling?"

"I have just heard from the king." Roger repeated to her what he had just told Simon.

"Didn't the men from the garrison return from the town to try to win back the castle?" Nell demanded.

Roger began to reroll the missive. "As soon as the castle guard was overcome, William of Roumare moved in with armed troops. Rannulf let them into the castle. It was very cleverly done. At this point, according to the king, Chester and Roumare are in full control of Lincoln Castle." He looked at Nell. "And they have declared for the empress."

Sir Simon swore.

"Precisely," Roger said.

"This is what you have feared," Nell said breathlessly. "That some great magnate would go over to the empress."

"Yes," Roger said grimly. It was precisely what he and all of Stephen's true adherents had feared.

"What is the king going to do?" she asked.

He looked at her and thought, *She isn't going to like this.*

He said, "He wants me to bring my feudal troops and meet him outside of Lincoln Castle to retake it. And he wants to move quickly."

Nell's hand went to her throat. "Dear God."

"The king is right," Sir Simon said. "The castle must be undermanned—there is no way Chester and Roumare could have brought in enough troops to hold it. If you besiege it right away, it should fall."

"That is my thought also," Roger said. "I'll send out notices to my vassals to raise their men and go directly to Lincoln Castle. I myself will leave immediately with half the castle guard."

"Good," said Sir Simon. "We should be able to hold Wilton if it comes to that."

Nell had been standing silently, listening to the men talk. She was very white. Roger turned to her. "I truly don't think there will be any trouble at Wilton, Nell. Everyone's energy right now is focused on Lincoln."

She nodded. "We will be fine." Her voice was quiet but firm.

Relief washed through Roger. *Thank God Nell isn't going to make a fuss about my going,* he thought.

He got up from his chair. "I'm going to tell the knights to make ready."

"When will you be leaving?" Nell asked.

"As soon as it's light tomorrow morning," he replied, and left the Great Hall to go down to the guardroom.

I must be strong, Nell told herself as she climbed the stairs to her bedroom. *I can't weep and make him feel badly about leaving me. He needs to know that I am perfectly able to keep the castle functioning while he is gone. I have to remember that I am his assistant, as well as his wife.*

But she was terrified. A siege! He would be wearing armor, but an arrow could penetrate a hauberk. What would she do if anything happened to him?

There was nothing she could do to keep him home. She knew that. The king had called and he must go. After her maid had undressed her and she was in her night robe, she went to the side of the bed and knelt down on the cold floor to pray for Roger's safety.

She had just finished saying her prayers when he walked into the room. He had changed into his own dressing robe, with his feet in furred slippers. He was carrying a candle.

Roger said, "What are you doing out of bed? You should be under the warm covers."

"I'll get in bed now," she said. "Is everything ready?"

"Yes. We'll leave at first light."

Nell went to her side of the bed and slid under the warm wool and fur covers that were piled upon it.

Roger blew out his candle, leaving the bedside candle as the only light in the room. He came over to his side of the bed, shed his robe and joined her. "I can't believe that Chester and Roumare have declared for the empress," he said after he had pulled the covers up around his bare shoulders.

Nell's mind was not on political matters, but she made a sound of agreement.

He went on, "Chester was angry with the agreement that the king made with David of Scotland giving David Carlisle. Chester thought he had rights to Carlisle. I think that had as much to do with this defection as losing the earldom of Lincoln did."

Nell moved until she was touching him. He felt so solid against her. So alive. She said, "What does it mean, to besiege a castle, Roger? What will you be doing? Is it safe?"

He reached an arm around her and drew her closer. "This siege should be relatively easy, sweeting. Stephen will bring up his throwing machines, the trebuchets, and use them to rain lumps of rocks at the defenders on the walls. Once we've killed and injured enough of them, we'll put ladders up against the walls and use the battering ram to take down the gate. As I said, Chester doesn't have the numbers. The castle will fall."

It sounded simple to Nell. Too simple. They would be shooting arrows from the walls. What if Roger should be hit by an arrow?

She shut her eyes. She could feel his heart beating under her cheek and thought again, *What will I do if something should happen to him?*

She squeezed her eyes together. *Don't think that way. Not now. Now is the time to be strong, to show him how much you love him.*

"I love you," she said out loud. "I will pray constantly for your safety, Roger."

"I'm happy to hear that," he replied soberly. "I think you have a special relationship with God, Nell. I truly think God listens to your prayers."

"He listens to everyone's prayers," Nell said.

"But I think he specially listens to yours. It's because you are so good."

She didn't answer.

His lips moved from the top of her head, down the side of her face, to her cheek. He nuzzled her. "Hmm," he said. "You always smell so good. I'm going to miss you, Nell."

His lips traveled across her cheek and down to her mouth. Then he was kissing her, long and deeply, and she opened her lips and kissed him back. Their bodies fitted together and Nell's head fell back against his shoulder, pressed there by the urgency of his kiss. She felt his body coming over hers and she ran her hands up and down his back, feeling the powerful muscles under her fingers.

He was so strong, she thought. Not one of his knights could stand against him.

But an arrow could take down anyone, no matter how strong.

She held him tighter. *Roger,* she thought with anguish. *Roger, please take care of yourself.*

He continued to kiss her and caress her until all thinking stopped and she was aflame with passion, arching up against him, her hips seeking him, her mind drowned in the white-hot need of pure desire.

They consummated their love and when it was over Nell held onto him as if she would never let him go.

I love him so much, she thought. *Roger. Please, dear God, bring him back safely. Bring back the father of my child.*

Roger finally fell asleep, but there was no sleep for Nell this night. She lay awake, her cheek pressing against his bare back, and she prayed.

The following morning she stood with Sir Simon in the outer bailey and watched as Roger and his castle guard rode out. The scarlet banner with its insignia of a leopard flew proudly in the cold breeze and the knights rode two by two, holding their great kite-shaped shields, the nose pieces on their helmets pulled down. Nell had eyes for no one but Roger, riding Bayard at the head of his men, looking invulnerable in his polished armor.

But he was not invulnerable. The scene before her blurred but she fought back the tears. Then she felt Sir Simon's arm come around her shoulders.

"Come inside, my lady," he said kindly. "It is too cold for you to be standing out here."

The last of the men had ridden under the portcullis and over the moat when Nell let Sir Simon steer her back into the empty castle.

Thirty

The king was set up before Lincoln Castle when Roger rode in. Stephen was happy to see him and Roger was equally happy to be there. He was finding that the prospect of action after so many months of stalemate was invigorating.

"The rest of my troops should be here in another day or so, Your Grace," Roger said as he met with Stephen in the reception room of the bishop's guesthouse.

"Good, good," the king said. "Most of my earls are here, but they have few of their feudal troops. Your men will be much appreciated."

"The siege is going well?"

"Yes." The king was jovial. "The poor citizens of Lincoln were overjoyed to see us! They have opened the town to our men. I foresee that this siege will take us but a week, particularly after your men arrive. I thought it was appropriate that your men should be among those who liberate Lincoln, considering that you are the earl."

"We are happy for the opportunity, Your Grace," Roger said truthfully.

"Chester and Roumare are seriously under-manned," the king revealed. "We captured a large number of the garrison when we took the town. All that is left in the castle is the remnants of the garrison and the men that Chester and Roumare managed to sneak in."

"It sounds promising," Roger said.

After leaving the king, Roger climbed the hill that led to the castle and surveyed the busy scene. The king's engineers had set up several trebuchets on three sides of the castle walls and the machines were being loaded with stones, which were then being hurled at the castle walls. There was only an occasional glimpse of men on the walls inside. The king's archers occasionally got close enough to the walls to rain down a spray of arrows inside, hoping to catch anyone who was unfortunate enough to be underneath them.

Roger thought the king was right. It would not take much to storm this under-defended castle and retake it. Once his own men had arrived, the king would have the numbers to attack.

Instead of having to camp in a tent, Roger was put up in a room in the bishop's guesthouse. The king had told him that most of the earls were present, but Roger was surprised to see how many were actually there. The night he arrived, they all gathered in the bishop's reception room.

The conversation revolved around the siege, and Roger waited for a lull before he asked the question that had been on his mind. "Are Chester and Roumare's wives still in the castle?"

"Yes," said the king.

Roger looked around the circle of men. "Isn't Chester's wife the daughter of Robert of Gloucester?"

"What of it?" asked the Earl of Worcester.

"You don't think there's any possibility that he will try to rescue her?"

"He won't try to enter Lincoln," the king said positively. "He doesn't have the manpower."

That was Thursday.

On Saturday, the last of Roger's men arrived in Lincoln and joined the king's men in the siege. The king started to make plans to storm the castle.

On Sunday, word came to the king that the Earl of Chester was not in Lincoln after all, that he had in fact slipped away before Stephen got there and returned to his extensive lands to collect an army. He had also sent word to his father-in-law, Robert of Gloucester, who himself had collected an army, including Welsh troops from his conquered lands. At the moment, both armies were marching on Lincoln with the intention of doing battle with the king's much smaller force.

The entire military situation had changed, Roger

thought with dismay after he had heard the news of the oncoming army. His were the only feudal troops in Lincoln; none of the other earls had their men with them.

It is essential that we convince Stephen to withdraw, Roger thought grimly as he prepared to go to the meeting the king had called. *We cannot risk a battle right now. We have enough men to besiege an undermanned Lincoln Castle, but we don't have enough men to meet Robert of Gloucester's entire army, reinforced by the army of the Earl of Chester. The situations of the two sides have completely changed, and the advantage now lies with the empress.*

The last thing Roger thought as he walked into the bishop's reception room to meet with the king and his earls was that Stephen wouldn't be foolish enough to risk a battle. Hard as it may be, they needed to retreat and collect a substantial army of their own.

The earls and the king sat in a circle of chairs and, to Roger's consternation, the king announced he was looking forward to meeting Gloucester in battle. "They have slipped away from us whenever we tried to confront them before," Stephen said. "Now we will finally be able to meet them face-to-face, and I am not giving up this opportunity. We have the chance to defeat two of the empress's main supporters, the earl of Gloucester and Rannulf of Chester. The whole backbone of the empress's military power is coming against us. If we defeat them, the war will be over."

Roger argued against the king's decision, as did the

other earls, everyone pointing out how disastrous a defeat would be for the king's side. But there was nothing they could do to change Stephen's mind.

Roger did not sleep well that night. He thought of Nell and of how terrified she would be if he were captured. He was not afraid of dying—he was far more valuable as a hostage than he would be if he were dead. But the stress on her would be terrible if he were captured. And she was with child!

And of course, there was always the chance that a stray arrow could bring him down.

There's nothing to be done, he thought grimly. The king was set on battle, and battle it would be.

The king's army deployed an hour after dawn before the west walls of the city, where Stephen had chosen to make his stand. They waited for a few hours until Roger saw the empress's army come into view on the other side of the ford across the River Witham. Stephen sent troops to attempt to stop Gloucester and Chester from crossing the river, but the king's men were unsuccessful. By afternoon the two armies were fully deployed, facing each other outside the west wall of the city, with the grassy verge that led down to the Witham separating them.

It was a clear, cold winter day, and the sun felt pleasantly warm on Roger's armor as he stood with the king and the rest of the earls in front of the army, surveying the enemy. Roger was shocked by the large number of cavalry troops that the empress had. It looked as if they must outnumber the king's cavalry by at least five to one.

The king began to speak. "It is time for the battle speech," he said. "My lord of Wiltshire and Lincoln, will you do the honor?"

Roger was deeply surprised. "Surely Your Grace should be the one to do that," he said.

"I have not a loud enough voice," Stephen returned, "and you are the earl with the most men present. I think the honor of making the battle speech should fall to you."

None of the other earls disagreed. They melted away to their commands, leaving Roger and the king alone in front of the army. Roger looked at the men massed in front of him and felt a slightly hysterical urge to tell them that they were facing certain slaughter and should immediately flee the scene. But obviously he could not do that. He pulled himself together and lifted his own voice, which was clear and strong and distinct and carried to even those who were farthest away.

"Men of England," he shouted. "Today is the day we strike a blow at the heart of this vicious rebellion. Today all of our enemies are gathered before us—all of the self-seeking, self-serving men who would tear our country apart for the sake of their own ambition. Today is the day we strike them down. Today is the day we strike a deadly blow for King Stephen, our rightful king. Today is the day we destroy the armies of the empress and force her to forever leave our shores. A victory here at Lincoln will be the turning point in this war."

He paused and looked from left to right at the mass of faces that were turned to him. "Men of England," he said again. "I know that King Stephen can depend upon you to stand fast and fight with all your strength against the traitorous forces of the Earl of Gloucester and the Earl of Chester. Let us but hold our ground, hold our courage, remember we are in the right, and victory will be ours!"

A great cheer went up when Roger had finished speaking.

"Well done," the king said to him heartily

"Thank you, Your Grace," Roger said gravely. Turning away, he mounted Bayard and went to join his men.

Stephen's battle dispositions were thus: In the middle was the king, on foot, along with a host of other dismounted men and the royal household guard. The left wing was cavalry, commanded by William of Aumale along with William of Ypres, the king's chief military adviser, and Roger. The right cavalry wing was commanded by Hugh Bigod and contained a whole handful of earls with their small followings.

Both of these wings were but two lines deep.

Roger ran his eyes over the empress's far more substantial army, and judged by the flags who was where. It looked like Miles of Gloucester was leading the left, the Earl of Gloucester was in the center, and Rannulf of Chester was on the right.

In the vanguard of Gloucester's two side wings were the Welsh, who were on foot.

As Roger scanned the empress's army, he wondered where his father was. He was in no doubt that Guy was present somewhere in that mass of armed men.

For a long moment the scene was like a painting, each side holding its position under the deep blue winter sky. Then the horns blew and the empress's troops raised their voices in a shout and began to advance.

The Welsh infantry troops came first, directly at Stephen's two cavalry wings. To Roger's horror, the men around him instantly began to race forward to cut the Welsh down.

"Back!" he screamed. He held tight to his own reins, to keep Bayard from charging with the rest of the horses. "Stay back! Hold your formation!"

Roger's household guard obeyed his command, but many of his vassals and their men rushed forward, eager to cut down the poorly armed Welsh. But the Welsh were followed by the full force of the empress's cavalry, thundering forward in tight formation, swords at the ready. The dispersed and unformed troops of King Stephen's two thin wings were in no shape to withstand the powerful charge. They splintered totally and were quickly overwhelmed. It was only minutes before the broken line of the king's cavalry turned away and fled from the field as quickly as it could.

Roger tried desperately to hold his own men together as riders raced precipitately by them. To their credit, a number of them came to his cry of *A moi, de Roche,* and with their horses shoulder to shoulder, they lined up to withstand the advance of the empress's cavalry. Roger took a quick look around and saw that his two other commanders, William of Aumale and William of Ypres, neither of whom were cowards, were no longer on the field. All around him, men were escaping as fast as they could.

He turned in the direction of the king and there saw a sight that left him aghast. Instead of chasing after the king's fleeing wings, the empress's cavalry was now turning against the center, where Stephen stood. A few lords were around him, fighting at his side, but the enemy was closing in inexorably. The king was fighting ferociously with his sword, but Roger could see that his capture was inevitable.

A phalanx of Gloucester's cavalry was galloping toward Roger and his men.

I have to save my own men, Roger thought desperately. *I can't leave them here to die or be captured in a hopeless cause.*

"Retreat!" he yelled at the top of his voice. "Retreat!"

In an instant, the men of Wilton swung around and drove their horses forward, galloping away from the battle at full speed. It was a wild scramble, with horses jumping over fallen men and horses on the field. Roger stayed a little behind his men, making sure that everyone was getting away safely.

As he had feared would happen, the battle was a rout. Roger turned his head and saw that Stephen's sword had broken. The king went to a battle-ax. It wouldn't be long before he was overcome.

The empress's cavalry pursued Roger's men for a short space and then turned back toward the battle. Once he was sure that the pursuit had ended, Roger pulled Bayard up and let him walk to catch his breath. He was out of sight of his men, who were well ahead of him, and he patted Bayard's neck and stared grimly at the small copse of wood through which he was walking.

Jesu! he thought. *What are we going to do with the king captured? What an utter disaster. Stephen made a catastrophic mistake by authorizing this battle.*

He was so deeply involved in his somber thoughts that it was a few moments before he realized that someone was calling his name. The voice came from behind him and he put his hand on his sword and looked over his shoulder. A rider was approaching, a rider who had his nose guard up.

Roger's heart leaped into his throat. It was his father.

His first impulse was to put Bayard into a gallop and ride away, but he would not give Guy the satisfaction of running from him. He stopped Bayard and turned him to face the oncoming rider.

Guy trotted forward steadily, halting when he was a few feet away. The two men faced each other. There was no one nearby.

"Your king has been captured," Guy said. His teeth flashed white in a triumphant smile. "The war is over."

"Those of us who are sworn to the king will remain faithful to him, even if he is in captivity," Roger said evenly. "I will continue to hold Wilton for Stephen. While I live, the empress will never get her hands on Wiltshire."

Guy's sapphire eyes glittered. Sensing his rider's tension, his horse pawed the ground. "Don't you understand?" Guy spat. "The war is over. You've lost. Wilton is mine now."

"Wilton will never be yours," Roger snapped. "This battle is only a temporary setback. The queen is still free, and she is as competent to run a war as was the king—perhaps even more competent! The empress still has a long way to go before she can claim victory."

Without another word, and with incredible swiftness, Guy raised high his sword and swung it down at Roger's neck.

Roger was unprepared. It was Bayard who saved him, leaping aside as he saw the weapon coming so that it only glanced off Roger's armored arm.

Roger pulled Bayard out of the range of his father's sword.

"You're mad!" he cried. The blood was thundering through his veins. He could feel it pounding in his head. "No wonder my grandfather banished you."

Guy lowered his nose guard. "If you will surrender Wilton to me, I will let you live. If you refuse, then I fear you must perish."

He wants to fight me in single combat, Roger realized with stunned amazement.

He said over the pounding of his heart, "I don't want to fight my own father, even if he is a maniac. I don't want your blood on my hands."

Guy threw back his head and laughed. He sounded

genuinely amused. "Do you know who you're talking to? The greatest champion in the world, that's who. You don't have a chance, boy. Give in to me and let me have Wilton."

Roger's golden eyes narrowed. "Never," he said through his teeth.

The sun glinted off Guy's armor. He shortened the reins of his horse. "Then prepare to die," he said.

Something deep inside Roger was appalled by the thought of his father's blood on his hands. He didn't want to fight Guy. He didn't want to be a parricide.

"I'm your son," he said.

"Your birth was the worst thing that ever happened to me," Guy said. His expression was concealed by his nose guard but his tone was hostile. "I could see from the minute that you were born that my father was setting his hopes on you. He would stand and watch you for hours. I could see it on his face—my disinheritance and you in my place. I tried to do away with you once, you know. I held a pillow over your face, but the old man came into the room too soon. That was the final straw for him. That was what caused him to cast me out."

Roger felt sick to his stomach.

"Just another minute, and it would all have been over," Guy said bitterly. "I never had any luck."

"You tried to smother me when I was a baby?" Roger didn't even recognize his own voice. He stared with horror at the armored man before him. "Have you no conscience at all?"

"Conscience is something the church invented," Guy scoffed. He lifted his sword. "Most men are like me— they look out for themselves." And then he was on Roger, sword raised and already striking. It was only Roger's quick reflexes that allowed him to get his shield in place. The blow was so strong, it numbed his whole arm. Clearly Guy had earned his title of champion of the French tournaments. Roger spun Bayard and rode a little distance away.

"Don't think you can escape me," Guy said. His teeth showed in a satisfied smile. In full charge, he came at Roger, standing in his stirrups, his sword raised. This time Roger raised his own sword to see if he could get inside the other's long, protective shield.

The two men met with a clash of arms and Guy was rocked back a little in his saddle. He backed up.

"Not so bad," he said through his teeth. "You appear to have inherited some of my talent."

"I don't want to have inherited anything of yours," Roger retorted furiously. "You're a monster."

Once more Guy drove his horse forward, his large broadsword poised to get Roger's face.

Roger aimed for the part of Guy's shoulder that was not protected by his shield. As the two men came together, Roger ducked away from his father's sword and slammed his own sword hard against the mail covering of Guy's right shoulder. For a moment, Guy lost his balance in the saddle. Roger swung Bayard around and cut hard at Guy's unprotected back. With a clanging and rattling of metal, Guy fell off his horse and onto the ground.

Roger felt a flash of triumph and gave silent thanks to his grandfather for all of those lessons from experts over the years. Then, afraid that Guy would skewer Bayard from the ground, he dismounted, as well.

Guy scrambled to his feet to face him. "A lucky blow," he panted. "Now we'll see who is really the man here."

The huge broadswords rang in the silence of the woods as did the grunts and heavy breathing of the men as they sought to bring each other down. Guy was immensely strong, but Roger was younger and quicker. They battered at each other until the sweat was pouring off both of them and their breathing was coming hard, causing white moisture to hang in the cold air.

"Give it up, Father," Roger said at last. His chest was heaving. "You can't kill me and I don't want to kill you. Give it up and go back to Gloucester."

"I will never give up Wilton," Guy panted back. "Once you're dead, your vassals will automatically turn to me."

He thrust swiftly, and Roger felt the point of the sword through his armor. He jumped back.

Guy laughed.

"Neither one of us will kill the other," Roger said. "We are too well matched, too well armored. Give it up."

"I'll knock you down and rip your helmet off," Guy said viciously. "A sword through the head will finish you off."

Another sword thrust came at Roger and he took it

on his shield. His shield arm was aching and with every blow it became harder to hold it up.

"I will say this for you," Guy said. The sweat was dripping from his chin. "You're putting up a good fight. But it's all for nothing, you know. I always get my man."

"Not this time," Roger said grittily and aimed his next blow low. But the Norman shield covered Guy completely and he just staggered back a little bit before he caught his balance once more.

On and on the battle went, until both men were staggering with exhaustion. Roger could scarcely see through the sweat that blinded his eyes, even in the cold air, and both his arms were trembling with the continued force of Guy's massive blows. He was afraid that it was not going to be long before he did fall to the ground, and then Guy would have him.

He was so focused on Guy and on their exhausting battle that he didn't hear the sound of horses approaching. Then, suddenly, through the trees came three men. They pulled up abruptly when they saw what was before them in the glen.

"My lord!" The voice belonged to Thomas. "What is going on here? We were looking for you."

"Get away," Guy snarled. "This is a private duel. You are interfering."

"Who is this man, my lord?" Thomas asked.

"My father," Roger said exhaustedly. He never took his eyes off Guy as he spoke.

His knees began to tremble. *It's over*, he thought.

With three of my men here, the battle is finished. We can take Guy captive. I won't have to kill him.

"I am very glad to see you," Roger said to his men.

"When we couldn't find you, we got worried and decided to come back to look," Thomas said.

Roger nodded. He said to his father, "The duel is finished. I formally take you prisoner. You will have your wish—you will see Wilton again. But this time you will see it from the dungeons."

"Coward," Guy said. "You're afraid to keep fighting me."

A muscle twitched in Roger's jaw, but he didn't reply.

The knight sitting next to Thomas had a bow across his saddle and he picked it up now and aimed it at Guy. "Get back on your horse," he said. "Thomas, go and tie his hands."

Roger reached up and took off his helmet, running his shaking hands through his matted, sweaty hair. With a lightning quick move, Guy leaped forward, sword raised and aimed to come down right on top of Roger's unprotected head.

An arrow sung through the air and buried itself in Guy's breast. Norman armor was not strong enough to resist the power of the shot. The sword slipped from Guy's hand and he folded forward, around where he had been pierced. Then he fell to the ground.

Roger leaped forward to bend over his father's prone body. It did not take him long to see that the arrow had gone through the left side of his chest. Guy was dead.

Thirty-One

It took Roger and his men three days to return to Wilton. They had to stop to buy a coffin for Guy and a wagon to pull it. By the time they rode in under the castle's great portcullis, all of the other knights had arrived, bringing news of the rout.

Nell was frantic. All of the men reported having seen Roger alive, but no one knew why it was taking him so long to reach home.

"When my lord called 'retreat,' we all just ran, my lady," one of the knights explained apologetically. "I know he was with us as we cut our way out of the empress's cavalry, but once we were free I didn't see him again."

"Was the empress's cavalry chasing you?" Nell asked. "Could he have been caught?"

"They were too concentrated on capturing the king to chase us, my lady," the knight replied. "I truly don't think Earl Roger was captured. I honestly expect he will be home soon."

Nell stood in front of the fireplace, addressing the group of four knights who had just arrived. "How could you just have left him there?" she asked furiously. "How could you have come away without him?"

"It was a rout, my lady," one of the men said miserably. "We stayed with Lord Roger for as long as he was fighting, but once he called the retreat, it was every man for himself. Besides, he was right behind us! I saw him as I was leaving the field."

"An arrow could have brought him down," Nell said.

The men looked at their feet and didn't reply.

Nell wanted to scream at them, to beat on their chests with her fists. They should have stayed with Roger! They should have protected their lord!

"Very well," she said in a tight voice. "You may go down to the guardroom and get cleaned up."

"Thank you, my lady," they said in low, uncomfortable voices.

It was a very long night. Nell went to bed, but she lay awake, her eyes wide open, her whole being concentrated in prayer.

Please, dear Lord, send him back to me. I will do whatever you want me to do, be whatever you want me to be, if you will only send Roger home safe. You made this marriage between us. I did not want it at first, but you made it. Now that we have come together, do not tear us asunder. I don't think I could bear it, to be with-

*out Roger. Save him, dear Lord. Save my husband. Save
the father of my child.*

Over and over she repeated this prayer. Always before when she had prayed she had received comfort, had at least had the feeling that God was listening to her. Tonight that comfort was denied to her. Tonight, for the first time, in her direst extremity, she had the feeling that she was sending her words out into a dark universe, that Roger's fate had already been sealed, and that no matter how hard she prayed, nothing would change it.

The castle was at breakfast the following morning when the door to the Great Hall opened and Roger and his three knights walked wearily in. Nell froze in place for a moment. Then she was out of her chair and racing across the floor, not caring who was watching her. "Roger!" she cried. "Thank God." She threw herself into his arms.

They closed around her and held her tight. It was uncomfortable, being pressed against a mail hauberk, but Nell didn't care. He was home. Roger was home. Everything was going to be all right.

Suddenly, and without control, she began to sob.

"Don't, sweeting," he said. "It's all right. I'm fine."

"You didn't come and you didn't come," she sobbed. "All the other knights were here but not you. I thought…I thought…" Her voice died away and she began to sob again.

He bent his head and kissed her forehead. "I'm perfectly fine." His voice was firm. "Try to get a hold of yourself, Nell. I'm home and I've not been injured."

"I'm s-sorry," she said. She made a heroic effort to get control of herself. "I—I'm better now."

"That's a good girl." He loosened his grip on her but still kept one arm around her shoulder. He looked over the hall. "Who didn't get back?" he asked.

Three men were missing. Two had been unhorsed during the cavalry charge and gone down under the horses' hooves. One man was unaccounted for.

Roger's mouth set in a grim line. They never should have fought this battle in the first place.

"Come and have something to eat," Lady Mabel said. "You must be starving."

Roger shook his head. "We have a burial to attend to first." He looked at his priest. "Father Ralph, will you see to it for me?"

"Certainly, my lord. But who is the victim?"

"My father." Roger's voice was harsh and short. "I do not want him laid out, I want him buried immediately. Have some of the workmen dig a grave in the cemetery that overlooks the river. We will bury him this afternoon."

There was dead silence in the room.

Then, "I will see to it, my lord," the priest said.

"Come upstairs with me, Nell," Roger said.

"Bring a tray of food up to the family solar," Nell said to one of the pages and the little boy ran off to the kitchen to do her bidding.

Slowly, side by side, Nell and Roger walked to the stairs that led up into the tower that contained their rooms. There was complete silence in the Great Hall as everyone watched them go. Finally, when they were out of sight, the knights turned to Thomas and his companions to find out what had happened and how Lord Roger happened to be bringing the dead body of his father home to Wilton.

Upstairs, in the solar, Nell helped Roger out of his armor. It was a measure of how upset he was feeling that he didn't even want to send for his squire. Nell took his helmet and his gloves and then unbuckled the hauberk that came off over his head. She helped him strip his mail leggings off until he was left in nothing but his shirt and his hose.

"It's cold in here," she said. "Let me get you your bed robe."

He put on the wool robe she brought him and by that time there was a knock on the door and a page came in carrying a tray of food. Nell had him put it on the table and he left quickly.

"Have some ale," she said. "You must be thirsty."

He accepted the cup from her, took a sip, then another, then he drained it.

She drew up a chair close to his. "What happened?" she said quietly.

"The battle was a disaster," he said. "All of the earls opposed it, but the king was adamant. They had almost five times the number of cavalry that we had. Our men gave way on the first charge and fled the field, leaving the king fighting dismounted in the middle."

"Did you flee, too?" Nell asked.

"No. At first I tried to hold my men together, to make some kind of a stand against the empress's cavalry. I could see that things were going badly for the king. He was surrounded by his household guard, but they were being swamped. I couldn't get to him and I finally realized that if I wanted to get my men home alive, we would have to get away. So we retreated."

Roger's voice was bitter as he said the last word.

"Don't blame yourself, my love," Nell said softly. "Your staying to die or to be captured would not have helped the king at all."

"I know. The battle should never have been fought. Stephen made a huge mistake when he ordered it. We should have retreated and continued the siege warfare that was wearing Gloucester down. Now he not only has Lincoln and Chester, he has the king himself!"

Nell sighed. "What a catastrophe."

"Yes." He picked up a soft white roll and took a bite.

"What will happen next?" she asked.

He chewed on his roll. "The whole tide of the war has changed, Nell. Now the empress is in the ascendancy. We will have to wait to see what she will do. We still have the queen, at least. She will not give up easily."

Roger took another bite of his roll.

Nell looked at him. He looked so weary. So sad. She

poured more ale into his cup and said quietly, "Roger…
how did you come home bearing your father's body?"

Roger put the roll down. The corner of his mouth
twitched. When he spoke, it was with difficulty. "It was
a terrible thing, Nell. He followed me off the battlefield
and caught up with me as I was following my men in
the retreat. We…fought."

Nell didn't say anything; she just picked up his hand
and held it in both of hers.

"He wanted me dead so he could have Wilton." His
mouth twitched again.

Nell's hands tightened on his.

"We fought for perhaps an hour. It was the worst hour
of my life. He was immensely strong and quick. I was
growing exhausted from holding him off."

"But you beat him.…" Nell said softly.

He shook his head. "Thomas, Philip and John came
back, looking for me. I thought that was the end of the
fight, and I was so hot I stupidly took off my helmet.
When Philip saw my father coming at my bared head
with a raised sword, he shot him in the chest with an
arrow. It killed him."

Nell's face was white, her eyes enormous. She said
in a low voice, "It is hard to believe that he wanted to
kill you. His own son."

Roger rubbed his eyes. "Oh, he wanted to kill me all
right. And what was even worse, I found out the reason
that my grandfather banished him all those years ago."

"What was it?"

"He tried to smother me when I was a babe."

Nell's mouth dropped open. She stared at him in horror. "What!"

He picked up his cup in the hand she wasn't holding and took a long drink of ale. When he had put the cup down again, he said, "He told me himself. He said that he saw me as a rival from the time that I was born. He tried to smother me with a pillow."

Nell gasped. Her eyes were enormous. "What stopped him?"

"Apparently my grandfather caught him holding the pillow over my face. That was when he banished Guy."

"That is a terrible story," Nell breathed.

He rubbed his hand over his eyes again. "What kind of blood do I have running in my veins, Nell? The man was scarcely human!" His voice was anguished.

"He had no conscience," Nell said. "That is not true of you. You think about other people beside yourself. Your father didn't. The only good he saw was what was good for him. You're not like that, Roger. Don't worry about having 'tainted' blood. You carry your grandfather's blood and your mother's blood. Your father was an aberration. Something was wrong with him. It had nothing to do with you."

His eyes searched her face. "Do you really think so?"

"I know so. You are nothing like your father. Don't ever worry about that."

"I was trying to kill him," he said. "I was trying to kill my own father."

"He was trying to kill *you*, Roger. He didn't give you much choice." Nell's mouth set into an unusually hard line. "I'm glad Philip shot him. I'm glad he's dead. He would have been a danger to you for as long as he lived."

Roger gave a ragged sigh. "I'm glad Philip killed him, too," he said. He looked at Nell with troubled eyes. "I'm glad he's dead and I'm glad I wasn't the one who had to do it."

She moved to stand in front of him and reached out her arms. He slid forward on his chair, wrapped his arms around her waist and buried his head in her breast.

"I'm glad, too," she said. "It is easier for you, thus."

He closed his eyes, reveling in the softness that was cradling him.

The charcoal brazier glowed bright in the silence. Then Nell said, "What about your mother, Roger? What is she going to do now that your father is dead?"

"Would you mind if she came here to us?"

"Of course not. And then there is my own mother. The empress will make William of Roumare Earl of Lincoln—my mother won't be able to stay there."

"She can come to us, as well."

"Will *we* be allowed to stay here?"

"I'm not sure." Roger sounded grim. "We may well have to fight to keep what we have."

"Well, that's a worry for another day," Nell said. She looked down at the dark gold head resting against her breast. "Did you get any sleep last night?"

"No," he admitted.

"Then try to rest for a few hours. It will take the men some time to dig the grave and you look exhausted."

He sighed and straightened up. "I am tired," he agreed.

"Come along, then."

He followed her into the bedroom and folded himself wearily onto the bed. He looked up at her. "Lie down with me for a little?"

"All right." Nell slipped off her shoes and got into bed beside him.

"Let me hold you," he said. "I know I need a bath, I know I probably smell, but I want to hold you, Nell."

Nell went willingly into his arms and he snuggled his cheek against the smooth, round top of her head.

"It's good to be home," he said.

Tears stung Nell's eyes and all she could do was nod.

Epilogue

After her decisive victory at Lincoln, the empress clapped Stephen in chains. Then she entered London. Her attempts to impose large taxes on the citizens of that city did not make her popular, however, and when Stephen's wife, Queen Maud, along with Stephen's army, surrounded the city, the citizens of London rose up and forced the empress to flee. The rousing welcome they gave to Queen Maud made it look as if everything were not lost for the king.

After being chased from London, the empress and her brother Gloucester went to Winchester, where they captured the castle and began to besiege the bishop's palace of Wolvesey.

In retaliation, Queen Maud's forces surrounded Winchester and blockaded it, keeping out all the provisions needed by the empress and her men. This forced Gloucester to realize that his only recourse was to get his sister and his army out of the city. To do this, Gloucester made a feint attack to draw the attention of the blockading army, thus giving the empress an opportunity to escape from Winchester disguised as a man.

Gloucester's attempt to cover his sister's escape cost him dearly, however. His force was small and the royalists were able to attack him from both sides. In the ensuing chaos, Roger and a detachment of his men managed to capture Robert of Gloucester himself.

The rout of Winchester was as great a disaster for the empress as Lincoln had been for Stephen. Without her brother, the empress was helpless. As a result, the two sides signed the Treaty of Winchester, agreeing to a "mutual exchange" of the major prisoners: Robert, Earl of Gloucester, for King Stephen.

For all intents and purposes, the war was back to where it had been before the Battle of Lincoln had ever been fought.

It was a beautiful October day and Nell was nursing her baby when her mother appeared in the solar and said, "Roger is home."

Nell's head jerked up and the baby lost the nipple and began to cry. Once she had reconnected him, she looked back to her mother. Nell's face was radiant. "I will come as soon as William has finished nursing," she said.

The baby was still feeding a few minutes later when the door opened again and Roger was there.

"Nell," he said, and came across the floor to bend over her and kiss her cheek. Then he touched his lips to the fuzzy baby head nursing at her breast.

"I am so glad to see you!" Nell said. "Is the exchange done? Is it all finished?"

"The exchange is done. We have Stephen back and they have Gloucester."

Nell sighed. "Thank God."

William made a loud sucking sound and Roger laughed.

"Does this mean that you will be able to be at home more?" Nell asked. "The way you were before Stephen was captured?"

Roger squatted down next to them so that his head was on a level with Nell's. "I think so," he said. "We still have a long way to go, but I think any chance that the empress had of winning this war has been lost. She had a perfect opportunity, and she turned London against her. Foolish, arrogant woman."

The baby had finished and Nell lifted him to her shoulder and began to pat his back gently. Roger watched in fascination. He had come home briefly when William had been born, but he hadn't seen his son since.

"He's so much bigger than he was a few months ago," he said.

"He's growing very well," Nell said.

The baby burped. "Good boy!" Nell laughed. She turned to Roger. "Would you like to hold him?"

His eyes shone. "Could I?"

"Of course." She got up. "Sit down and I'll give him to you." Roger took her seat and reached up for the baby. Nell placed the small bundle tenderly in his arms. They cradled the child instinctively and Roger looked with wonder into the small face of his son.

"He has your beautiful blue eyes," he said to Nell.

"Yes, I think they are going to stay blue."

Roger made a small rocking motion with his arms. A corner of the baby's mouth flew up, as if in a grin.

"He likes it!" Roger said delightedly.

Nell decided not to tell him that the grin probably denoted some gas.

"He knows his papa," she said softly.

Roger looked at her. "I am so sorry that I had to be away for such a long time, Nell. I'm so sorry that you had to go through this pregnancy and childbirth by yourself."

"I wasn't alone," she said. "I had my mother and your mother to help me. It wasn't so bad. But I missed you very much."

He let out a long breath. "It is so good to be home! Home to my wife, my child, my castle…"

She sat on the floor at his feet. "We managed while you were gone, but the heart of our world was gone. Now that you are back, all is well again."

He cradled the baby with one arm and reached out his hand to lay it on her head. "We're a family," he said softly.

She rested her head against his knee. "Yes," she said. "We are."

They remained that way for a long, silent moment, then William began to grunt.

"What is he doing?" Roger asked.

Nell laughed and took the baby from him. "What goes in must come out," she said. "I will have one of the maids change his clothes. In the meanwhile, would you like me to have a bath brought upstairs for you?"

"That would be wonderful," he said fervently.

"Is Richard with you? Would you like me to send him to you, as well?"

"Thank you, Nell."

She bent down to kiss him gently on the mouth. "I am so glad that you are home."

That evening Nell lay abed, waiting for Roger to finish undressing and come to her. She had not missed lovemaking during the months of heavy pregnancy, but now that the baby was born and she was well again, she found her whole body quivering, waiting for Roger to take her into his arms.

These months of warfare between the forces of the empress and the forces of the queen had taken a toll on Nell. She had known that Roger was in the thick of the fighting and she had almost worn the skin off her knees praying for him. It was like a miracle, to have him back again, to have things go back to the way they had been before Lincoln. Or maybe things were even better—that was what Roger had seemed to imply when he'd said that the empress had missed her chance in London. And, too, there was no longer any danger from Guy to fear.

Life was very good, Nell told herself as she waited for her husband. Her mother and Roger's mother had blended right into the ways of the castle—in fact, they had become good friends. And Lady Mabel had mellowed considerably and was obviously fond of William.

Thank you, God, she prayed. *Thank you for my husband and my baby and for all the many blessings you have bestowed upon me.*

The door to the bedroom opened and Roger came in wearing his bed robe. He crossed the floor with a few swift steps, pulled his robe off, tossed it on the bottom of the bed and got in beside Nell.

He reached for her. "Nell. God, it has been so long. I have missed you so much."

"And I have missed you," she returned softly.

His mouth took hers and his kiss was deep and hard and demanding. She slid her arms around his neck and opened her mouth for him, returning his kiss with all the ardor that was in her.

"I thought about you every night," he said in her ear when he finally lifted his mouth. "I would lie awake, and think about you, and then I wouldn't be able to sleep."

"That doesn't sound good," she said.

"It wasn't good. It was awful. But now I have you back again and I'm going to make up for lost time."

"Go right ahead," she invited him. "I have some making up to do myself."

They caressed each other all over, growing more aroused the more they touched. Finally Roger groaned, "I don't think I can wait another minute."

"Come," Nell said, and opened her legs for him.

He drove into her and the power of his coming was so strong it was almost painful. But then he began to move back and forth, and the tantalizing tension that had been building in her loins began to ratchet higher. Her fingers pressed into his shoulders and she wrapped her legs around his waist. She felt open and vulnerable, her hips arched toward him, waiting in incredibly pleasurable torment for the orgasm to peak and explode. And when it finally did, her whole body shook with the intensity of the experience. She held him tight as he drove again and again until his seed was released and he cried out with the power of his own release.

They lay together for a long time, still joined, their bodies pressed together, their arms around each other, Nell's loose hair streaming all around them. Finally Roger said, "Not even my most vivid dreams were as good as this."

"Mmmm," she agreed drowsily.

"I love you so much," he said. "Do you know that, Nell?"

She opened her eyes and tried to wake up. "Yes, I do," she replied. "And I love you the same way."

He kissed the top of her head. "Do you remember how frightened of me you were when first we met?"

She smiled, her cheek moving against the bare skin

of his shoulder. "Yes. But it seems like such a long time ago. It seems like I was someone else then."

"We've both changed," he said. "I suppose love can do that to a person."

She reached up and ran her hand through his golden hair. It felt so good, thick and smooth and familiar as it slid through her fingers. "I was so afraid for you, Roger," she whispered. "I prayed so hard for your safe return."

"And I'm sure God heard your prayers, Nell."

A little silence fell as they lay quietly in each other's arms. Then she thought of something she wanted to tell him. "I have gained somewhat a name as a healer. I've been called to minister to a number of folk in the village, as well as some on the outlying farms."

"Good," he said. She heard him yawn. "That is what you wanted, isn't it?"

"Yes."

There was a pause. Nell thought of all the things she had to tell him about what had gone on around the castle. One of his favorite gyrfalcons had died, but she decided that that news could wait until the morrow.

Under her cheek, his breathing was coming slow and steady. After a few minutes, she raised herself on her elbow and looked down into his face. His long lashes lay upon his cheeks; he was sleeping.

"Good night, my love," she whispered, and bent down to drop a light kiss on his cheek. Then she leaned over and blew out the candle.

Afterword

The Battle of Lincoln took place on February 2, 1141. I have pushed it forward in time to accommodate the exigencies of my story.

The name of Stephen's queen was Matilda. I have called her Maud to avoid the reader's confusing her with the Empress Mathilda.

*The second book of the passionate Bride's Necklace trilogy
by* New York Times *bestselling author*

Kat Martin

The necklace promised great happiness or great tragedy—
and nobody could elude its power...

To Ethan Sharpe, Grace Chastain is nothing but a pawn for
vengeance against Harmon Jeffries, the traitor responsible for his
brutal years in prison. Believing Grace to be Jeffries' mistress, he
plans to humiliate his enemy by seducing her.

Grace fears her priceless heirloom necklace has begun to live up
to its curse when Captain Sharpe makes her his prisoner aboard
his schooner. But Ethan quickly realizes that she is not the wicked
woman he imagined her to be. Now Ethan must decide: can he settle
the demons of his past and follow the destiny his heart commands?

**"Martin adroitly balances the passion and intrigue
and provides vibrant characters and a satisfying
resolution of the necklace legend."**
—*Publishers Weekly* on *The Bride's Necklace*

JODI
THOMAS

32064 FINDING MARY BLAINE   ___ $6.50 U.S. ___ $7.99 CAN.
66715 THE WIDOWS OF
      WICHITA COUNTY   ___ $6.50 U.S. ___ $7.99 CAN.

(limited quantities available)

TOTAL AMOUNT $ _____
POSTAGE & HANDLING $ _____
($1.00 FOR 1 BOOK, 50¢ for each additional)
APPLICABLE TAXES* $ _____
TOTAL PAYABLE $ _____

(check or money order—please do not send cash)

To order, complete this form and send it, along with a check or money order for the total above, payable to MIRA Books, to: **In the U.S.:** 3010 Walden Avenue, P.O. Box 9077, Buffalo, NY 14269-9077; **In Canada:** P.O. Box 636, Fort Erie, Ontario, L2A 5X3.

Name: _____
Address: _____ City: _____
State/Prov.: _____ Zip/Postal Code: _____
Account Number (if applicable): _____

075 CSAS

       *New York residents remit applicable sales taxes.
    *Canadian residents remit applicable GST and provincial taxes.

MIRA®
www.MIRABooks.com

MJT0805BL